Michael had forgotten how it felt to be aroused.

Pain and pleasure. Sweet and bitter. Full of promise. Anticipation. Connection. If he could make love to Valery Navarre, he could feel alive again.

He could find hope—hope that, if his emotions weren't dead, maybe his spirit had also survived. That maybe someday he would be whole again.

If he could make love to Valery Navarre. To the stranger who had invaded his mind days before intruding into his life. To the woman he had promised against all his better judgment to protect.

If he could make love to Valery Navarre.

Which, of course, he couldn't.

He shouldn't....

Dear Reader,

Welcome to another month of fine reading from Silhouette Intimate Moments. And what better way to start off the month than with an American Hero title from Marilyn Pappano, a book that's also the beginning of a new miniseries, Southern Knights. Hero Michael Bennett and his friends Remy and Smith are all dedicated to upholding the law—and to loving the right lady. And in *Michael's Gift,* she turns out to be the one woman he wishes she wasn't. To know more, you'll just have to read this terrific story.

The month continues with *Snow Bride,* the newest from bestselling writer Dallas Schulze. Then it's on to *Wild Horses, Wild Men,* from Ann Williams; *Waking Nightmare,* from highly regarded newcomer Alicia Scott; *Breaking the Rules,* Ruth Wind's Intimate Moments debut; and *Hear No Evil,* a suspenseful novel from brand-new author Susan Drake. I think you'll enjoy each and every one of these books—and that you'll be looking for more equally exciting reading next month and in the months to come. So look no further than Silhouette Intimate Moments, where, each and every month, we're proud to bring you writers we consider among the finest in the genre today.

Enjoy!

Leslie J. Wainger
Senior Editor and Editorial Coordinator

Please address questions and book requests to:
Silhouette Reader Service
U.S.: 3010 Walden Ave., P.O. Box 1325, Buffalo, NY 14269
Canadian: P.O. Box 609, Fort Erie, Ont. L2A 5X3

AMERICAN HERO

MICHAEL'S GIFT

Marilyn Pappano

Silhouette

INTIMATE MOMENTS

Published by Silhouette Books

America's Publisher of Contemporary Romance

SILHOUETTE BOOKS

ISBN 0-373-07583-9

MICHAEL'S GIFT

Copyright © 1994 by Marilyn Pappano

Books by Marilyn Pappano

Silhouette Intimate Moments

Within Reach #182
The Lights of Home #214
Guilt by Association #233
Cody Daniels' Return #258
Room at the Inn #268
Something of Heaven #294
Somebody's Baby #310
Not Without Honor #338
Safe Haven #363
A Dangerous Man #381
Probable Cause #405
Operation Homefront #424
Somebody's Lady #437
No Retreat #469
Memories of Laura #486
Sweet Annie's Pass #512
Finally a Father #542
*Michael's Gift #583

*Southern Knights

Silhouette Books

Silhouette Christmas Stories
1989
"The Greatest Gift"
Silhouette Summer Sizzlers 1991
"Loving Abby"

MARILYN PAPPANO

has been writing as long as she can remember, just for the fun of it, but a few years ago she decided to take her lifelong hobby seriously. She was encouraging a friend to write a romance novel and ended up writing one herself. It was accepted, and she plans to continue as an author for a long time. When she's not involved in writing, she enjoys camping, quilting, sewing and, most of all, reading. Not surprisingly, her favorite books are romance novels.

Her husband is in the Navy, and in the course of her marriage, she has lived all over the U.S. Currently, she lives in North Carolina with her husband and son.

For Dale McCann,
one of those rare souls

Chapter 1

Michael Bennett knew he was in trouble when the visions started again.

There was little of substance: the whisper of a voice, the flash of a face, the feeling of fear. They came at different times—asleep or awake, at work or at rest. He could be lost in a book, and her face would appear on the pages. In the middle of his favorite TV shows, the actors' voices would fade away to be replaced by hers. After three hours of sound, restful sleep, he would awaken, his heart thudding, his chest tight, fear spreading slowly and insidiously through him with every pained breath. Because *she* was afraid.

He stood in front of the easel that, along with a table, a cabinet and a chest, filled one corner of his living room and made up his studio, and he studied the portrait there. *Her*. He knew she had blond hair, fair skin and blue eyes. He knew her hair was long, practically to her waist, soft and straight and heavy. He knew her forehead was high, her lower lip fuller than the top one, and that her nose was probably the most perfect nose he'd ever seen.

He knew all that without ever having met her, without ever having seen her except in those brief flashes. He didn't

know her name. He didn't know who she was or why she
was bothering him.

But he knew a few other things. He knew she was afraid.
He knew she was in danger.

He knew she wasn't going to leave him alone.

Muttering a curse, he turned away from the canvas and
went outside onto the balcony. It looked down on New Orleans' Jackson Square and Decatur Street, on the Café du
Monde and St. Louis Cathedral and the mighty Mississippi. There were few tourists in the square. It was January,
a Thursday afternoon, cool and uncomfortably damp from
the drizzle that coated everything with a slick, wet sheen. He
liked rain, liked to lie in bed and listen to it on the roof, liked
to watch it drip from the iron-lace balcony. He liked the fact
that it kept all but the hardiest of tourists away from the
Quarter. He liked—when it was warm and the air smelled of
flowers and spring—to walk in the rain, block after block,
until he was soaked clear through his clothing, until his
shoes were so wet that they would need a week to dry out.

Until he'd been washed clean.

But he wasn't in bed, it wasn't warm, and the sins he carried now could never be washed clean. He had to work tonight, and rain usually made working hell, so he wished to
God that it would stop before it was time to hit the streets.

Wished to God.

It was just a phrase. It didn't mean anything to him, not
anymore. Once he'd been a God-fearing man. He had been
raised in church, had dressed in black trousers and a short-
sleeved white shirt every Sunday morning and sat in the pew
in front of his mother. He had sung the hymns and prayed
the prayers and had believed—oh, yes, had believed with
every fiber of his being—that there was a good and benev-
olent God taking care of them all.

When he'd grown up and moved away from home, he had
cut back on the churchgoing, but he hadn't quit believing.
He had still believed in right and wrong, good and bad, angels and demons, God and Satan, heaven and hell. He had
still believed in the power of prayer, the power of healing,
had still believed in the promises of the Bible.

And then Evan had died. He had lost one of his best friends, his partner, and he had lost his faith. All those beliefs his parents had instilled in him since infancy had gone right out the window... except one.

He still believed in hell.

He was living in it.

His expression hardening into a scowl, he focused his gaze and his attention on a woman in the square below. She was tall, slim, had long heavy blond hair. Although she wore a trench coat buttoned from neck to hem, her hair was uncovered, left to soak up the water, to grow heavier as it became saturated. She reminded him of the woman in his vision, although he knew it wasn't her. In spite of the rain, this woman was strolling across the square, in no hurry to get where she was going, unconcerned about whether she got wet on the way. His vision from hell was too afraid to stroll. If she dared to go out at all, she would rush, scurrying from here to there, clinging to the shadows, looking over her shoulder.

He wasn't going to think about her. He couldn't keep her out of his mind in those odd moments when the visions—the hallucinations?—started, but, damn it, he did not have to think about her any other time. He couldn't. That was how things always started: the visions first, followed by the desire to help, followed by the obsession. Soon someone would show up—maybe Remy, maybe Smith; it often used to be Evan—and he would be pulled into something beyond his control, something reckless, something dangerous.

Something evil.

But not this time.

He wouldn't be drawn in this time. The cost the last time had been too high. That child, sweet and innocent though she was, hadn't been worth Evan's life. He couldn't risk it again. He would simply learn to cope with the visions. Maybe one day they would fade—when she escaped whatever danger she was in, when the cops who had to, helped her or if she never escaped, when she...

Died.

Savagely he hit the rail with the heel of his open hand. He wouldn't think about her, damn it. He would pretend the visions meant nothing, would pretend that everybody had them. He would ignore them and continue with his life.

He would.

Damn it, he would.

Turning, he focused his gaze on the painting. Three days ago he had never seen the woman. If he had passed her on the street, had met her through the course of his work or had been introduced to her by mutual friends, he would have thought she was pretty and then immediately forgotten her. But he hadn't met her in any of the usual ways. She had invaded his mind, and for that reason, he would never, ever forget her.

He remembered them all—the eight-year-old girl kidnapped by the perverted bastard who had rented the upstairs half of their house from her mother. The seventeen-year-old boy who had gotten involved with a satanic cult, who had been running scared after witnessing a ritual murder. The young woman taken at gunpoint by the stranger who had stalked her, who had terrified her, for two years. He remembered them and each of the others. Their faces and their problems had become a part of his life. Their fears had become his fears.

But no more. This pretty blond-haired woman would have to get by without his help. He didn't have anything left to give.

Rain dripping from his hair, he at last went back inside, but he left the double French doors open. In the kitchen he put water and coffee grounds into the battered aluminum pot and turned the burner on; then he went into his bedroom, where he stripped off his wet clothes and dressed for work in jeans, a T-shirt and a wrinkled button-down shirt in muted green and khaki stripes. For five years he'd worn the uniform of the New Orleans Police Department—dark trousers and light blue shirt—and then he'd made detective. For the next five years he'd worn suits to work every day, fitting in—appearance-wise, at least—with Remy and Smith for the first time in his life.

Now he worked drugs. Jeans, good running shoes and a shirt or jacket that would cover his weapon were all he needed. No more uniforms, no more routine haircuts or, for that matter, regular shaves, were necessary. Hanging out in the areas where he hung out, being clean-cut could get you made for a cop, and being made for a cop could get you dead.

Evan had worked drugs, too, had worked most of Michael's cases with him. They had gone through college together, the four of them: him, Evan, Remy and Smith. Remy and Smith had gone on to law school—Remy here at home in Louisiana, Smith back east at Harvard, where all the Kendricks sons went—and Evan and Michael had joined the NOPD. They had gone through the academy together, had worked down here in the Vieux Carré District together, had in the early days even lived together in a shabby two-bedroom place on Dauphine.

After law school, Remy and Smith had joined them in New Orleans, Remy with the FBI and Smith with the U.S. Attorney's office. They had stood up at each other's weddings—Evan's first, then Michael's—and they had been there through Michael's divorce. Evan's marriage had lasted nine years, until a spray of bullets brought it to an end. Michael still occasionally ran into his widow around town.

They had always thought that, if they died young, it would be because of the job. Drug dealers could be vicious. When a single shipment up from Mexico or South America could net a profit in the millions, when even the small-time dealers could rake in hundreds of thousands of dollars, the stakes were high. What was one cop's life compared to such easy money?

But it hadn't been the job that had killed Evan. It had been Michael and the nightmare he'd dragged his friend into.

The aroma of coffee drifted into the bedroom as he went to the closet. From the shelf he took down his Beretta and the leather holster that clipped on to the waistband of his jeans, a couple of extra clips for the pistol and his handcuffs. There was something comfortingly familiar about the

solid-steel cuffs, although these days they often made so
many arrests that instead they used flexible cuffs, unbreak-
able bands of plastic that could be slipped into place and
tightened in an instant. He had a stash of those, already
linked together in pairs, in the trunk of the undercover car
he drove.

Back in the living room, he laid everything on the table
alongside the heavy black flashlight he carried, then poured
himself a cup of coffee. He added nothing to it but half a
spoonful of sugar. Good coffee shouldn't need doctoring
with sugar and cream, Evan's aunt Sirena insisted. She had
taught them both to make coffee, jambalaya, shrimp *étouffé*
and crawfish gumbo. Michael had turned out to be a pretty
good cook, better by far than the woman he'd married eight
years ago. Like Evan's wife, he still saw his ex around town
occasionally, too. She had married a man with some money.
With their two children—children she had insisted to Michael that she would never have—they were the perfect little family.

He had just set his coffee on the table when the doorbell
rang. His friends were welcome, but because his work hours
varied, no one ever dropped in without calling first. If the
answering machine was on, it usually meant he was sleeping in after a late night at work.

Since the visions had begun three days ago, he'd left the
machine on all the time.

Moving to the easel, he carefully draped a piece of cotton sheeting over the painting there, then opened the door.

Remy Sinclair walked inside, looking every bit the fed in
an expensive steel-gray suit, white shirt and conservative tie.
He could pass as a respectable and thoroughly harmless
businessman in the outfit, but give him a pair of jeans, a
loud shirt and a camera, and he made an equally good
tourist. With a little rattier change of clothes and a splash
of booze on a French Quarter street corner, it would be hard
to pick him out from the winos.

He didn't speak right away. He walked to the middle of
the room and turned around, his gaze settling on the easel.
He didn't go to it, although Michael knew he wanted to.

Instead he shrugged out of his coat, folded it neatly and laid it on the sofa. "You look like hell."

Michael dragged his hand through his hair, leaving it standing on end. "I haven't been sleeping."

Remy ignored his scowl and sarcastic tone. He was good at that, Remy was—good at ignoring anything that might not set right with him. "Why doesn't that surprise me?"

Settling at the table, Michael ignored his remark. Insomnia had long been one of his problems. Of course, the business he was in didn't help any.

Neither did the visions.

"You have anything to drink?"

With a careless wave, Michael gestured toward the kitchen. He didn't have to play host for Remy. His friend knew what he would find—fresh coffee, soda and juice—and where to find it. He knew he wouldn't find any booze, not even a beer, and he knew why. He'd sat through some hellacious times with Michael when he was trying to sober up and regain control after Evan's death.

Remy returned with a mug of coffee, doused with so much cream that its color resembled the nearby river. He sat down across the table and, for a moment, looked at the easel again. So that was why he'd come. He knew something about the woman—probably knew plenty about her, except where she was—and he hoped that Michael knew something, too. He hoped that, like so many times in the past, he could say, "I have a case." Hoped that, like so many times, Michael would reply, "I know. I had a vision."

Michael felt sick inside, a queasy sort of nausea that made his stomach churn and brought a sour taste to his mouth. He didn't want to have this meeting. He didn't want to hear whatever his friend had to say. He didn't want to know anything about that woman. He didn't want to see the photograph that Remy was sure to have, didn't want to hear what terrible thing had happened to her, didn't want to know why she was afraid.

Remy didn't waste time on small talk. He didn't try to pretend that his visit was anything other than what it was:

business. The FBI wouldn't officially ask for his help—they tended to want hard-and-fast explanations, to be a little skeptical of anything that couldn't be explained—but Remy would ask. He didn't care about jurisdiction or boundaries. He cared about solving crimes and saving lives and locking up crooks, and he counted on Michael to share those feelings.

And Michael always had before. But not this time.

"Can I see the painting?"

Michael didn't respond, and Remy took that as a yes. He walked to the easel, lifted the cover and for a long time simply stood there, hands in his pockets, studying the woman's face.

Michael was a reasonably talented artist. He could, if he didn't mind giving up the expensive apartment, earn a living selling his work in the square, as so many other local artists did. He was better with scenes than with people, but this painting had turned out better than usual. Maybe because the image of her was so strong in his mind. Maybe because this time, in addition to feeling her fear, he had fears of his own.

Remy reached into his shirt pocket and removed a small flat item, balancing it on the easel against the portrait and then returning to the table and his coffee. The photograph. Oh, yes, there was always a photograph.

He wasn't going to look at it, Michael swore. Damn it, he wasn't. He didn't need to know how perfectly he had captured the woman's likeness. He didn't want to know her name, didn't want to hear how old she was or which anxious family members were waiting hopelessly for her safe return.

He stayed where he was, leaning back comfortably in his chair, his foot propped on another. He refused to get up and cross the room to the easel. He refused to show any interest at all in the woman. He refused to even look in that direction.

But his mind kept seeing that small photograph propped against the painting.

"Her name is Valery Navarre," Remy said quietly. "She witnessed that murder three days ago over on Chartres Street."

Three days ago. The visions had started three days ago.

Michael closed his eyes, wishing he could cut off his hearing as easily as his sight. If he listened, if he heard even a few of the details, she would cease being a nightmare vision and become a real person, someone deserving of help, but, damn it, he couldn't be the one to help her. He *couldn't.*

"She spoke to the police after the shooting. She was obviously upset and very afraid. There were a few other witnesses—mostly tourists down the street who weren't paying attention—but she was standing right beside the guy when he was shot. She was less than ten feet away from the men who shot him. She was the only one who could positively identify them."

Remy spoke in quiet, emotionless tones, but Michael knew if he looked at him, he would see regret in his friend's face. He didn't want to do this to Michael, but he had no choice. Valery Navarre had no choice. No hope. Just him.

And right now, that was worse than no hope at all.

"She left the police station before we got there to question her. That was about this time Monday. No one has seen her since."

Michael stood up and walked to the French doors. The rain was coming down harder now. In weather like this, business was slow for him and his partners; even the damn addicts didn't want to come out in heavy, cold rain.

"Her car was found on Rampart Monday evening, the door standing open, her purse dumped on the seat. Her apartment has been searched. She hasn't shown up for work all week."

Michael stared out the door, wishing for a cigarette or, better, a bottle of whiskey. Failing that, he wished Remy would go away and leave him alone.

Seventy-two hours. That was how long Valery Navarre had been out there. Had she been kidnapped by whoever was responsible for the murder, as the discovery of her car seemed to indicate? Or was she still out there, running, trying to hide?

He didn't know and, damn it, he couldn't care. Not wouldn't—it wasn't a matter of free will, of choosing to help this woman, of doing what his friend wanted. He *couldn't*. After what had happened last time, he could not do this again.

Remy waited, watching him patiently. He could be so damned patient, Michael thought ruefully. Sometimes, when he'd been working on a particularly tough case or when Michael had been trying to quit drinking, Remy's patience had been a blessing.

At times like this, it was a curse.

The silence grew, along with the tension that was making his head ache. He turned around and returned Remy's steady gaze. The desire for a drink—not a need, no longer that, but just the wanting—made his throat dry. What he was being asked to do made his hands shake.

"I can't do it," he said at last.

Remy didn't reply.

The queasiness in Michael's stomach increased until he thought he might lose the spicy shrimp and rice he'd had for lunch. The visions were always uncomfortable—having someone else in your mind, feeling someone else's feelings—but they'd never been this bad, this repugnant, this unwelcome. "You know what happened last time."

Remy's only response was a nod. Of course he knew. He'd been there, too—at the hospital through Michael's surgery, through Evan's funeral and, afterward, in every sleazy dive within walking distance of here.

"I can't do it. Damn it, you don't know what it's like."

"Okay. No problem, Michael." Remy got to his feet and put his coat on, straightening his tie, smoothing his shirt collar. He started toward the door, then slowly, hesitantly, turned back. "What happens if you don't help, Michael?" he asked, his voice oddly pitched. "Do the voices eventually go away? Do the visions disappear? Or does she have to die before you get any peace?"

His hands clenched into fists at his sides, Michael refused to answer.

He didn't have any answers, save one, and it mocked him.

I can't do this.

I can't, I can't, I can't....

The hotel room was tiny and smelled of must and mildew, but Valery didn't mind. She felt relatively safe here—safe enough to spend another night—and it was cheap. She sat in the dark, the lone chair pulled close to the window, the vinyl-backed drapes drawn shut but for a crack in the center. From here she could see the front door of the hotel, could watch who came and went. She wasn't sure exactly who she thought might follow her here—the bad guys or the good guys. She wasn't even sure there were any good guys this time.

Oh, God, she wasn't cut out for this. She managed a shop in the Quarter, a tiny little place on Royal Street that specialized in wearable antiques—clothing, jewelry, shoes. She wasn't a criminal. She wasn't supposed to have to go on the run to stay alive. She wasn't the sort to be interrogated by the police. She had no experience with crime, and certainly not with murder. She'd never even gotten a speeding ticket.

She never should have become so accustomed to habit. If she hadn't, maybe she wouldn't even have been on Chartres Street Monday. But, no, she had to do things just so. She had to leave work at exactly three o'clock every afternoon. She had to follow exactly the same route to the lot where she left her car. She had to turn onto that particular block of Chartres at exactly that particular time.

Why hadn't she varied her routine even the slightest? Why hadn't she worked just a few minutes late? Why hadn't she walked down one more block before turning? And why had she responded at all to that man's apologies when he bumped into her? Why hadn't she simply nodded, accepted the purse she'd dropped and gone on? Why had she let him walk alongside her toward the end of the block?

She never should have formed such rigid habits.

She never should have been standing less than three feet away from that man when the two other men shot him.

Leaning across to the bed, she snagged the spread and pulled it toward her, then wrapped it around herself. She'd been getting chills at the oddest times lately. Whenever she remembered the sudden appearance of those two men on the sidewalk ahead of them. The sound of the gun. The startled, betrayed sort of look on the man's face. The words the two men had spoken after he'd fallen.

Those words... She got plenty of chills when she thought of them. They were the reason she hadn't been entirely truthful with the police. The reason she had slipped out of the police station as soon as the detectives' backs were turned. The reason she had gone into hiding. She needed some time to consider what she'd heard. She needed to make some decisions. She needed to figure a few things out.

Still shivering underneath the bedspread, she watched the rain and the empty street outside. She felt lost, pretty much the same way she had when she was eleven years old and her parents had split up. Then she'd had a place to go and family—Aunt Marie, Uncle George and Remy—to take care of her, but she'd still been afraid. She had cried every night for months—for her mother and her father, for the security of her own bedroom, and for the familiarity of her own neighborhood, her own friends and her own school.

Now she had no place to go. Home—Aunt Marie's—was definitely off limits, as were her friends. Her life was in danger, and she couldn't expose any of the people she cared about to that danger.

She couldn't even go to the one person—her cousin—who she would have turned to naturally under the circumstances, because Remy—FBI agent, one-time best friend, one-time betrayer, but still, always, her cousin—was a part of it. He was supposed to be one of the good guys.

But she was terribly afraid he might be one of the bad.

Watching the rain, she wished she had grabbed her trench coat from the back seat when she'd abandoned her car. The rain had started sometime Tuesday, and it seemed as if it would never stop.

She wished she knew what to do.

She wished she knew who to trust.

She wished she wasn't so afraid.

Wearily she shifted position so she could rest her head on her knees. Tomorrow morning she would have to leave this hotel and find another. The thought of leaving its dark, grimy safety for the openness of New Orleans's streets frightened her, but she couldn't stay in one place too long, and she'd been here two nights already. She couldn't run the risk of anyone getting curious about her.

She would go to the Quarter.

The thought, quiet and calm, seemed to come from nowhere, and it brought her upright in the seat. Go to the Quarter, where all her troubles had started? Where she had seen a man gunned down on the sidewalk? Where she had stood close enough to two murderers to be able to describe them down to the last detail? She was never going there again—provided that she lived long enough to refuse the chance. No, what little sleep she got now was disturbed by nightmares about the place. She would never feel safe there again.

But she would go there, some part of her insisted, and she would be safe. Until this mess was all sorted out, until the bad guys were caught, until her questions were answered, it was the only place she would be safe.

With a grimly mocking smile, she shook her head in protest. "Jeez, girl, you're losing it," she murmured, her voice loud in the still of the night. She wasn't going back to the scene of the crime. People were looking for her—the killers, the cops, the FBI. Some of them wanted to know what she knew, and some of them wanted to make her forget it—permanently. The problem was, she wasn't sure which group wanted what.

Go back to the Quarter?

She didn't think so.

Not in this lifetime.

Friendships were strange things sometimes, difficult to explain. Michael had never had any problem figuring out his friendship with Evan; they were both from small, average families in small, average towns. Michael's father was a preacher and part-time farmer in southern Arkansas; Evan's had been an insurance salesman and part-time Little League coach in northern Louisiana. Michael had two younger sisters, and Evan had had three younger brothers, and they had both worked to put themselves through college.

Even his friendship with Remy was relatively easy to understand. There weren't many similarities in their backgrounds—Remy was an only child, and his parents had enough money to comfortably maintain the old family plantation home on the river between Baton Rouge and New Orleans—but they were both cops, after all. They understood and respected each other's work. And, in spite of the privileges the Sinclair money had given him growing up, Remy was really just an average guy—as common as Michael and Evan and just about everyone else.

But Smith Kendricks was a puzzle.

Michael liked him—truly, sincerely liked him—even though they had nothing in common besides the somewhat tenuous connection of their jobs. Michael was a cop; Smith was a prosecutor. Michael caught the bad guys, and Smith sent them to jail—although rarely the *same* bad guys. Smith worked in the U.S. Attorney's office and prosecuted federal cases, while Michael's cases were usually handled by the district attorney.

But as far as Smith Kendricks ever being an average guy... not even when hell froze over. He came from back East somewhere—Connecticut, Michael thought, or Rhode Island—someplace where his family had settled two hundred years ago and built their own small empire. Why he'd decided to attend college in Louisiana was anyone's guess, although his choice of law schools—Harvard—and jobs—government service—hadn't been a surprise. The Kendrickses were old money with a social conscience. Every young Kendricks was expected to devote a portion of his life—five, ten or fifteen years—to the service of others, after which time it was perfectly acceptable to become selfish and gather his own fortune. Michael had no doubt that in ten or twenty years, Smith would be, if he chose, one of the wealthiest and most successful men in the country.

And yet they were friends.

Just as Remy's visit yesterday hadn't been casual, neither was Smith's today. He had called first, though, getting the answering machine and leaving a clipped message that he was coming over at lunchtime, that they could go somewhere. Michael had already been cooking a pot of jambalaya, so instead they were eating here.

Michael hadn't asked Remy what the FBI's interest in the Chartres Street murder was. He hadn't wanted to know if it was connected to one of their cases, if it was important, if there was some particular reason why Remy wanted his help on that particular case. Now, after exchanging nothing more than pleasantries and small talk with Smith, he knew the answers. Something *was* going on, something more than a woman witnessing a murder.

Now that lunch was nearly finished, Smith got to the point of his visit. "Have you been following the Falcone case?"

Michael shrugged. He and Remy had discussed it a few times. Jimmy Falcone was a very rich, very powerful man, only, unlike the Kendrickses, he'd gained his money and power through illegal means. For fifteen years he'd been satisfied with what he had, but lately he'd begun expanding. He was buying into honest businesses and not so honest politicians. Just about every crime in the United States Code could be laid, if not directly at Jimmy's feet, then indirectly so, and yet now he was verging on respectability.

If he ever got it, he would be untouchable.

"You know Remy's in charge of the investigation into Falcone's activities."

Michael nodded. It was a big case, probably the biggest of Remy's career. If he nailed the bastard, he would succeed where all other efforts had failed. It would be a boost to an already-illustrious record.

"The man who was killed Monday was one of Remy's sources."

And no cop liked to lose his sources. It tended to scare other people away—which, of course, was the purpose behind killing them. "Listen, Smith, I'm sorry, but—"

"Did he tell you about the woman—the witness?"

"Some." More than he'd wanted to know. Now that she had a name and a story to go with the visions, Valery Navarre haunted him more than ever. So did Remy's last question: *Does she have to die before you get any peace?*

Smith pushed his plate away, neatly folded his napkin and laid it on the table. "Did he tell you—" He broke off, glanced at the portrait across the room, then grimly continued. "Did he tell you that she's his cousin?"

Michael left the table and carried their dishes into the kitchen, setting them down harder than necessary. Damn it, he didn't want to know this. He didn't want to hear anything that would change his mind, that would take away his choice, on this matter.

"Valery's father is Remy's mother's brother," Smith said from the table, watching him. "Her parents divorced when she was eleven, and she went to live with the Sinclairs. She and Remy haven't been on the best of terms the last fifteen years, but they *are* family. They were more or less raised together. And now she's in danger, and he needs your help to find her."

Michael's chest tightened with every breath he took. He couldn't stand this. He'd sworn he wouldn't get involved, had promised himself that nothing could change his mind, but, damn it, this did. How could he say no? After all Remy had done for him, how could he tell him that he wouldn't help find his cousin? How could he tell him that he would rather let her die than deal with the visions, with the danger, with the risk?

He had to help her, for Remy's sake if not her own.

He had to get involved, no matter how much he didn't want to. No matter how adamantly he'd promised himself he wouldn't. No matter how badly even the idea frightened him.

He had to do it.

For Remy.

Damn him.

Lifting the pot from the stove, he filled it with water, then measured coffee grounds from a tin bearing the Café du Monde label. After he returned the pot to the burner, turned to high, he leaned against the counter and faced Smith. "Why didn't he tell me?"

"He didn't want you to feel pressured. He understands that you don't want to be burdened with this..." he chose his word carefully "...this gift anymore."

"So why are *you* telling me?"

Smith shrugged. "I thought you would want to know."

And, damn it, of course he did. Remy had saved his life. He owed him.... God, he owed him big time.

Looking away, Michael rubbed his neck with one hand. The muscles there were stiff and tight, and he had a hangover sort of headache. He'd felt rotten since the first time he'd seen Valery Navarre. Early this morning he had lain in bed, unable to sleep, and focused on her, tried to force something even though he knew his gift—as Smith so cautiously referred to it—rarely, if ever, worked that way. He had concentrated until he felt sick; then, finally, exhausted, he'd fallen asleep, only to dream of her.

"She has black hair now," he murmured.

"What?"

He glanced at Smith again. "Her hair. It's black. And shorter."

"Which suggests...?"

"That she's probably hiding somewhere. That she knows people are after her, so she's trying to disguise her appearance."

"She manages some clothing store. How good can she be at hiding?"

Michael shrugged. Granted, her job certainly hadn't prepared her for this turn of events, but if she was bright, if she was logical and sensible, if she could think on the move, she just might be all right.

Without his help? Was he trying to reason his way out of this, trying to convince himself that if Valery Navarre was bright and logical, she could take care of herself and wouldn't need him?

It wouldn't wash. Because she was Remy's cousin, he had to help whether she needed him or not. Because of a coincidence of birth, he was in this until the bitter end.

The coffee ready, he poured two cups and set one on the table for Smith. He carried his to the French doors and gazed out across the square. It was raining again, a relentlessly hard rain that was bringing the usual flood warnings. It didn't take a lot of rain to put the better part of the city underwater, and they'd had just about enough.

"Why hasn't she gone to Remy for help?" he asked absently as he watched a lone figure below, dressed in jeans and a wildly colored jacket that was much too big. It was a woman, he thought, even though he couldn't see a face or any hair. It was the way she moved, the way she stood when she stopped. Those natural, unconsidered motions were thoroughly feminine.

"We don't know. As I said, they aren't close. I don't know the reason. He didn't volunteer it, and I didn't ask."

To a cop's eye, the behavior of the woman down below was curious . . . but curiosities were part of what the Quarter was all about. There was a freedom to be found in these few city blocks, a sort of anything-goes attitude. Besides, what was so curious about a woman wandering through Jackson Square, looking up at the apartments that bordered the two sides?

Wandering—that was what. Through pouring rain. On a nasty chilly day.

She was probably a tourist, he thought, from Kansas or Arizona or some other such state. She had probably saved all year for a week-long excursion to the most exotic of all American cities and, by God, a little rain wasn't going to dampen her enjoyment of it.

"What about money?"

Smith's chair squeaked as he changed positions. "She makes a living wage. She was her mother's sole heir when she died a few years ago, but unfortunately, she didn't have much to leave."

Still staring outside, Michael shook his head. That wasn't what he wanted to know. "When was the last time she got any money from the bank? What is she living on right now? Is she using credit cards?"

"No. She got cash advances on two credit cards Monday afternoon at different banks a block apart—a total of three thousand dollars. It was just before closing time. She must have gone straight to the banks from the police station."

So she was bright, Michael acknowledged. She had realized right away that she was in trouble, that she had to hide, that she would need money. She'd gotten the cash, then ditched her car and disappeared. She knew better than to use her credit cards, knew that the paper trail would lead the cops, the feds and, likely, Jimmy Falcone's people straight to her.

The woman below left the square through the Decatur Street gate, and Michael abruptly closed his eyes. His head was really throbbing now. The more he thought about Valery Navarre, the more he considered what had happened to her, the worse he felt. The more hopeless he felt. The more despairing.

God help him, he couldn't do this.

But he had to.

For Remy.

He took a drink of coffee to wash the sour taste of fear from his mouth. "I'll need to see her apartment and her car."

"All right."

"I want to see whatever reports you have on the shooting."

"No problem."

No problem. It was so easy for Smith to say. Other than an occasional threat, he didn't deal with the seamier side of life. He saw the reports, photographs and evidence that made up his cases, but it was all sanitized for the courtroom. He never saw the actual killings, never took part in the actual investigations. He never got dirty, never risked his life, never risked his friends' lives. He'd never killed anyone, and he'd never gotten anyone killed.

No problem.

Well, Michael had problems. He had lots of them—the insomnia, the booze, the guilt. The sorrow, the blame and the loss of faith. How it would hurt his father, pastor of the Titusville, Arkansas, First Assembly of God, to know that his only son had quit believing in God. But a merciful God wouldn't have let him live while Evan died. A compassionate God wouldn't let people do the things they did to other people, to innocent people, to children and the good, decent men who tried to help them.

"I have to go to work this evening," he said, turning at last to face Smith again. "I'll see about getting some time off. I'll do this. I'll do whatever I can to help." Whatever the hell that might be; he never knew until he was doing it. "But I'll do it on my terms, Smith. Alone."

Smith looked as if he wanted to protest, but after a moment he simply nodded. His expression showed all too clearly that he understood what Michael was thinking, that if he didn't let anyone else get involved, then he couldn't be responsible for what might happen. If he hadn't asked for Evan's help in rescuing that little girl, then maybe Evan would still be alive.

Maybe.

But Michael wouldn't be.

And, more than likely, neither would the girl.

"I'm sorry, Michael," Smith said quietly as he stood up. "I know this isn't easy."

"I'll deal with it. Tell Remy to give me a call."

He walked to the door with Smith, said goodbye and locked it behind his friend, then went into the bathroom to start dealing with his decision.

He threw up.

Chapter 2

Valery huddled on the steps leading to a lace shop, her jacket pulled tight, shivering uncontrollably in the cool night air. The rain had finally stopped a few hours ago, but not before soaking her clothing all the way through. It was after midnight now, and she was cold, hungry and more tired than she'd ever been. She'd taken a cab from her dingy hotel around eleven this morning and had spent the last thirteen hours walking around the Quarter.

She didn't know why she was here, exactly where she didn't want to be. She had started walking away, back toward Canal Street, a dozen times, but every time something stopped her. Every time something drew her back here to Jackson Square.

She put little faith in her judgment. She'd made major mistakes in judging people and situations ever since she was a kid. She had misjudged the men she'd dated, had misjudged Remy—heavens, she had even misjudged her own parents. The parents whom she had believed loved her more than life itself had both abandoned her—her mother for another man, her father for...

Well, he'd had his reasons. She'd been nineteen before she'd found them out, and it had been Remy who had told her. Remy who had willfully destroyed what was left of her childish illusions.

Remy. For half of her life she had loved him dearly, then, for a time, she had hated him. In the past fifteen years she hadn't even spoken to him, even though they lived in the same city, even though she occasionally saw him around, even though his face and name were in the news from time to time.

And now he was back in her life.

A wind swept across the square from the river, making her nestle deeper inside her sodden jacket. She had started to check into a hotel this evening, had gone so far as to walk inside the brightly lit lobby and request a room. The two clerks behind the desk had given her a long, measuring look—at her ragged hair, her ill-fitting clothes and her overall bedraggled appearance. With no more than those looks, they'd made it clear that she didn't belong in the elegant home-turned-inn, and she, embarrassed and uneasy, had abruptly turned and walked out.

She had come back here to sit and wait—for what, she wasn't certain, although her attention kept wandering to a set of dimly lit third-story French doors. Something about that apartment...

She had walked through the square today, over and over, studying each of the apartments. She hadn't understood why and had been too weary to try to figure it out. All she knew was that one of those apartments was significant for her. She had a *feeling....*

If she hadn't been so miserable, she would have laughed. She wasn't psychic, not by any means, but she occasionally had these...premonitions, for want of a better word. Sometimes when the phone rang, she knew before she answered who it would be. All too often she'd known something special was going to happen before it did, had known that a particular man was going to ask her out before he did. She sometimes knew things that she couldn't possibly know, sometimes felt things she shouldn't possibly be feeling.

And for about twelve hours now she'd had a feeling about that apartment, the corner one with the sort of dim lighting a person would leave on so he wouldn't have to come home to a dark place. That apartment—or, rather, the man who lived there—was the reason she'd come back to the Quarter today. She didn't know how she knew that, and she didn't know why. All she knew was that he could help her.

He could keep her safe.

This time, in spite of her misery, she did laugh, a choked, bitter sound. With all the trouble she was in, she would be crazy to go to a place she didn't know and a man she'd never met and ask for help. If she had any sense, she would get herself out of the city. She could head west, get lost in Texas, maybe even slip on down into Mexico. Sooner or later this mess would get straightened out. Either the killers would be caught and punished, or, when the leads ran out, the murder would be forgotten. *She* would be forgotten.

Another chilly blast of air came across the river, sending ripples across the puddles a few feet in front of her. She was so cold that she hurt inside, so exhausted that she felt sick. She hadn't slept well since Monday, hadn't been able to grab more than a few hours of rest here and there. Inevitably, when she dozed, the dreams came—the gruesome replays of the man, a real charmer, laughing and talking, of his smile fading into bewilderment and betrayal as the two other men stepped onto the sidewalk in front of them. She dreamed about the grim expressions the detectives had worn as they'd talked about protection for her, about security. She dreamed about how easily the men could have killed her, too, how one of them had even, for a moment, taken aim at her before his partner had pushed the gun away.

She dreamed about dying.

She couldn't even remember the dead man's name. Too afraid of seeing her own name, her own face, she had avoided the papers, had refused to watch the news on the snowy black-and-white television in last night's room. She didn't know why he had died, didn't know if the men had been caught.

She did know, from the detectives' talk among themselves, that Jimmy Falcone was involved.

She knew that Jimmy Falcone's philosophy of business was simple: If someone was standing in his way and he couldn't pay them to move, he removed them. Permanently.

She knew that she'd never been so afraid.

A half-dozen tourists, inebriated and enjoying their Friday night in the Big Easy, passed only a few yards away. Instinctively Valery pushed herself back against the concrete steps, trying to make herself smaller, less noticeable. When they passed without looking her way, she breathed a sigh of relief, then glanced once again at the apartment and became still.

There were more lights on inside, and the French doors had been opened. Billowy white curtains moved in the breeze, but the shadowy figure on the balcony didn't move at all.

He was the one.

Without questioning that knowledge, without once doubting the certainty of it, she rose from the steps and started toward the building. Her first steps were painful ones; her feet ached, and her joints were stiff. As she moved out of the shadows and into the pale glow of the streetlamp, she pulled the jacket hood over her head, tugging it forward so it left her face in darkness.

Refusing to think, to consider the folly of what she was doing, she circled the park, its gates locked against vandals. She entered the building, climbed the stairs and approached the door at the end. For a moment she simply stood there, her hand pressed flat against the door. This was crazy, she grimly acknowledged. Sheer lunacy.

Then, shrugging away that certainty, she rang the bell.

There was a brief silence, then the sound of locks being undone. In a flash of panic, she considered fleeing down those long stairs and back out into the night. But her body wasn't able, even if her spirit was willing.

The door opened, and the man she'd seen on the balcony stood there. He was a stranger to her, no one she'd ever met, but she knew with a certainty that strengthened her that he was what had drawn her back into the Quarter.

He was the one who would help her.

He was the one who would keep her safe.

He didn't speak. He simply stood there, one hand on his hip, the other out of sight behind the door, and he waited. He seemed calm enough, not overly curious about this unexpected, late-night visit.

Until she pushed the hood off.

Until he saw her face.

Then his own face turned pale, his fingers curled into a fist and he softly, savagely whispered, "Sweet Jesus."

Michael didn't mean the words as an oath. He might have stopped believing, but his father's teachings were still there deep inside him. *Thou shalt not take the name of the Lord thy God in vain.* Rather, it was ... not actually a prayer. He hadn't prayed since Evan had died. A plea. Yes, it was a plea, instinctive, impulsive, to the all-powerful deity he had once had complete faith in.

He just wasn't sure what he was pleading for.

In spite of the eight inches of hair she had cut off, in spite of the change in color from ethereal blond to night-black, he would have recognized her anywhere. In the past few days he had become that familiar with her, that intimate.

That intimate ... with someone he was meeting face-to-face for the very first time.

"I—" Her voice was small, trembly, exactly the way it had sounded in his head. She cleared her throat, closed her eyes for a brief moment, then tried again. "I know it's late—"

"Valery." It was all he could say, that soft whisper of her name. It was enough to stop her in midexplanation, enough to make her gaze lock with his, her blue eyes search his. She hadn't expected him to know her, hadn't thought he might be expecting her. Of course, he hadn't been, not like this. He had intended to find her, but he had never thought she might find him. That wasn't how it worked. Not ever.

There were questions he wanted to ask. What had brought her here? How had she found him? What did she think, feel, know about him? But before he could put his thoughts into any coherent order, before he could organize the words into a logical structure, she swayed toward him. She was dead on her feet. He winced at the phrase and corrected it. She was exhausted, liable to collapse at any moment. Returning his pistol to the holster he still wore in the small of his back, he took her arm, drawing her inside, supporting her until the unsteadiness passed.

For a moment she simply stood there, her waterlogged jacket dripping on his rug. He recognized the coat—a man's jacket, bright colors, much too big for her. She was the woman he had seen in the square this afternoon, studying the apartments opposite his so intently. Had she been looking for him then? And why hadn't he known her then? She had been on his mind, had been the topic of conversation between him and Smith, and yet he had looked at her, had watched her, without sensing anything.

He closed and locked the door, then faced her. "You're soaked."

She neither agreed nor disagreed with his statement of the obvious. She just waited, submissive and still.

"Let me take your jacket."

It took her a few seconds to respond to that, but finally she began undoing the buttons that ran down the front. Once they were open, she could reach the zipper inside. She shrugged out of the garment and shivered.

He took the jacket into the bathroom, then detoured through the bedroom for a blanket. By the time he returned, she had removed her shoes and socks, as well, but she hadn't stepped off the small woven rug where he'd left her. Standing there like that, barefoot, wet, her carelessly cut hair dripping down her neck, she looked vulnerable. Fragile.

She roused feelings that he didn't want to feel anymore. Sympathy. Concern. The need to protect.

His hands clenched into tight fists around the blanket. It was all he could do these days to take care of himself. He didn't have it in him to care for someone else.

But he had to.

For Remy.

When she became aware of him again, she didn't speak but only looked at him. There was confusion in her eyes. Bewilderment. Wariness. Fatigue. Curiously fear was missing.

Not so curiously, so was trust.

"How do you know my name?" she asked as he offered her the blanket, draping it around her shoulders.

She had been hiding for four days now—not only from Falcone's people, but also from the police and the FBI. Did she know she had come to a cop? Maybe. Maybe not. Deciding he could wait until later to find out, he answered with a question of his own. "How did you know to come here?"

As he'd done only a moment earlier, she curled her fingers tightly around the blanket, then answered in a whisper. "I don't know. I just . . . knew."

Just knew. The way he'd known things about her? The way he'd known she was pretty and blond and afraid? The way he'd known the sound of her voice? The way he'd known that she'd colored and cut her hair? Did Valery Navarre have an unwanted gift of her own?

"You . . . I don't know . . . I'm not—" She broke off the confused rambling, took a deep breath and spoke in a voice so calm that he knew it was sheer will holding it together. "Who are you?"

"Michael Bennett."

She repeated his name with a sigh, so soft, so delicate. It wasn't quite the answer she wanted, he knew. It didn't tell her that he was a cop. That he and her cousin Remy were friends. That he was unofficially involved in her case. It didn't tell her that she'd been haunting him for the past four days.

Feeling the need to do something, to put some distance between them, to distract himself even for a moment, he started toward the kitchen. "Make yourself comfortable, and I'll make coffee."

The last glimpse he had of her, she was moving toward the sofa, her bare feet noiseless on the wood floor.

At the sink, he ran water into a pan and watched it splash because his hands were unsteady. Abruptly he shut off the water, set the pan in the sink and laced his fingers tightly together. He wasn't ready for this. He had agreed only this afternoon to find her, and here she was. *She* had found *him.* He had agreed to the game only if he could make the rules, but she had broken them. She had changed everything.

Then, forgetting that small, unnerving detail, he considered the bigger, more important implications. He had done what he'd promised Smith he would do. He had fulfilled his obligation to Remy. Valery Navarre was here, and she was safe. All he had to do now was turn her over to Remy. The government would protect her, Remy would make his case against Falcone and Michael would be free and clear. He would be out of the game.

It had never been so easy before—just a few days' discomfort, a few days' dread, and now it was over and done with. Now he could relax.

Then he moved to the end of the galley-style kitchen where he could see the sofa. Where he could see Valery, lying down, knees drawn up, clutching the blanket tightly as if it were a lifeline. Where he could watch her, as delicate and fragile as an antique china doll, asleep and so damned vulnerable, and he knew it wasn't going to be so easy.

He knew there would be more to come.

He knew there was no way he could relax.

Not yet.

Valery awakened to the smell of coffee brewing and gentle sunlight on her face. She kept her eyes shut, savoring the normalcy of it—a comfortable bed, coffee, sunshine after endless days of rain—and she wished she could stay there, snug and safe and warm, forever.

Then, abruptly, memory came rushing back, ripping away the veil of normalcy. She was in a strange man's apartment. She had come here in the middle of the night, had invited herself in and fallen asleep on his sofa.

Her life might never be normal again.

When she forced her eyes open, he was the first thing she saw, sitting in the armchair across from the sofa, silhouetted by the morning light. He wasn't doing anything—just sitting there and watching her. He still wore the jeans and knit shirt he'd had on when she'd arrived last night, leaving her to wonder if he'd gotten any sleep himself or if he had watched her all night. Oddly the idea of this man, this stranger, watching her while she slept, while she was at her most vulnerable, didn't make her uncomfortable. Instead she felt...

Safe.

He made her feel safe.

She wondered why that was, wondered *Why?* about a lot of things. Why had he let her sleep here? Why hadn't he thrown her out? Why had he even let her in the door?

And then she remembered: he had expected her. He had known her name. He had known they would be meeting.

So he "knew" things, too. But exactly how much did he know? How much better was he at this than she was?

She wasn't sure she wanted to find out. Maybe he'd known only that they would meet. Maybe he didn't know that she was wanted by the police. Maybe—likely—he didn't know that there were people looking for her who might want her dead.

Maybe he wouldn't have been so willing to take her in if he knew all that.

For a time they simply watched each other. Sunlight made his features indistinguishable. She couldn't see his expression at all, couldn't read anything in that oh-so-still posture of his.

Finally he left the chair and went into the kitchen. Free of his watchful gaze, Valery sat up, running her fingers through her hair. She would give half of the nearly three thousand dollars she had for a shower, a toothbrush and some clean, dry clothes, she thought wistfully. But she couldn't ask a stranger for the use of his bathroom, his toothbrush and his closet...not even if she *had* wandered in in the middle of the night and fallen asleep on his sofa.

The mere idea of what she'd done made her shake her head in disbelief. She must have been more exhausted than she'd realized—or maybe just crazier. Her actions in the past twelve hours had gone from frightened and desperate to totally off-the-wall.

But *he* didn't seem to think so.

He had somehow expected her.

To keep from examining that thought too closely—to keep from examining *him* too closely—she turned her attention to the apartment. The ceiling was high, the floor wood. One wall was mostly brick, old and a deep rusty hue, while the others were painted a pale, pale rose, really more just a suggestion of color rather than an actual shade. The French doors and tall windows were curtained with white sheers, and the furnishings were sparse, mostly soft fabrics and old woods. The overall effect was pretty without being frilly, elegant without giving up comfort. She would have assumed a woman—perhaps a professional decorator—was responsible, if not for the art supplies in the distant corner.

So he was an artist. He understood color and texture, what worked together and what didn't, what complemented and contrasted and clashed.

She liked his work space, the only area of the room that was cluttered. There was an oak table, bearing tubes and pots, brushes, rags and splatters of every shade of paint known to an artist. Against one back wall was a short, squat chest, also oak, its drawers closed on the supplies it held and, set at an angle across the corner, was an armoire. Unlike the table and the chest, it was a fine piece, old and lovingly cared for. There wasn't a splatter of paint anywhere on it, no defects at all that she could see from here.

And, of course, there was an easel, situated close to the table, the canvas it held covered with a heavy piece of fabric.

It was a portrait, she realized, a shiver passing through her.

A portrait of *her*.

"Do you want to see it?"

Startled, she looked back to find him—he had a name, she reminded herself: Michael—standing directly in front of her, two mugs of coffee in hand. He didn't wait for her answer but set one cup on the table between them before returning to the armchair with his own. She glanced at the easel one last time before deliberately turning her back on it and reaching for the coffee. "No," she said shortly. She didn't want to see a picture of her own face painted by a man who hadn't yet seen it.

The coffee was fragrant, mild and liberally laced with cocoa, brown sugar and cinnamon. The cocoa reminded her of all the nights when she'd gone to live with the Sinclairs and Aunt Marie had brought hot chocolate to her room. For years she had associated the drink with tears and abandonment.

This morning, though, it was exactly what she needed: warming. Soothing. Worth savoring.

Unless it was Michael who'd created those comforting sensations.

Refusing to explore that line of thought, she settled back comfortably on the sofa and faced him. "I'm sorry about last night."

He simply shrugged.

"I've never done anything like this before."

"You've never had to go into hiding to stay alive before."

That answered a few questions, she thought, wrapping both hands around the hot mug and sipping. He knew. He knew she was in danger, and he had taken her in anyway. The knowledge made her feel a little bit safer and, at the same time, a little more uncomfortable. What else did he know about her? Just how finely tuned was this gift of his?

"Are you hungry?"

Pulling back from her own thoughts, she didn't need even a moment to consider his question. "Yes." She hadn't eaten at all yesterday, hadn't managed more than a few bites of anything since Monday. Yes, she was hungry, too hungry to be embarrassed about it.

"The bathroom's through there." He gestured with one hand toward a short hall as he got to his feet. "There are towels in the linen closet and toothbrushes in the medicine chest. Go ahead and clean up, and I'll get breakfast."

This time she watched him walk into the kitchen, noticing that his hair, brown and thick, was long enough in back to cover his collar; that in spite of his spending the night in his clothes, his shirt was neatly tucked in, his jeans too soft and faded to wrinkle.

She also noticed the pistol he wore and wondered why. Was he concerned for her safety, or for his own safety as long as she was around? Was he a cop, a crook, or just an extracautious citizen who knew he lived in a dangerous world?

Right now she didn't care. If she could trust him—and that weird sixth sense of hers said she could—that was all that mattered.

Untangling herself from the blanket, she left the sofa and went to the hall. It was less than ten feet long, with a single door at each end and a third one—a closet, she guessed—right in the middle. The open door at the right led into his bedroom. She caught a glimpse of a neatly made bed, a thick crimson comforter and a hunter-green wall.

The door on the left opened into the bathroom. It was a big, square room with a claw-foot tub, a pedestal sink and cut-crystal knobs on the doors. Although her own bathroom was as modern as any apartment in New Orleans—or perhaps because it was—Valery had a deep appreciation of old tubs and sinks, of their graceful curves and arches, of beauty combined with function.

The mirror over the sink was old, beveled and fronted a recessed medicine cabinet. Some of the silver in the corners had flaked off, leaving the reflection slightly distorted in places. She sighed, wishing she could blame the way she looked on those minor flaws, but these flaws were all her own. Her hair, damp when she'd fallen asleep, stood on end, and her face was seriously devoid of color, except for the dark shadows beneath her eyes. She looked thin. Pinched. Pathetic.

Inside the cabinet she found a tube of toothpaste and two new brushes. She used one, then gathered towels and a washcloth from the small closet built into one corner. It took only a moment to locate a bottle of shampoo, only a moment more to uncover a disposable razor and a can of shaving cream. Clean up, he'd said, and he very well might have meant wash your face and hands and brush your teeth. But after last night—after the last four days—she needed more than a washcloth, a bar of soap and a toothbrush. She needed a hot bath.

She needed rejuvenation.

Letting the water fill the tub, she peeled off her jeans, stiff and still damp on her legs from yesterday's hours in the rain, then paused to secure the lock on the door. It wasn't much of one—an old-fashioned hook that fit into an eyelet screw; she'd grown up with similar locks on the screen doors—but it added a degree or two to her comfort level. Then, as the last of her clothing hit the brightly woven mat, she sank into the warm water, letting it seep higher around her, letting it warm and soothe her.

She was past crazy, she acknowledged, nudging the handle with her toe to make the water hotter. Based on nothing more than a feeling, than premonitions that might very well be little more than lucky guesses, she had come to a total stranger, had invited herself into his home for the night and was now soaking in his bathtub. Desperation had taken her from a boringly normal life to utter madness.

But maybe madness wasn't so bad, she reflected.

At least she felt safe.

With breakfast cooked and warming in the oven and a fresh pot of coffee brewing on the stove, Michael picked up the cordless phone and settled into the armchair. He'd spent the night there, had slept the few hours between three o'clock and dawn with his feet propped on the coffee table and his head cushioned on a thin tapestry pillow. The rest of the night and all this morning, he had watched Valery. He had sat there for the better part of ten hours and simply watched her.

He had decided that he liked her hair black, liked it better than the angelic blond that was her natural color. He had seen that she needed rest, food and, most of all, a sense of security. A moment's freedom from fear. He had realized that she was prettier than he'd given her credit for, that if he had passed her on the street, he would have noticed her, and his interest would have been more than casual. If he had made contact with her, if their gazes had met or they had spoken or even simply bumped, he would have felt...

Just the right word with all the right connotations eluded him. Attraction was too simple, lust too one-dimensional. He would have felt something strong. He would have been *touched*.

He *was* touched, he thought with a cynical smile, or tetched, as his grandmother would say. He was touched in the head.

Turning the phone on, he began dialing Remy's number. On the last digit, though, his finger hovered above the button. He owed Remy this call—had owed it to him ten hours ago when he'd opened the door and found Valery standing there. Remy wouldn't have minded a middle-of-the-night call. He would have been grateful to find out that his cousin was alive and safe, would have been eager to get her into FBI custody, where they could ensure that she stayed that way.

But Michael hadn't made the call. He'd wanted to talk to her first. He'd wanted to ask her questions that he knew she had no answers for. He'd wanted to explore the mental connection, however tenuous, that linked them.

And he'd wanted to watch her. Just for a while. Just for a few peaceful hours. Lately they'd both had so few of those that it had seemed a shame not to savor them.

He didn't call now, either. Disconnecting before the call could go through, he laid the phone on the table and pushed it out of reach.

From the bathroom he heard the sounds of water draining from the bathtub, the splashing as she got out, and an image formed in his mind of Valery, naked and wet, reaching for a thick towel. It wasn't a vision, wasn't anything so intimate and accurate, but rather the product of imagination—of an imagination too long unused, of a libido too long unsatisfied.

In other words, he thought with a genuine grin as he headed for his bedroom, for the first time in a long time he was thinking like a man. An ordinary man.

He found a pair of sweatpants in the back of his closet, old and too snug for him, and pulled a T-shirt from its hanger. At the opposite end of the hall, he tapped once on the door, then hung the clothes over the doorknob and returned to the kitchen. A moment later he heard the door open, then close again. He imagined he even heard the scrape of metal on metal as the lock was refastened.

Another ten minutes passed before she finally emerged from the bathroom. His clothing was too big for her, naturally, but at least it was clean and dry. It was something to wear until she got settled wherever the FBI took her.

Her hair was wet and combed straight back; even so, he could see that she'd taken advantage of the mirror and a pair of scissors to even the ragged edges, to shape the blunt cut. She was still pale, though, and still reminded him far too strongly of a delicate china doll. All she needed to complete the image was an antique dress of the sort she probably sold in her shop.

Thank God all he had for her was sweats and a T-shirt.

She came to the table, to one of the two chairs where he'd set places, and rested her knee on the seat, watching as he carried their plates, filled with eggs, bacon and French toast, from the kitchen. "I don't know why you're doing this."

Her voice was stronger. Under better circumstances, he imagined *she* was stronger. Maybe, now that she was off the streets, she would find that strength again.

Deliberately misunderstanding her comment, he shrugged. "I almost always eat around this time."

"I meant letting me stay here. Being polite. Acting as if I'm a perfectly normal guest instead of a complete stranger who came uninvited into your home."

"You're not a complete stranger."

"I'd never seen you before last night."

His mouth began curving in what would be a bitter smile if he let it form, but he didn't. "I've been seeing you for four days."

Sliding into the seat and scooting it closer to the table, she continued to watch him thoughtfully. She understood, at least to some extent, what he was saying, knew what he meant by *seeing*. Because she shared the same sort of ability?

The idea interested him as much as it repelled him. He'd never known anyone else who experienced visions, foreknowledge, clairvoyance. He had never sought out anyone, had never wanted to expand his own knowledge and understanding of the visions that haunted him. He had dealt with them on his own terms, hadn't shared them—not even their very existence—with anyone but Evan, Remy and Smith. He had never wanted to know more, had never wondered why the ability had been conferred on him instead of someone else, had never wanted to know anything but how to get rid of them and, failing that, how to live with them.

And now, sitting across from him, was someone with a power, a gift—a curse—all her very own.

"I know about the murder."

She nodded calmly. Of course, his statement meant nothing, proved nothing. Everyone in the city with a newspaper, television or radio knew about the murder.

"And that people are looking for you."

She didn't respond to that. Instead she picked up her fork and poked the pile of scrambled eggs, onions and sweet peppers that filled half her plate.

"You're the best witness the cops have."

She took a bite of eggs, washed it down with coffee and poured syrup over her French toast. "This is good. I don't believe I know many men who cook."

He started on his own meal, barely tasting the food. After a few moments of silence, though, he spoke again. "I like your hair better this way."

Gazing at him, she ate one strip of bacon, then another. At last she asked, "Better than what?"

"Long and blond."

"There have been pictures of me in the paper?"

"No. Only in my head."

She glanced over her shoulder toward the easel. The portrait intrigued her, but, at the same time, he thought, it frightened her. She might be more comfortable with the idea of visions than he was, but she wasn't sure how she felt about being the subject of them. She wasn't comfortable with how well a stranger could know her without even meeting her.

She used the growing silence to eat, to think and to study him. He knew well what other people saw—shaggy dark hair, dark eyes, a generally tired, grim expression. He couldn't help but think, though, that Valery Navarre would see more. More than he usually shared. More than he cared to see himself. Still, he let her look. He didn't try to distract her.

Finally she laid the fork down and pushed the plate away. It was empty but for the last bite of syrupy French toast. "This has happened to you before, hasn't it?"

His first impulse was to pretend to misunderstand her question, to dismiss it with a flippant response. *Eating breakfast? Yes, I've done that before. Sharing a meal with a lovely woman? That's happened a time or two.* Instead he simply, shortly answered, "Yes."

"You have…premonitions? Prescience? Second sight?"

He shrugged. "I call them visions, although I don't know if that's strictly correct. I not only see things—people—but I also hear voices, sense feelings."

"Visions can be auditory and sensory as well as visual," she remarked, her tone conversational and casual, as if she wasn't the subject of the aforementioned visions.

"So can hallucinations."

She smiled faintly, and damn her if she didn't suddenly look fragile again. "I assure you, I'm not a hallucination." Then, for the first time showing a little feminine vanity, she ran her fingers through her sleek hair. "I'm not much of a vision right now, either," she said with another smile and a tinge of regret.

He didn't say anything, didn't assure her that she was as appealing with her self-cut hair and too-big clothes as any other woman would be dressed to the teeth. He didn't tell her that she had been lovely when he'd opened the door last night and was growing even lovelier as the exhaustion, the tension and the fear drained away. He didn't even want to notice those facts himself, much less point them out.

Although, of course, he did notice.

"So..." She sighed. Unlike last night, when her sigh had been so whispery, so vulnerable, this one was a strong exhalation. "What happens when you have these visions?"

He thought of Evan, and his expression darkened, closed in. He'd gotten his best friend killed—that was what had happened last time. He'd saddled himself with a burden he would never escape from. He'd destroyed lives—his, Evan's, Evan's wife's.

Forcing the guilt and the sorrow back where they belonged, where they lived, he concentrated on providing a satisfactory answer. "I only have visions of people in trouble, people who need help."

"And you help them." Her tone wasn't exactly skeptical, but more curious. More wondering exactly what it was he could do for her.

"Yes." So far he'd managed to help every single one of them—except Evan. It was odd. He'd had countless visions of strangers, of people he'd never met, people he didn't know and didn't—in anything other than a broad humanitarian sort of way—care about, but he hadn't had any visions of Evan. He hadn't known that his best friend was in trouble until he was already dead. Until he had sacrificed his own life to save Michael's and that little girl's.

"And how will you help *me*, Michael Bennett?"

He smiled cynically. He would help her—and would help himself at the same time—by getting her out of his life and out of his head. It was simple: all he had to do, all he was obligated to do by either his own code of ethics or his obligation to Remy.

"Easy," he replied. "I'm turning you over to the FBI."

Chapter 3

Valery sat motionless. He made it sound so obvious, as if once she was placed in FBI custody, everything would be all right; she would be safe from harm. Of course, he didn't know that one FBI agent might have reasons of his own for finding her, reasons that had nothing to do with wanting her testimony in court but rather exactly the opposite. He didn't know that Remy—her own cousin Remy—might very well be involved with the murder from the wrong side. He didn't know that FBI Special Agent Remy Sinclair might—*might*—want her dead.

And she couldn't tell him. She couldn't tell anyone. If Remy was innocent—God, how she prayed he was!—even the suggestion of misconduct would be enough to irreparably damage his career, and that would be enough to irrevocably destroy the last of her family.

And if he was guilty?

It was possible. Much as she wanted to believe otherwise, it *was* possible. People changed. Kids grew up, and sometimes the adults they became had little in common with the children they had been. The Remy she'd known for the first eleven years of her life had been mischievous and rowdy but basically decent, had stood up for kids younger or weaker. The teenage Remy she had lived with after her parents' divorce had been sullen, resentful, with rarely a kind thought or word for the cousin whose presence in his home he so deeply resented. And the adult Remy...

She didn't know him at all. He was more of a stranger to her than the man across the table.

Maybe the man Remy had become *was* capable of murder. Maybe he was capable of having *her* killed. Maybe he no longer had a conscience to bother him with right and wrong.

She didn't know. And she didn't know what she was going to do about him. She just knew she needed time. She had a hard decision to make, and she needed the courage of her convictions, still lacking, to make it.

Most of all, she needed not to have her choices taken away from her. She needed not to be taken into protective custody by the FBI.

Abruptly rising from her chair, she moved toward the door. Her tennis shoes sat on the braided rug where she had removed them last night, and her socks were draped over a branch of a small potted tree near the door. They were stiff and dry when she picked them up, but they wouldn't stay that way long, not once she put on her shoes, soaked clear through, squishy and cold.

"What are you doing?" Michael asked, leaving the table and coming to stand between her and the door.

She sat down on the nearest chair, a solid wooden piece that reminded her of the library back home, and she tugged on one sock. "I'm leaving."

"You can't—"

"I can't go to the FBI."

"Why not?"

She simply shook her head.

There was irritation in his voice, darkening his eyes. "You can't go back out on the streets, Valery. People are looking for you—people who most likely want you dead."

"You think I've forgotten?" The second sock slid on, rough and uncomfortable, and she shoved her foot into her shoe, barely suppressing a flinch at the wet chill that instantly soaked through her sock and, it seemed, into her very skin. "I'll take my chances out there."

"You'll *die* out there."

She put the second shoe on, then stood up. "Where's my jacket?" She would leave without it except that her money, just under twenty-eight hundred dollars, was tucked in an inside pocket. With the money, she could make it. She could slip out of the city, could hide wherever the cash would take her. Without it, she was sunk. She might as well just throw herself off the bridge into the river, because she very well might end up floating there anyway.

"You're not leaving."

For the first time since he'd mentioned the FBI, her control snapped. Her voice was shaky, and so, she realized, was her body. She hugged herself tightly to still the tremors. "I won't be turned over to the FBI!" she insisted. "If I wanted to be in police custody, I never would have left the police station Monday! I wouldn't have stayed in those shabby hotels or been afraid every moment of the last four days! I won't go! Do you understand? I'll leave town before I'll let anyone make me go to them!"

He regarded her with such calm that, slowly, bit by bit, she began feeling foolish for the outburst. She wondered if he was trying to read her, trying to judge just how serious she was, wondered if he could even do that. Well, she *was* serious. She was leaving—leaving the apartment, the Quarter, the city, maybe even the state. She was going to find someplace safe on her own, someplace that met *her* requirements, someplace where she could—

"All right."

She blinked and weakly echoed his words. "All right?"

"I won't call the FBI."

"Or the cops?"

"Or the cops."

"Promise," she demanded.

Closing his eyes briefly, he pressed his fingers hard against his temples, as if trying to ease an ache there—an ache, she suspected, that *she* was responsible for. Then, with a heavy sigh, he opened his eyes and fixed his dark gaze on her again. "I promise. You'll stay here, and I—" It was almost as if it hurt him to say it. "I'll find some other way to help. But you have to trust me, Valery. You have to do what I say."

Trust him. He wasn't at all shy about asking for impossible things, she thought. The last person she had trusted fully was her father, who had waited exactly two days after her mother took off to dump her on his sister's family. And as much as she'd loved Aunt Marie and Uncle George, she had never totally trusted them, either. She had lived with the fear that one day *they*, like her mother, like her father, would decide they didn't want to be burdened with her any longer, that, like Remy, their love would turn to something else, something less.

And here was this man, this stranger, Michael Bennett, asking for her trust.

Because he was waiting for a response, because she had to give an answer, because he made her feel safe, she nodded solemnly. She would trust him.

As much as she was able.

Looking suddenly haggard and bleak, he shook his head in dismay. "Damn it," he said softly, without feeling. "I knew it couldn't be so easy."

She felt a swift regret for involving him in her problems, even though it hadn't been deliberate on her part, even though, through the visions that haunted him, he had been involved almost since the beginning.

And he *was* haunted. A person didn't have to be sensitive to otherworldly gifts to see it in his eyes, to recognize his sorrow. He had lost something—someone?—important, and it had almost cost him more, she thought, than he could afford to pay. *Almost.*

He shook off the bleakness, the dismay, hiding them from her sight, and offered her a taut smile. "Make yourself comfortable while I clean the kitchen."

"I can help."

Turning down her offer with a shake of his head, he gestured instead toward the hall closet. "The laundry room's through there if you want to wash your clothes. Later I'll go out and pick up whatever you need.''

She nodded and kicked her shoes off again, peeled off her wet socks. She waited until he was about halfway to the kitchen before she spoke. ''Are you a cop? Or a crook?''

His fingers brushed lightly, familiarly, across the pistol in its holster before he turned to face her. ''Which one would be the lesser evil right now?''

She thought once more of what she'd seen Monday afternoon, of what she'd heard. ''I'm not sure.''

Like her, he took a moment to consider his response. When it came, it was flat, bare, laid out without excuses. ''I'm a cop.''

A knot formed in her stomach, a queasy Oh-God-what-have-I-done? sort of knot. A cop. God help her, after hiding from the police for four days, she had followed her silly little premonitions right into a cop's home.

A *cop.* That could explain how he'd known about the murder. How he had known her name. Why he had let her spend the night. It could explain everything he had supposedly learned about her from his so-called visions.

Then she remembered the dark, anguished look that had come into his eyes when he'd spoken of his visions, and she knew beyond a doubt that he did indeed have some sort of psychic power, as surely as she knew he didn't want it. It was nothing to joke about, nothing to lie about.

You have to trust me, Valery.

Hadn't she already shown some measure of trust in even coming here? Hadn't she trusted him enough to spend the night here?

So he was a cop... a cop who hadn't yet turned her in. Who could have picked up the phone at any time in the last ten or twelve hours and been rid of her. A cop who had said he would find some way to help her, some way that didn't involve bringing in the police or the FBI. He had *promised* her.

''Are you willing to help me because it's your job?''

''I'm willing to help you because it's the only way I know to stop the visions and because...'' The bleakness reappeared for an instant, then was gone again. "Because I owe it to a friend."

She stood motionless for a long time, and Michael watched her, waiting for her response. He'd taken a chance with the last part of his reassurance. If she knew that the friend he owed was Remy—her cousin, yes, but also a fed with the very agency she was determined to avoid—she would be out the door in a flash. She wouldn't bother with shoes and socks, wouldn't wait to find her jacket with its twenty-seven hundred seventy-odd dollars and change in the pockets.

But if she demanded an explanation, he had another to give. He owed Evan, too—owed it to his old friend and partner to see that his visions didn't get anyone else killed. He owed it to Evan to get Valery Navarre—and himself— through this alive.

"You won't turn me in." She said it as a statement of fact, but there was a faint questioning tone in her voice.

"I told you I wouldn't."

She stood there for a moment longer, then, with a shake of her head, she laughed. It was a queer, bitter and, at the same time, amused sound. "A cop. Damn. First a soon-to-be-dead guy, and now a cop. Can I pick 'em or what?"

He watched her turn toward the bathroom to retrieve her discarded clothing, and slowly, when she was out of sight, he went into the kitchen. A soon-to-be-dead guy and a cop. He could think of a thousand other pairings she could have made that wouldn't have given him a moment's pause. But he had more than a passing familiarity with death. He had a great guilt for causing it, a great sorrow for not being able to prevent it.

Death was just a passing, he'd been taught, from one realm to another, from one imperfect place to—for God-serving Christians, at least—a better, happier one. He'd had no doubts when he was a kid that heaven and hell really existed, that those who believed would be rewarded in heaven and sinners would be punished in hell.

Now all he had, it seemed, were doubts. Good people suffered and died, and sinners lived long, healthy, wealthy lives.

He had just started filling the sink with hot, soapy water when the phone rang. Drying his hands, he found the cordless phone in the living room where he'd left it and, under Valery's watchful gaze from the utility closet, he took it back into the kitchen to answer, pitching his voice so she couldn't hear.

Remy wasted no time with greetings. "I talked to Smith this morning."

"Did you?" Michael wasn't surprised. The three of them talked on a regular, almost daily, basis. They talked about unimportant things like the weather and the Saints and where they should meet for dinner, and about the important stuff, too. Investigations. Arrests. Trials. Problems. Families.

Families. In the nineteen years they had been friends— best friends, damn it—Remy had rarely talked about his family, and he'd never mentioned his cousin at all. Not once.

"He said he told you about Valery."

Why didn't *you* tell me? he wondered. Not two days ago, not Thursday afternoon, when Remy had come over to talk about the Chartres Street murder. He understood perfectly well why Remy hadn't wanted to pressure him then. But at some time in the past, any of the times when he and Remy, Smith and Evan had talked about their families, why hadn't Remy mentioned Valery then? It wasn't as if she were just a cousin, a not-too-distant relative whom he saw on holidays and at family get-togethers. She had lived in his house, had grown up with him, must have been more a sister than a cousin to him, and yet he had never told them—his best friends—about her.

"I'm sorry, Michael," Remy went on. "I didn't tell you because I didn't want you to feel obligated."

Which, of course, he did. "You didn't tell me because you knew I couldn't turn you down. But you should have told me anyway."

"I remember how bad it was last time."

Michael smiled bitterly. Yes, Evan dead certainly qualified as bad. "How do you think I would have felt if I had ignored her and she...?" *And she died, too?* If he'd been somehow responsible for someone else's death—for Remy's cousin's death—it would have been enough to send him crawling back into the nearest bottle.

And this time he wasn't sure he would have crawled back out.

"I know. I'm sorry." Remy sounded regretful. "I want to help you—"

"No."

"Michael, she's *my* cousin, and Falcone is my case. I have to help."

"No," he repeated, stronger this time. "I don't want you or anyone else calling or coming around. When I find out something, I'll let you know."

"Damn it, I don't want you in this alone."

"Alone is the only way I can do it." Michael sighed wearily, then ended the call with an abruptness that was rude and with the certainty that Remy wouldn't take offense. "I'll be in touch."

When he returned the phone to its base on a small Queen Anne table in the dining room, he saw that Valery was sitting on the sofa, hugging a pillow to her middle. "Who was that?"

He didn't mind the question, didn't mind the suspicion that prompted it. "Someone I work with." Gathering dishes from the table, he returned to the kitchen.

She hugged the pillow tighter. "Another cop?"

"Yes."

"Did you tell him about me?"

Pressing his palms flat, he rubbed his eyes, his temples, then combed his fingers through his hair. Damn, he was tired. He wished he could go to his room and shut the door—shut out the world and shut *her* out, too—and sleep the rest of the day away. But to do that, he would also have to shut himself out, and he hadn't yet learned how to do that.

With a sigh, he focused his gaze on her. "No."

"You didn't tell him I'm here?"

"I said no, Valery."

Now it was her turn to sigh. "I'm sorry. I don't mean to be so suspicious. It's just ... hard."

He didn't respond to her apology. He simply returned to the kitchen and the dishes waiting there. A moment later she appeared in his peripheral vision, this time sitting cross-legged on a seat at the dining table. "When do you have to go to work?"

"I generally work evenings, but I took some time off."

"Why?"

He gave her a sidelong glance. "To find you."

"And how were you planning to do that?"

"I've never failed before." Turning away, he murmured, "Not at the finding, at least."

Though the words weren't intended for her, she heard them. "What have you failed at? The helping? The keeping safe?"

He didn't answer. Laying out his role in Evan's death for her examination—for her condemnation—wasn't part of the bargain. For all he knew about her, she was still a stranger, and he didn't share his private hell with strangers.

"Considering that you expect me to trust you with my life, you aren't forthcoming with many answers," she commented dryly.

"I wasn't planning on being entrusted with your life," he replied, his tone equally dry. "I was planning to turn you over to the FBI and let *them* protect you." It took only a few minutes to wash the dishes, to rinse them and leave them to drain on the counter. He dried his hands, then joined Valery at the table, choosing a chair at right angles to her, facing her. "Do you want to talk about that?"

"About what?"

"Who's not forthcoming now?" He didn't wait for an answer. "About why a law-abiding, upstanding citizen is scared senseless by the idea of being taken into protective custody by the FBI. You have something personal against them?"

"They're a bunch of strangers. How could I have something personal against them?"

Michael was neither surprised nor disappointed by her lie. He was a cop; he'd been one nearly half his life. He was used to people lying to him. He *was* interested, though, in the reasons behind the lie. Why was Valery denying that she knew an FBI agent? And why hadn't that agent been the first person she'd gone to after fleeing the police station Monday? Granted, Smith had said that she and Remy weren't close, that they hadn't been for fifteen years. But he was still her cousin. He was still family. He was still the logical choice to ask for help.

But he knew all too well that logic wasn't always reliable. *Logically* he knew he wasn't really responsible for Evan's death. Evan was a cop. Cops risked their lives to help and protect others. Even if he hadn't worn a badge, Evan would have done everything exactly the same that night. He would have protected Michael. He would have put himself in danger to save that little girl. He would have died so that she could live. It was the kind of cop he was.

It was the kind of man he was.

But none of that lessened Michael's guilt for being the one to draw him into the case in the first place.

"They could protect you," he said, putting Evan out of his thoughts. "You could be someplace safe and comfortable."

"I'm someplace safe now."

What she didn't say said a lot. Safe, but not particularly comfortable. At first glance—and maybe even second—no one would know by looking at her that she wasn't comfortable. Her hair was drying, a few wisps stubbornly standing straight up. Her clothes—*his* clothes—were slouchy and well-worn. Her posture was outwardly relaxed—feet on the chair, legs crossed, hands loosely clasped.

But there were lines on her face—at the corners of her eyes, around her mouth. There was a certain wariness, a certain tension, in her body, as if she were prepared to take flight at any moment. And her eyes... A man could read a lot in those blue eyes of hers. Exhaustion. Stubbornness. Determination. Caution.

Distrust.

She had said she would trust him, and he believed she did—as much as she was capable of trusting any stranger. But she was holding some part of her trust—and her self— back. She was waiting for him to prove himself worthy of total faith. What she didn't know, and he knew all too well, was that he *wasn't* worthy. Only a short while ago he'd made her a promise—that he wouldn't tell anyone she was here— that he knew he wouldn't keep. And sooner or later she was certain to find out about his friendship with Remy. She was sure to discover that one of his best friends was the cousin she wouldn't—or couldn't—go to for help.

It was best that she didn't trust him fully.

Even if some part of him wished she did.

"So..." She blew her breath out with a force that shivered through her entire body. "What do we do now?"

"What exactly is it you want?"

Valery answered immediately, without hesitation. "For the past week to never have happened."

"Sorry. Time travel is a little out of my field." He almost smiled. She would have sworn it. "You can't go back and change the past, and you won't go to the authorities. So... what *do* you want to do?"

It was a good question. Living here secretly for the rest of her life was obviously out of the question. So was running away—avoiding the issue and thereby avoiding a decision about Remy that she didn't want to have to make. What she wanted was time... but how could she explain that to him without telling him what she needed it for?

And how could she possibly trust this stranger—this cop—with that?

"Have they caught the two men?" she asked, absently drawing her fingertip along the beveled edge of the table.

"No."

"But they know who they are."

"Your identification was as positive as it gets. They also know where the guys live and who they work for, but New Orleans is a big city. There are plenty of places to hide."

"If they're even in the city."

He nodded in agreement. "Right now they could be anywhere in the world."

"What about the man they killed?" In avoiding the news reports on the murder, she had not only avoided any possible mention of her own name, but she'd also kept herself in the dark about the other details. The two detectives who had interviewed her at the station Monday had told her his name, had repeated a few minor facts about his life, but she had still been shaken, hadn't paid much attention. She didn't remember any of it.

But she would never forget his death.

"His name was Simmons—Nate Simmons. He was thirty years old, single, came here from Pensacola. He had an extensive criminal record—had been in prison in Florida, Georgia and Alabama. He was a burglar of dubious skill, was slightly better as a thief, but he preferred the con. He could charm a lady out of whatever she held most dear with no more effort than it took to breathe."

Interesting. Her first impression of the man had been that he was handsome, her second, that he was a charmer. His smile had been quick, practiced and slick, but no less potent for that slickness. He'd been a toucher, too—brushing shoulders, bumping against her, touching her hand. She'd been warned about such people since she was a child, had been taught—especially in the Quarter—that the man bumping against her in the crowd might be the innocent tourist he seemed, but could just as likely be a pickpocket. Her first instinct, in fact, when the man—when Simmons—had knocked her purse to the ground, then handed it back, was to feel it to make certain that her wallet was still inside.

"Did he have any family?"

"I don't know."

"Do *you* have any family?"

For a time she thought he wasn't going to answer, and she didn't blame him. It was a nosy question and tactlessly asked. She had already intruded into his home—into his mind, if his talk of visions was true, and she believed it was—but that didn't give her the right to barge into his personal life.

But when she was about to apologize—again—he spoke. "Yes, I do."

"Here in New Orleans?"

"That depends on your definition of family." He leaned back in the chair, gazing somewhere over her head. "My parents, grandparents, sisters and their families all live in Arkansas. That's where I'm from—a little town called Titusville, right across the state line. I don't see them often."

"And here in New Orleans?" she repeated.

"I've got friends—good friends. None of us has anyone here, so we're each other's family."

Feeling a twinge of envy, Valery left the table and went to stand near—not in front of, but near—the French doors. "That's nice," she remarked, gazing out across Jackson Square to St. Louis Cathedral through the filmy white veil of the curtains. "I've never had friends like that." With a backward glance that didn't connect, she sent a smile his way. "I mean, I have friends—people to go out with, to go shopping or to dinner or a movie—but not anyone close enough to consider family."

"But you've got family nearby."

This time her glance did connect. His eyes were dark, shadowy, impossible to read. "How do you know that?"

He shrugged. It was a simple gesture, a slight lifting and falling of his shoulders, but it was eloquent. It told her what he clarified with words. "You wanted to go home, but you couldn't. You were afraid to get them involved."

Afraid. Heavens, yes. Aunt Marie and Uncle George deserved so much in return for everything they'd given her—a home, love, acceptance—but she had managed to give them only heartache. She was responsible for their fifteen-year estrangement from their only child. She couldn't also be responsible for bringing danger and possibly even death into their lives.

Could she, if it became necessary, be responsible for permanently destroying not only their relationship with their son, but also for destroying Remy himself?

She didn't know.God help her, she didn't know.

"So where is home?"

She turned her back on the square and the church. "Halfway between New Orleans and Baton Rouge. In Belclaire."

"Your parents live there?"

"No. My aunt and uncle. They raised me after my parents divorced. My mother is dead now, and my father..." Her voice trailed off, the next words refusing to come. It was a simple little story, the Sinclair-Navarre version of her life. *My parents divorced, and my mother left me with my father, who left me with my aunt and uncle. My mother is dead now, and my father lives with his second family up in Vicksburg.* Told with just the right touch of carelessness, it generated nothing more than an equally careless *I'm sorry* or *Too bad.* It didn't give a hint of the pain she had suffered at her parents' abandonment. It didn't hint at the turmoil she had eventually caused in her aunt and uncle's lives.

It didn't do much more than even hint at the truth.

Copying his shrug and borrowing his last comment about his own family, she abruptly finished. "I don't see my father often." At least, not in the past fifteen years.

Looking around the apartment for a likely change of subject, her gaze swept across the paintings on the wall. They were mostly French Quarter renderings, not the familiar places that any tourist could identify, but smaller, more intimate scenes that only someone who knew the district well would find. He was talented, no denying that, but so were most of the numerous artists one could find around the square every sunny day. He liked to paint, and he was good, but for him art was a pastime. It wasn't his passion.

She wondered what was.

"You aren't married." She said it as a statement, full of certainty even though she wasn't. It was apparent that he lived here alone, and obviously last night had passed without a wife's presence, but she still wanted to hear him say it. She wanted to know for sure.

"I was."

"What happened?" she asked, looking at him, seeing that his attention, as hers had been, was on the paintings.

"You don't ask easy questions, do you?"

"I'm sor—"

"Stop apologizing," he interrupted, his tone underlaid with impatience. "'Sorry' is the most worthless word in the English language."

She watched as he drew his hand through his hair. It was too long, but so well cut, so thick, that each strand fell right back into its proper place. Pretty hair.

Pretty man.

"What happened to my marriage?" He shrugged, with the same degree of carelessness that usually accompanied her partially-true story about her parents. "She was a lousy cook. I was a lousy husband." First answer, the easy one. Flippant. Then he added what she thought was probably closer to the truth. "She wasn't cut out for being a cop's wife, and I wasn't cut out for being anything else."

"How long were you married?"

"Not long enough. Too long."

She waited for him to ask her about that aspect of her own life, but he didn't. Instead he rose abruptly from the table, got a pad and pen from the phone table and came toward her. "Make a list of what you need, include your clothing sizes, and I'll go shopping."

She took the pad reluctantly. Of course she needed clothes, and she would like to have her own brands of shampoo and toothpaste, and some makeup and a bottle of her favorite perfume sounded wonderful. But she hated to spend a penny of the money she had secreted away on nonessentials—after all, she still might have to leave here. Even if she didn't have to flee, even if Michael was able to resolve her problems, that money would have to be repaid to the credit card companies, and at fifteen percent interest.

"Couldn't you just go to my apartment and pick up some things?"

"Your apartment was broken into Monday evening." Michael saw the pad tremble just a bit in her hand. "It's possible it's being watched now."

"Watched by who—the police or the killers?"

He shrugged again. "We don't want either one to know you're here."

His words seemed to reassure her that they were on the same side, which, of course, they were. They both wanted her to survive this mess that she'd found herself in through no fault of her own. There, though, their ideas went different ways. She thought she was safest with him.

He knew she wasn't. He had let Evan die. It was entirely possible that he could get her killed.

And if that happened, he would have to die, too, because he couldn't live with another life on his conscience.

Couldn't live with another death on his hands.

However, in the interest of safety, it might be interesting, he decided, to see if someone *was* watching the place. If it was the cops, he had Smith's permission to be there, and the assistant U.S. Attorney's okay went a long way. If it was Falcone's people . . . well, he knew how to lose anyone who might try to follow him. Then he would know who to look for around here. "Do you have the key to your apartment?"

His question surprised her, and she simply nodded in response. He'd already known she did, had come across it when he'd gone through the pockets of the coat she'd been wearing last night. She had abandoned her car on the street Monday afternoon, but she'd taken the keys with her. Old habits were hard to break, even when you were in a panic.

He got the jacket from the closet, and she gave him the keys, along with her address. "Anything in particular you want?" he asked as he shrugged into his own jacket.

"My pillow." Her smile was faintly embarrassed. "I sleep better on my own pillow."

After a long, still look, he nodded, warned her not to answer the phone or the door, and left the apartment. Watching her sleep last night, damp and fully dressed on his sofa, had been interesting enough. Valery sleeping in a bed—*his* bed—was a thought best not pursued.

Her apartment was an easy fifteen-minute drive away. The complex was typical, two-story town houses, probably ten to twelve years old, reasonably maintained but showing wear and tear. The parking lots in front of the buildings were about half full, since it was Saturday, but there was little activity outside. He parked in a lot down from her building and simply sat there for a time, keeping an eye on the traffic, studying the cars parked nearby and watching the occasional resident's trip outside.

If her place was under surveillance, he decided, the watchers had taken up residence in one of the other apartments, and if that was the case, there was nothing he could do about it. They would just have to watch him walk in.

Driving slowly, he moved his car to the space directly in front of her door. There were tall glass panels on either side and no dead bolt. Breaking in must have been a piece of cake for Falcone's people. Before all this was over, he would have to give Valery a short lesson in security. She should be more careful with herself.

He unlocked the door, slipped inside and closed it behind him. For its two stories, the apartment was small, the layout simple. A hall extended straight ahead, leading to the kitchen and a door with a four-paned window in the back. The living room opened on his right and led into the dining room, which connected to the kitchen. There were two narrow doors in the hallway ahead, one leading to a bathroom, he assumed, the other to a coat closet.

Although there were signs of a search, the rooms were relatively neat, relatively...empty. He had no sense of her living in these rooms, stretching out on that couch, sitting down to eat at this table, cooking in this kitchen. Coming back down the hall to the front door, he found himself at the stairs and started up.

At the top he found a bathroom, large and cluttered, and two bedrooms. One was apparently used for a little bit of everything: boxes were stored, along with unused suitcases, in one corner; a sewing machine sat on a table against the far wall; a tiny student's desk with a high-powered lamp was on the opposite wall; an exercise bike, untouched long enough for a heavy layer of dust to form on the seat, was near the window.

The other room was hers.

Valery's.

As he stopped in the doorway, an image of her flashed into his mind. Vision, memory or yearning, he didn't know—and he wasn't sure he wanted to. So this was where she spent most of her time. There was a television on the bureau, a stack of videotapes beside it. A quick glance showed that most of them were movies she had recorded herself, although there was one that she'd purchased. *The Big Easy*. Life and love, murder and betrayal, in New Orleans. The hero was a dirty—although later reformed—cop. Was that part of her problem with cops? he wondered. Did she look at the NOPD and—guilt by association—all other law enforcement agencies in Orleans Parish and see corruption, greed, dishonor?

Maybe.

But he suspected there was more to her reluctance to turn herself over to their safekeeping than that.

Slowly he turned to take in the rest of the room. It wasn't overly large and held only a few pieces of furniture—dresser, bureau, bookshelf, nightstand, bed—but it looked cluttered. Probably because of the books that spilled off the shelves and were piled on the floor. Or the magazines that were untidily tucked into baskets on both sides of the bed. Or the framed snapshots that filled almost every available space on the dresser top.

Family pictures. The aunt and uncle she'd mentioned.

And the cousin she hadn't.

He glanced at a few of the pictures. Remy looked so young. So invulnerable. Michael had never known him when he was like that. By the time they'd met, resentment—and, later, sadness—had already been a well-entrenched part of his friend's life.

Michael had never known what it was Remy had resented, what had made him sad. Best friends half their lives,
and there were still secrets between them.

Like Valery.

Returning to the other bedroom, he found an empty box
and, back in her room, began filling it with clothing. Her
closet held plenty of jeans and sweats, T-shirts and simple
cotton shirts. He placed three outfits in the box, then started
to close the closet door. The sight of a dress made him stop.

It hung on a padded hanger on a hook screwed into the
wall. It was the sort of dress she sold in her shop, precisely
the sort of thing he was grateful she hadn't been wearing
when she showed up at his place. He didn't know enough
about fashion to date it, other than to say it was old, but in
this case, older was definitely better. The fabric was soft and
light, giving the suggestion of sheerness even though it
wasn't, and there was lots of lace, delicately made with cut-
outs and embroidery.

It was a lovely old-fashioned dress, the kind he would
choose for a model if he were inclined to place a model in
one of the old courtyards he often painted. It was exactly
what he didn't want to see Valery wearing . . . but at the moment, it was the *only* thing he could see her in.

Carefully he slipped it off the hanger and folded it neatly.
He had to be crazy to take it. There was something so airy
about it, so romantic, so damn angelic. Yes, that was it;
when her hair was long and blond, she must have looked so
damn angelic in the ivory-hued dress.

But her hair wasn't long and blond anymore.

And as long as a man didn't make the mistake of believing that angels existed, what could it hurt if Valery looked
like one?

Leaving the dress on the bed, he took canvas sneakers and
ivory leather ballet slippers from the closet floor. Those
went into the box, along with socks and lingerie. There were
piles of it in the drawer, all soft, silky and sexy as hell. He
took the first sets his hand touched, making certain they
were ivory or white, that none of the jewel tones she seemed
to have a fondness for were included. It was too easy to

imagine her in this emerald-green set or that one in crimson. It was entirely too easy to see her—all pale skin and long, blond hair—in these bits of royal blue satin and lace.

Maybe he'd been wrong when he told her he preferred her hair short and black.

In a hurry to get out of her apartment—even though the only place he could go was back to face her in person—he quickly finished the packing. Bathroom articles went into a white plastic trash bag, then into the box. He grabbed one of the pillows off the bed, from the side where the night table held the phone and a lamp for reading, carefully slid the folded dress inside the pillow case, and carried them and the box downstairs.

For a moment he stood by the door, looking out through the narrow window. Again he couldn't see anyone overtly paying attention. There was a guy in the next lot washing his car and a cranky-looking woman waiting impatiently for her toy poodle to finish its business in the grass. No one else was around. No one else caught his attention. But then, anyone who was good at his job wouldn't be noticeable.

To be on the safe side, though, he braced the box against the wall, drew his pistol from the holster and laid it on the pillow. When he left the apartment, locked the door and headed for his car, he could feel the gun there, pressing against his chest, within easy reach should it be necessary.

It wasn't, but that didn't mean he could relax. Now he had to go home, taking a circuitous route to make certain no one was following him.

And even after that, he still couldn't relax, because then he would be with Valery. Talking to her. Protecting her. Watching her.

Hell, yes. Watching her.

Chapter 4

For a long time after Michael left, Valery remained exactly where she was, standing rather helplessly in the middle of the living room, as if afraid to make even the smallest move. While she tolerated helplessness fairly well in others, she despised it in herself. Being afraid was one thing. Being unable—or, worse, unwilling—to do anything about it was another.

Now she roamed the apartment, opening doors, peeking into closets, touching nubby fabric and old wood. She liked the contrasts—soft pastels in the living room and rich, masculine tones in the bedroom, turn-of-the-century fixtures in the bathroom and up-to-date appliances in the kitchen, the open airiness of the main rooms and the soothing closeness of the bedroom.

All in all, she decided as she drew her fingertips along a dust-free mahogany dresser that she dated mentally to the late 1800s, it was a lovely, comfortable, cozy place. It was exactly the sort of home she would like to have for herself. Exactly the sort of home she couldn't begin to afford on her salary, not if she also wanted food, electricity and transportation.

How could Michael?

She had no idea what kind of salary cops made, but she didn't imagine it was enough to pay for an apartment like this ... which meant he needed another source of income. Maybe he was on the take. Maybe he and the cops he worked with had their own little widows and orphans fund, generously if somewhat unwillingly supplied by the very people they were sworn to protect.

And maybe her imagination—her suspicions—had been working overtime lately. Maybe he had family money that helped income meet outgo. Or maybe it was his paintings. Maybe he sold enough to cover incidental expenses ... like a gorgeous apartment.

Leaving his bedroom, she returned to the main room. The only area she hadn't yet explored—hadn't yet snooped into, she admitted with a wry smile—was the corner studio. It was the painting on the easel that kept her away. That damned portrait of herself.

Slowly she moved to the armoire. Its doors opened with a slight tug on the curved wooden handles. Inside were a supply of blank canvases and, more interesting by far, a few finished paintings. Kneeling, Valery reached for the first one. It was small, no more than ten by thirteen inches, and showed a little country church. The building was white, the windows stained glass, the tulips and daffodils around the foundation bloodred and yellow. It was a pretty scene. Peaceful.

Until she noticed that the doors were open and the church was totally empty. That the stained-glass windows were cracked, the colors bleeding together, distorting the biblical scenes. That the wispy white clouds in the sky overhead formed changing images—from this angle an angel, from that one something darker, more threatening. Peaceful changed to disturbing, welcoming to warning.

The part of her that admired talent admired what he had done, taking a pretty little picture that could have been painted by any intermediate art student and giving it such power, such strength. But the part of her that considered churches holy places, places to worship, to find peace and fellowship and love, disliked it. She disliked it intensely.

With a barely suppressed shudder, she put it down, facing away from her, and reached for the second canvas. This one was also a church, St. Louis Cathedral across the square. She'd seen the cathedral thousands of times, had seen hundreds of paintings and postcards of it, but she had never once seen it like this—dark, distant, distorted. There was such a degree of despair about the painting that she felt it deep inside. Such sorrow and anguish. When had Michael painted it? she wondered. Why? What had been going on in his life at the time he'd created such a troubling work?

Leaving the other pieces untouched, she returned the two canvases to the cabinet, then closed the door. For a moment she poked around among the items on his worktable. There was such a jumble there, everything lying where it was carelessly dropped—tubes of paint, mixing tools, rags and cleaning solvents. The brushes, in contrast, were meticulously cleaned and stored, handles down, in an upright position, grouped together by type and size.

Contrasts. He was definitely a man of those.

At last she was in front of the easel. She stared at the sheeting that covered it and wondered how he had depicted her. With the same sense of despair as he'd shown in the paintings of the churches? If she lifted the cotton and looked at herself, would she see fear on her own face? Would his aversion to the visions that haunted him come through on the canvas?

She reached out, touched the fabric, felt its rough texture between her fingers, then drew her hand back. She wasn't sure she wanted to know what he saw when he saw her. She was afraid of what darker part of himself might have come through into the painting.

She was afraid.

Of a portrait.

Painted days before the artist had met her.

She was turning away from the easel when, at the same time, the phone rang and the lock rattled at the door.

Catching her startled cry, she listened to the answering machine click on and watched as Michael opened the door. His gaze, dark and steady, came straight to her as the message being taped filtered into the air. The voice was masculine, strong, New England softened by Old South. "Michael, it's Smith. Call me." As abruptly as the machine had started, it whirred to a stop.

Still shaken—by the churches, by the portrait, by the innocent scare—she weakly asked, "Smith who?"

Michael came on into the apartment, shifting the box and her pillow to one arm so he could close and secure the door behind him. "Smith Kendricks."

That was a name she knew. Her impressions had been on target. Smith Kendricks, of the U.S. Attorney's office, was definitely masculine, strong and powerful, and had spent roughly half of his life in New England and the other half here. "You work with him?"

"Occasionally." He laid his load on a chair, slipped off his jacket and hung it on the back of the same chair. "We're also friends."

Contrasts, Valery thought again. She had never met Smith Kendricks, but she'd read about him often in the pages of the *Times-Picayune* and local magazines. He was as much a fixture of the hard news stories, prosecuting this criminal or that, as of the society pages, attending some charity event or squiring some beautiful, wealthy and sophisticated woman. He came from wealth and sophistication himself, was considered the best prosecutor in town—even better than his boss—and also the most eligible bachelor in the city, if not the entire state.

And he was friends with Michael. With this simple, private, intensely serious man.

She gestured toward the answering machine. "Is this call business or personal?"

His smile was faintly reproving. "I don't know. I'm not a mind reader."

"Not at all?"

He shook his head. "Was that the only call?"

She nodded.

"Come on into the bedroom. I'll find a place to put your stuff."

She had admired his bedroom earlier, had found it a safe place, but now she hung back. "I can put it in the closet over there. It'll be more convenient, since I'll be sleeping on the sofa."

Stopping in the doorway, he looked back at her. "I'll sleep on the sofa."

"No, don't be silly. This is your home. I don't want to put you—"

With a level, dry look, he stopped her in midprotest. She had already put him out, she realized, in ways far more serious, far more important, than where she slept. "I don't usually sleep much anyway," he said, further piquing her interest. "When I do, I can do it anywhere. You take the bedroom, where I won't disturb you."

But *she* would disturb *him,* she thought regretfully. She'd been doing it for the better part of a week.

She followed him into the bedroom and opened the box that he set on the bed. While he cleared a place in the closet and got her some hangers, she began unpacking, happy to see in the bag of toiletries her makeup kit and a cobalt blue atomizer filled with her favorite cologne. She spritzed her wrists and throat with the fragrance before setting it on the bed, pushing the pile of lingerie aside and removing two pairs of shoes.

The tennis shoes made perfect sense. The leather shoes she'd been wearing when she had arrived last night were still soaked, even though she'd stuffed them with newspaper. But the slippers? They were dressy, too dressy for the jeans and sweats he'd brought. She could imagine another man making such a mistake, but not Michael, with his artist's sensibilities, his unerring knowledge of what went together and what didn't.

She placed the shoes in the closet and hung her clothes on the rod he had cleared. As soon as he finished emptying one of the small drawers in the mahogany dresser, she carelessly, hastily dumped her lingerie inside and closed it. Leaving the bag of bathroom items on the bed, she knelt to push the empty box into the corner of the closet. When she stood and turned again, she came to an abrupt stop.

Her dress. He was holding her dress.

Her first impulse was to smile. She loved that dress and had paid a small fortune for it, even with the discount her boss had given her. She'd never regretted the purchase, even if it had made money tight for a while, even though she'd had few opportunities to wear it. It was beautiful, old-fashioned and, oh, so romantic, and it made her feel beautiful and romantic.

But the smile never quite formed. He didn't offer any explanations as to why he'd packed jeans, sweatpants and an antique lace dress, but she knew. The answer was in the fierceness in his expression. In the knowledge that he hadn't wanted to bring the dress, that he'd felt compelled to do so. In the certainty that he didn't want to see her wearing it . . . and that maybe he wanted it too much.

The ivory lace looked so pale against his skin, so fragile compared to the powerful hands that held it. As she studied the contrasts, as she considered his ambivalence, she found herself wanting to sway him to the wanting rather than the not wanting. She found herself wanting to wear it for him.

To feel beautiful and, oh, so romantic in it.

With him.

With a stranger.

She approached him slowly, one small step at a time, and Michael watched her. He knew he should keep her at a safe distance, should offer it to her, hand it over and walk away, but he didn't. He held it, feeling the texture of the lace and the finely woven fabric—linen, he thought, not sure and not caring—against his fingers, and he waited for her to come to him.

When she was right in front of him, she stopped. He could smell her perfume, a subtle floral fragrance, Oriental in flavor. He could see the distinct shadings of blue in her eyes. He could hear her soft, steady breathing, the measured sort of breaths that indicated a conscious effort to maintain control.

Without releasing his gaze, she reached for the dress, her fingers brushing across his, her careful and firm tug removing the garment from his hands. She didn't ask why he'd brought it, didn't point out that she was in hiding, that she wasn't likely to find an occasion to wear it while she was secluded in his apartment. He was grateful for that, because if she had, he might have responded that they could make their own occasion. He might have told her that he would be as appreciative of her appearance in the dress as any crowd could be.

He might even have told her that his primary interest in getting her into the dress would be the pleasure of then getting her out of it.

Such pleasure. Such foolishness. Such danger.

He wasn't ready for a relationship. There was too much sorrow in his life, too much emptiness. He barely managed to care about himself; he had nothing left over to give someone else. He had nothing to offer. No hope. No faith. No future.

At the same time, as if in silent accord, they both turned away, Valery going to the closet, Michael into the living room and onto the balcony that looked out over the square.

It was a typical winter Saturday afternoon. There were artists set up along the iron fence, selling their paintings and caricatures to tourists who came from places cold enough that they didn't mind the chill in the air. A smiling group of Japanese tourists posed in front of the statue of Andrew Jackson in the center of the square, and over in front of the cathedral a band consisting primarily of horns played jazz for donations.

He envied all those strangers down there without a care in the world, with nothing more important on their minds than where to go for dinner tonight or which sights to see next. He had felt like that the first time he'd come to New Orleans, but that had been so long ago. It had been another world, another life.

Another Michael.

Now he had cares. He had important things to think about—such as the woman in his bedroom. Such as his job to protect her—and his need to protect himself *from* her. Such as Remy and Falcone.

He would call Remy, he decided. Lying to his best friend didn't set well with Michael, and that was exactly what he was doing by not telling him about Valery. He would arrange a meeting, would explain everything. He would tell him that she was safe, that he was looking out for her, but that he had to deal with her on his own for now. Remy would understand. He would trust Michael to know what was right, then trust him to do it.

For one weary moment his fingers curved around the iron rail. He wasn't sure he wanted Remy's trust, wasn't sure at all that he wanted Valery's. Trust could be a gift to be well guarded. It could be a reward for hard work and effort. It could just as easily be a burden. Trust was what had brought him to where he was today. If Evan hadn't trusted him, he never would have offered his help last time and he wouldn't be dead. If Remy and Smith hadn't trusted him, they wouldn't have gotten him involved *this* time. They wouldn't have put Valery's safety—maybe even her life—in his hands, and she wouldn't be somewhere in his apartment, her clothes hanging in his closet, her pillow on his bed, her perfume scenting the air. She wouldn't be eating meals at his table or bathing in his tub.

She wouldn't be sleeping in his bed tonight.

But since she would be, he thought with a cynical grin, it was too damn bad that *he* wouldn't be. He could use the diversion of a few hours' pleasure, of mindless, meaningless sex. Unfortunately he'd never learned how to have mindless diversions or meaningless sex. Maybe it was because his father was a minister, and in their small town, everyone had expected certain standards of behavior from the preacher's kids. Maybe it had something to do with the fact that his parents had been happily married for more than forty years, maybe because commitment and devotion had always played such a strong part in his family's relationships. When a Bennett married, he did it for life, until-death-do-us-part. His had been the first—and still the only—divorce in family history.

Whatever the reason, he'd never had affairs—no one-night stands, no brief encounters. He'd never been to bed with a woman he hadn't been serious about.

And he sure as hell couldn't start with Valery Navarre.

As if summoned by his thoughts, she spoke from behind him. "Michael?"

He turned and leaned back against the railing, bracing his hands on each side. She was standing inside, well away from the door. He liked that about her—that she took her situation seriously, that he didn't have to remind her to stay out of sight.

"Do you mind if I make some cocoa?"

"No, go ahead." For a time he remained where he was, unable to see her but all too easily able to match her movements with the noises he heard—the opening of the refrigerator, the sound of the microwave, the clink of a spoon against a ceramic mug.

A moment later she reappeared in his line of vision, carrying two mugs. She offered one silently. Pushing himself away from the railing, he took it, then closed the doors and joined her in the living area. She went to the couch, making herself comfortable, propping her feet on the table and holding her cup in both hands. He sat down once again in the chair where he had spent most of last night.

"Do you have insomnia?" she asked as soon as he was settled.

"Why do you ask?"

"You said you usually don't sleep much."

So he had. She was observant, paying attention even to casual conversation. "Yes, I do." His trouble sleeping had started so long ago that now he couldn't recall exactly when. He had never tried to determine the cause, had never tried to do anything about it. He'd just learned to live with it, to sleep when he could and do something productive—read, usually—when he couldn't.

He'd read more than anyone he knew.

"When I first went to live with my aunt and uncle, I had problems sleeping." Her tone was casual, as if going to live with the Sinclairs hadn't been traumatic, as if her move to

Belclaire had been just a normal, everyday thing. But, in spite of her airiness, he didn't believe that was the case. Like him, Valery Navarre must carry some scars. She just hid them better than he hid his.

"You were going through some major changes," he remarked, his voice as neutral as hers had been.

She flashed a surface-deep smile. "Yeah, moving from the city to the country—and from a tiny two-bedroom apartment to a fourteen-room plantation house—*is* quite a change."

"To say nothing of being abandoned by your parents."

Her phony, glittering smile froze, then slowly faded. "I don't believe I said anything about being abandoned by my parents," she said slowly, warily.

"You said your aunt and uncle raised you after your parents divorced." He was observant, too. He'd heard what she had said in their earlier conversation. More importantly, he'd heard what she hadn't said. "It's customary in most divorce settlements for custody of the children to go to one parent or the other, not to an aunt and uncle."

After a moment, she sighed. "After nearly twelve years of marriage, my mother decided that she didn't want to be married anymore, and she didn't want to be a mother anymore. So one day, while my—my father was at work and I was in school, she packed up everything and left. And since he was no longer a husband, he saw no reason to be stuck playing father. He took me to his sister, and I lived with her family until I started college."

He wondered about the way she'd faltered in referring to her father. There was more involved, he suspected, than a man deciding to wash his hands of responsibility for his daughter. What was she leaving out?

He didn't press. There would be time enough for that later, if it became important, and the only reason it might was if *she* became important. *Too* important.

He didn't intend to let that happen.

"Did your aunt and uncle have any kids of their own?"

"One. A son." Her eyes darkened, and her manner grew stiffer, more guarded.

What was between her and Remy? Michael wondered. Why had they spent most of their adult lives not speaking? What problem could be so serious between them that, when her life was in danger, she couldn't turn to him for help?

"Sort of a big brother, huh?"

"No." She spoke very clearly, very firmly. "We didn't get along."

"Sounds like a little sibling rivalry."

"Rivalry, maybe. Sibling, no. Not at all."

Before he could consider that, before he could wonder at the implications of it, she smiled, *really* smiled, the sort of smile that could make a man stop dead still. "Enough about my cousin and me," she said. "Tell me about *your* siblings. Sisters, you said?"

Bedtime came too quickly to suit Valery. She should have welcomed it—God knew she was tired, and for the first night in a week she had a safe place to sleep—but she felt funny taking Michael's bed, having all that comfort and room to snuggle while he was making do with a blanket, a pillow and the sofa.

She felt even funnier thinking of him in the bed.

They'd had a quiet dinner—a spicy stew that he'd taken from the freezer and thawed in the microwave—and then she had watched TV while he had just sort of *watched*—her, the apartment, the square. It wasn't as if he were expecting trouble, but he would be prepared if it came. Now he was in the shower and she was in his room, preparing to get into his bed.

Alone.

When he'd packed her clothing at the apartment, he hadn't bothered with her robe, hanging on the back of the bathroom door. She wondered if he had seen it and decided it was too bulky, if he had intended to bring a nightgown instead. He wouldn't have found any nightclothes if he had looked; she didn't own any. Since she'd been seventeen or so, she had always found naked the best way to sleep—in her own bed. Until tonight she'd never tried it in a man's bed. Not when he wasn't sleeping with her.

She peeled off her socks and sweatpants, then turned back the covers. The sheets were hunter green, and the comforter was a matching green, navy and crimson, with strong stripes on one side and an intricate paisley design on the other. They were soft, top quality. Her cop had good taste.

Only he wasn't hers, she admonished herself as she stripped off the rest of her clothing. Not by any stretch of the imagination.

Leaving the bedside lamp burning, she slid between the sheets, tucking them around her, and rested her head on her pillow. It was interesting, this mix of old and new, of strange and familiar—his bed, her pillow. His bold, masculine linens and her feminine embroidered and lace-edged pillowcase. His scent on his bedclothes, her scent on hers.

She wished she knew him better, wished she had answers to questions she hadn't yet asked. After today's conversations he'd learned more about her—more, she suspected, than he'd wanted to know—and she had learned plenty about his home, his art and his family. But she knew practically nothing about *him*.

She didn't know why he was troubled. Why his eyes were so often bleak. What had driven him to create those troubling paintings of churches. She didn't know what sorrow haunted him.

She didn't really know anything at all—except that he was helping her. He was giving her the secure place she needed, the time she needed. He was making room for her—temporarily—in his life. He was prepared to do whatever it took to keep her safe.

She knew a few other things, too. That he was handsome. That in spite of the bleakness and the sorrow, she was attracted to him. That the attraction was stronger than with any other man she'd ever known. That there probably wasn't much that could come of it, because she couldn't trust him fully and he, she suspected, didn't trust himself at all.

Down the hall, even though two doors were closed between them, she heard the shower shut off. He would dry off now, get dressed and return to the living room, where he would spend most of the night not sleeping. She wondered whether he would watch television or read one of the novels that filled the corner bookcase. Or would he ignore the chill and stand out on the balcony again and stare at God knew what. The empty square? The occasional passerby? The Mississippi River bridge?

Or maybe the cathedral. The church that, judging from his painting of it, could offer him no peace. Did he want peace? Had he tried and failed to find it there? Was that why those two paintings had been filled with such hopelessness?

Her shiver made her burrow deeper beneath the covers until she was properly cocooned. Even though she had a million more thoughts to think, her eyes were growing heavy, her breathing slowing and evening out. She had survived another day. With Michael in the other room, she was safe. Tonight she could sleep, and he would worry for her.

Just before she drifted off, she mouthed a silent prayer—for her own safety, as she had done for the last five nights, and now for Michael's. She prayed that the men who had killed Nate Simmons would be caught and that this nightmare would end. She prayed for the guidance she needed to make the proper decision regarding Remy.

And she prayed for assurance. With all the problems Michael already had in his life, she asked God not to let *her* be one more than he could bear.

The apartment was quiet. Occasionally the refrigerator motor switched on for a moment or two, and less often the heat came on, sending a blast of warm air into the room, but for the most part it was quiet.

Michael was well accustomed to silence. Unlike most of his friends who lived alone, he didn't use the television or the radio to disturb his solitude, didn't need the distractions, didn't need to pretend that he wasn't alone. Most of his life he'd been comfortable with silence, maybe because he'd found so little of it. Growing up back in Arkansas, his sisters had ensured that there was always noise of some sort. In college, the dorm where he'd lived his first year and the apartment he'd shared with Evan, Remy and Smith the remaining three years had been busy places, with someone always coming or going, stereos blaring, arguments waging.

He'd taken his silence where he could find it—in the woods surrounding the fields he had helped his father farm. In a library alcove with built-in desks for serious studying. On long middle-of-the-night walks along the river when there was nothing but the lapping of water against the levee and the occasional passing car.

And in church. Every service he'd ever attended had included moments of quiet for reflection, for silent prayer, for communion. It had been easy back then, sitting on a padded wooden pew, touched by the multicolored light that came through the stained-glass windows, surrounded by belief, by faith, by reverence. Easy to believe in God. Easy to believe in prayer. Easy to believe in eternity and final rewards for lives well lived.

Good and evil. Salvation, damnation. Heaven and hell. Evan's death had taken more from Michael than his friend and partner, far more than the man he'd respected most and loved best. It had stolen the balance from his life, from his faith. Good no longer triumphed over evil. Salvation was an empty promise. And he'd found his own hell right here on earth.

Now he tolerated the quiet. It didn't comfort him, as it once had. It had become merely a respite from the noise of the world. It was no longer a time to reflect. To pray. To renew. It was simply silence. The same silence that had met his prayers for Evan. The same empty, unforgiving silence that had met his curses when his prayers had gone unanswered.

God had deserted him that night last spring, and he had repaid the favor in kind.

With a sigh, Michael rolled onto his side so he could see the kitchen clock: 3:21. He'd read for the five hours since Valery had gone to bed, but now, though he was no closer to sleep than he had been, his eyes were gritty and tired. He knew the routine. Now it was time to simply lie there, eyes closed, and relax. If he was lucky, soon he would drift off and sleep enough to take the edge off his weariness.

But there were things he had to do first. Throwing back the blanket, he got to his feet. He checked the French doors, even though he knew they were locked, and the front door, which was still as secure—lock, dead bolt and chain—as it had been the last two times he'd checked.

It was on his way back that he noticed the bedroom light was still on. He headed in that direction, hesitating a moment before tapping lightly at the door. When there was no answer, he twisted the knob and the door swung noiselessly in.

Valery was lying on his side of the bed, facing him, her black hair a dramatic slash across the snowy-white pillowcase. She was sleeping deeply, the kind of heavy, restorative sleep that he rarely got, the kind that she badly needed.

He wondered if he could find that sort of rest with her at his side.

For a time he considered staying, drawing a chair close and simply watching her as he'd done most of last night. If she happened to awaken and find him there, she wouldn't mind, not if he told her it was for her safety.

But then she shifted onto her stomach, sliding both arms free of the covers to pillow her head, and he realized that she was naked, and he knew he couldn't stay. Not with the arousal that simple glimpse—bare arms, bare shoulders—had awakened inside him. Not with the desire to see more of her. Not with the need to touch her that was as strong as his desire. Not with the hunger for intimacy that had gone too long unsatisfied.

Even knowing he had to leave, he delayed. It had been a long time since he'd experienced these particular emotions. Lately he'd just been too empty. Before that there had been the drinking, the grief, the sorrow. He had almost died when Evan had, had tried to finish the job with booze. Thanks to Remy, in particular, and to Smith, he had survived physically, but not emotionally. Not spiritually.

He had forgotten how it felt to be aroused. Pain and pleasure. Sweet and bitter. Full of promise. Anticipation. Connection. If he could make love to Valery Navarre, he could feel alive again. He could want. For a time, at least, he could give, receive and satisfy. He could prove that all the good hadn't gone out of his life, that not only the negative remained. Through intimacy with her he could once again become intimate with himself.

He could find hope—hope that, if his emotions weren't dead, maybe his spirit had also survived. That maybe someday he could find it again. Maybe someday he would be whole again.

If he could make love to Valery Navarre. To the stranger who had invaded his mind days before intruding into his life. To Remy's cousin. To the woman he had promised against all his better judgment to protect.

If he could make love to Valery.

Which, of course, in all fairness—to her, to Remy, to himself—he couldn't.

He shouldn't.

He wouldn't.

Chapter 5

"Tell me about the murder."

Meeting Michael's gaze, Valery slowly licked powder sugar from her fingertips, then wiped her hands on a paper napkin. She hadn't realized until this morning one of the tremendous advantages of living exactly where he did: fresh *beignets* and coffee from the Café du Monde any time of the day or night. Once a week she stopped by on her way to work and picked up a bag to share with her part-time help, but by the time she reached the shop, the *beignets* had cooled enough to become greasy, and the powdered sugar had collected in clumps. These, though, had been perfectly done when Michael returned with them.

"You've read the papers," she remarked.

"Yes, and I've seen the TV stories, but the reporters weren't there. *You* were. I want to know what you saw."

What she'd seen wasn't the problem, she thought grimly. What she'd *heard* was.

"You were leaving work."

She nodded.

"Why so early?"

"I work nine to three through the week and all day Saturday."

"So you always leave at that time."

"Always." It was her habit, and she had always been a creature of habit. The past week had made her value those habits even more. There was something reassuring about knowing that she would be home in time to see her favorite daytime talk show, that her house would be clean on Monday and her laundry done on Wednesday. There was a certain comfort in having *beignets* for breakfast on Thursdays, in knowing her route home so well that she could drive it with her eyes shut, in reading in bed to the accompaniment of David Letterman on weeknights. Routine was so familiar, so... well, *routine*.

"And you always walk the same route to your car?"

She nodded.

He shook his head, his expression faintly dismayed. "You're a single woman who lives alone in the nineties. Don't you know the world is dangerous? That you should vary your routine?"

"If you vary it, then it's not a routine anymore," she replied dryly; then, with a sigh, she answered seriously. "Come on, Michael, I'm a shopkeeper. I earn a living wage, I work six days a week, and I deal with antique clothing. It's not as if I'm important enough for anyone to care. There's not enough of a market for antique clothes for my job to be a danger, no one's going to kidnap me and hold me for ransom, and I certainly don't look prosperous enough to rob. How could my routine possibly matter to anyone?"

"There are a lot of motives for kidnapping besides ransom," he pointed out mildly, "and I've seen people killed for a few dollars and change." He emptied the last of the coffee into his cup and stirred a scant bit of sugar into it. "If you took a different route to your car every day, chances are five out of six that you wouldn't have been on that particular block at that particular time."

She couldn't even argue the point with him. Hadn't she berated herself only a few days ago for being so predictable? "All right," she said, giving in. "If I ever get to go back to my job—if I even have a job to go back to—I won't walk to the car the same way every day."

"So... tell me about that day. Tell me about Nate Simmons."

"I had turned onto Chartres. I was right in the middle of the block when a man—when Simmons came out of a store. He bumped into me, knocked my purse to the ground and picked it up."

"Did he palm anything?"

She smiled faintly, but it felt wrong—profane—when she was talking about a dead man. The smile faded as quickly as it had come. "That was my first thought, too, but no. He picked up my bag, handed it back to me and started walking with me. He was very talkative, very friendly."

"What did he say?"

"He told me I was pretty, asked if I was alone, if I was in New Orleans on vacation. He asked if I minded a little company." Again she smiled. He had been too brash, too confident—not her type at all. But she had found his obvious flattery charming, and she had been pretty confident that she could get rid of him when it became necessary. "I didn't see any harm in letting him walk with me. We were on a busy street in the middle of the French Quarter in the middle of the afternoon. What could possibly happen?"

Michael's voice was soft, his tone gentle, when he gave the obvious answer. "A man could get killed."

"Yes," she agreed in a whisper. Wetting her fingertip, she pressed it into the powdered sugar remaining on the plate between them, then licked it clean. She didn't want to continue this conversation any further, didn't want to get to the part where the man *did* get killed. She didn't want to remember her terror, so strong that she couldn't give voice to the scream rising inside her. She didn't want to feel again the nausea that had overwhelmed her when she'd recognized the stains on her clothing as the stranger's blood.

She didn't want to go through the whole story, to present it as the truth, the whole truth, while leaving out the worst part, the part suggesting that, while the dead man had been a stranger to her, the man who had ordered his death wasn't.

"What happened next, Valery?"

"We reached the end of the block." She spoke mechanically, forcing herself to recite facts without remembering emotion. "There was a car there, and these two men got out. The man—Simmons—he knew them. He wasn't surprised to see them. He grinned, called one of them by name—Vince—and started to say something to the other. I thought it was my chance to ditch him. I could leave him with his friends and go on to the lot and get my car. But before I could, he stopped in the middle of a sentence, and he swore, and that was when I saw the guns. That was when they shot him. He looked so...surprised." Not frightened. Not angry. Not disappointed. Just surprised.

Had Nate Simmons known, Michael wondered, why Falcone was turning on him? Had he been aware of whatever sin he had committed against his boss, or had he been caught totally in the dark?

"The two men," Valery continued. "Vince and the other guy—they were so calm. They didn't care that I'd seen them. They didn't care that there were other people down the street. They acted like nothing was wrong—just put their guns away, strolled back to the car and drove away. They never hurried. They were cool."

"When you kill people for a living, you learn to be cool about it," he said idly, his mind still on why Simmons had been killed. "If you panic, you make mistakes, and if you make mistakes in that business, you don't stay healthy long."

A shiver rippled through her, and she rubbed her arms to dispel it. "Why was he killed? And why like that—in public, with witnesses? Why not do it in private and dump his body someplace where it wouldn't be found for a while?"

"I don't know why. As for the method, maybe they wanted him to be found. Maybe they wanted someone to know how easily they could get rid of a problem."

"Maybe it was a message?" she asked.

He shrugged. "Or a warning. Or maybe it was just arrogance. Falcone thinks he's above the law. He thinks he can get away with anything."

She responded to his words more seriously than he'd expected. "So far he has. No one's been arrested yet. And even though the men work for Falcone, no one's been able to tie him to it, have they? All the crimes he's committed, no one's ever been able to tie him to any of them." She left the table, carrying dishes into the kitchen and rinsing them before returning. She didn't sit down this time, though; instead, she paced the length of the room and back again. "I wish we could go somewhere."

He didn't remind her that they couldn't—that *she* couldn't. Her tone made it clear that she was all too well aware of that, that it was merely a fruitless wish. She knew she had to stay inside, off the streets and out of danger.

"Those first few days, until I came here, all I wanted was to hide in a tiny, dark room where no one could find me. Now I'd like to take a walk, even if it's to nowhere. I'd like to join the tourists and window-shop, listen to some music and watch the river."

"Being safe gets boring, doesn't it?"

She gave him an unwilling smile. "I'm not bored—just restless. Given a choice, this is exactly how I would choose to spend a winter Sunday—inside with breakfast, a newspaper, someone to talk to and nothing to do. It's not having the choice that makes it hard." Dropping into one of the two armchairs, she dangled her legs over the side and swung her feet back and forth. "What do you normally do on Sundays?"

"Watch TV, go out with friends, paint."

"Tell me about your friends—the ones who are as close as family."

He thought of Smith, whose call he hadn't yet returned, and Remy, who he also hadn't yet called. Tomorrow, he promised himself. He would catch him on his way to work tomorrow and tell him all about Valery.

Tell me about your friends. She made the request so easily, so breezily, and it would be as easy for him to obey. But talk without names would rouse her suspicions, and giving her the names would endanger her trust. If she wouldn't accept protection from Remy, she likely wouldn't accept it from his best friend, either.

"I'd rather not," he replied, his gaze even, his tone deliberately bland.

There was a momentary flash of emotion in her eyes. Hurt, he thought with surprise. He had answered all her questions—maybe not fully, but he had answered them just the same—until now, and she was just the slightest bit wounded that he wasn't going to answer this one. But she was responsible for his refusal. Until she trusted him with the truth about Remy, he certainly couldn't bring him up.

"All right. I understand." Her voice was frosty, her expression just short of a pout.

"Valery, my friends are—"

"Personal," she interrupted. "And this is business."

"Honey, there's not much that's more personal than having you inside my head," he pointed out wryly.

Her bad humor forgotten, she smiled slowly, provocatively. From five feet away it touched him, warmed him, wrapped itself around him with a haze of exotic scents and subtle hints. With no more than that, she damn near seduced him, and her soft promise almost finished the job. "You're wrong, Michael. I can get *much* more personal than that."

Finding his throat dry, he swallowed. An image of her as she'd looked last night—soft and relaxed, her troubles eased by sleep, her skin winter pale—came back, accompanied by more than a twinge of the way he'd felt seeing her. Desire. It was a comforting discomfort. A welcome reminder from his body that he was still alive, that he still had needs. It was pleasurable just feeling those needs.

And outright torment thinking about fulfilling them.

Only this morning, standing in the stillness of his room and watching her sleep, he had accepted the reasons why he couldn't have an affair with her. Their circumstances were too tenuous to risk the distraction of a relationship. Getting through this stranger to stranger would be hard enough; he couldn't afford to make it personal. She deserved better than he could offer—any woman did—while he didn't deserve anything at all.

But could a man be held to decisions reached in the middle of a sleepless night, when all was quiet, when everything seemed possible and nothing seemed likely?

Yes.

But those decisions could also be changed. If Valery was willing. If they shared the attraction, the desire, the risks. If she knew exactly what she would get. If he knew exactly what he could take.

She might be willing. That smile—that promise—suggested she was. But she didn't know all the things he couldn't give her. She didn't know all the things he needed to take.

She didn't know him.

Didn't know his life. His failures.

She didn't know what an utterly empty man he had become.

Forcing his muscles to relax, his voice to remain neutral, he ignored their last exchange and returned to the topic preceding it. "Tell me about *your* friends. Who's worrying about you?" What kind of people appealed to her? What kind of women did she befriend and what kind did she avoid? What kind of men did she like, date, get involved with?

"I'm not sure anyone is, besides my aunt and uncle."

"And your cousin."

She shook her head. "I doubt that."

Although he knew she was wrong, he let the remark slide. It wouldn't be wise to show too much interest in Remy. "No girlfriends who miss you? No boyfriends?"

"No girlfriends. No boyfriends. No lovers."

His muscles began tightening again. "Why not?"

"Why not which one?" She shrugged. "I have friends that I see on a fairly regular basis, but it's not unusual for weeks to go by without any contact."

"You don't think they've heard about what happened and worried about you?"

"Maybe some of them. Most of them would say, 'Gee, too bad. I hope she's all right,' and go on with their lives." She drew her feet into the seat and wrapped her arms around her knees. "I told you, I don't have really close friends. My friends are people I like and enjoy spending a few hours with from time to time, but they're not that important in my life, and I'm not that important in theirs. I wouldn't wish anything bad on them, and vice versa, but we're not close."

"Why do you keep them at a distance?"

Valery fixed her gaze on the gauzy curtains at the window, watching as they swayed in the current from the heating vent below. "I don't—"

"Are you afraid they'll leave you the way your parents did?"

Ruefully she wished she'd echoed his response when she had asked him to tell her about his friends. *I'd rather not.* It would have been safer and more comfortable by far.

Was she afraid? She would like to think the answer was no, that she hadn't made many friends for the simple reason that she didn't need them. She was happy with her own company. She liked spending most of her evenings alone. She liked not having the responsibility that came with a serious friendship. She didn't want the benefits of real friendship—the caring, the sharing, the companionship—enough to meet the obligations—emotional support, giving in exchange for what she took, being there when things were bad, remembering special days, providing a shoulder to cry on.

She would like to believe all that was true.

But it wasn't.

Her mother, her father and Remy had taught her a simple lesson, one she had learned well: if she didn't let anyone into her life, then no one could abandon her. For that reason all her relationships were shallow, nothing more than surface deep, never involving any emotion stronger than liking. She liked the friends she went shopping with, the ones she saw movies with, the ones she shared dinners with. She liked the men she'd dated, had liked each one she'd gone to bed with.

She *liked* them, but she didn't need them.

She hadn't needed anyone since Remy.

Michael moved, a blur at the edge of her vision, from the table to the other armchair. That placed him in her line of vision, a still figure waiting patiently for her answer. She gave it with a shrug. "It's a matter of choice. You need friends in your life. *I* don't."

"You need me."

She shook her head. "I *want* you. I want your help. I want you to keep me safe. But there's a world of difference between wanting and needing. I don't need you. I don't need anyone."

He studied her for a moment, so quiet, so thoughtful. Whatever he saw—untruthfulness, deceit, vulnerability—he kept to himself. Instead, in a lighter tone—a damn near condescending tone, she thought with a scowl—he agreed. "Okay. So you don't need me. What would you be doing without me?"

"I'd be out of the city."

"And where would you go?"

"I don't know. Texas. Then probably Mexico."

"How would you travel? By plane? Bus? Are you sure no one's watching the airport or bus station?"

"Maybe I would rent a car—"

"How do you know the rental agencies aren't covered? And how can you rent a car without a driver's license? You left your purse in your own car when you ditched it. The FBI has it now."

She scowled harder. "Or borrow a car from a friend. Maybe I'd hitch a ride."

He simply gave her another of those long looks that made her shift uncomfortably. All right, she grudgingly, silently, agreed, maybe traveling wouldn't be so easy. But if her life depended on it, if it was a choice between managing to leave the state or facing Falcone's people—or Remy's—she could manage. Somehow.

"Say that you make it to Texas, to the Mexican border. How are you going to cross without some sort of documentation?"

Triumphantly she smiled. "I had a friend in college who was from San Diego. You can go across for shopping or whatever without any problem. All you have to do is show proof of residence when you come back."

"So you pretend to be making a day trip. You cross the border, then disappear. How?"

Because she had no answer, she didn't say anything. She hadn't thought that far ahead. All she had considered was escaping the panic and the fear. Minor things like details hadn't entered into it.

"Do you speak Spanish? How are you going to support yourself when your money runs out? How are you going to protect yourself down there? Falcone's men aren't the only people in the world you have reason to fear. A pretty, naive woman all alone in a foreign country, doesn't speak the language, doesn't even have the legal right to be there... You'd make an easy target, sweetheart."

The phone rang, and he glanced at it before rising to his feet. On his way to the table where it sat, he stopped in front of her, resting his hand lightly on hers. "Maybe you could make it on your own out there, Valery. Maybe it would get easier with time. Maybe you could run so far that you could outrun the fear, and maybe you'd get used to missing the U.S. and New Orleans, to spending holidays alone, to keeping your past a secret, to never being able to see or talk to or write to your family. But you don't have to find out. If you let..."

He hesitated. *Us,* he'd been about to say. She knew it. *If you let us help*... Him. The police. The FBI.

"If you let me help, we'll find a way out of this. We'll make it safe for you to stay here, to go back home, to go back to your life. I promise."

She didn't look at him. She couldn't.

After one last ring, the answering machine picked up the call. He withdrew his hand and picked up the receiver before the outgoing message was completed. "Hey, Smith," she heard him say as he walked toward the French doors. "I've been meaning to call you." Then he went out onto the balcony, and she couldn't hear any more.

Damn him for taking away her only other option, she thought, only mildly annoyed in spite of the curse. Now, if she changed her mind, if for some reason she had to leave this apartment, she would have to do some serious planning—planning that she wasn't sure she could manage on her own.

Of course, running away wasn't her *only* other option. There was always Michael's first choice: the FBI. She could always decide to hell with Remy and his career and their family. She could cast enough doubt on her cousin that he wouldn't be able to get within fifty miles of her, enough doubt that his reputation would be forever stained.

Even if she was wrong.

There was also one other choice: She could tell Michael everything. She could trust him enough to hope that he would believe her, could trust that he would give her his best advice. But he was a cop. If he believed her, he would have to take some action. Remy would be in just as much trouble, and their family would wind up just as irreparably damaged.

Those arguments aside, there was one even stronger reason for not confiding in Michael: She didn't trust him. Not enough.

Not yet.

Maybe not ever.

Michael was up early enough Monday morning to watch the sun come up over the river, but the rays couldn't cut through the heavy cloud layer and the rain that left the pavement shining under the street lamp. He was tired of rain, tired of winter, tired of gloom. He wished for summer, but knew he would complain then about the unbearable heat, the mugginess and the tourists who thronged the city. Sometimes, he thought with a wry smile, it seemed he could never be satisfied.

And then he thought of Valery, spending her second night in his bed, and his smile disappeared.

She could satisfy him.

After Smith's phone call had interrupted their conversation yesterday, the rest of the day had passed more quietly. They had read and watched old movies on TV and talked very little. As dusk settled, they had started dinner together, at Valery's insistence, until they discovered rather quickly that the kitchen was too small for both of them. It was impossible to maneuver without constantly brushing against each other, and the contact had left them both equally unsettled. Finally she had volunteered to set the table instead, and when that was done, she had sat there and waited.

After dinner she'd gone to bed early, a book from his shelves tucked under her arm. He wondered now as he watched the rain if she'd gone to sleep easily. If she'd noticed how big the queen-size bed was when she was in it alone. If she had entertained, even for a moment, the notion of sharing it.

Turning away from the door, he went to the kitchen and removed a roll from the microwave. Evan's aunt Sirena had taught him to cook but hadn't been able to interest him in baking, so she kept his freezer well stocked with cinnamon rolls, muffins and an occasional cake from her own kitchen. It made for an easy breakfast, especially when he had things to do.

And this morning he was meeting with Remy.

He had already called his friend, had asked for a meeting in Jackson Square at eight o'clock. He felt guilty about it—after all, hadn't he promised Valery that he wouldn't tell anyone where she was? He owed it to her to keep that promise.

But he owed Remy a whole lot more. Like his life.

He ate the roll while writing a note to Valery, then changed from the gym shorts he'd slept in to jeans and a T-shirt. Yesterday he'd moved some of his clothes from the bedroom to the laundry closet so he wouldn't have to disturb Valery—in truth, so he wouldn't have to disturb himself—by going into the room while she slept. This morning he was grateful for it. He didn't want to face her while he was getting ready to break his promise to her.

By the time he'd clipped his Beretta in place and put on a waterproof jacket, it was ten minutes till eight. He checked the locks on the French doors, propped up the note on the dining table and left the apartment with the only sound the necessary clicks of tumblers turning and locks relocking.

The rain had been falling hard enough and long enough to puddle in low-lying areas around the square. There would be no artists out today, no musicians playing for a few bucks. Some tourists would venture out, huddled under umbrellas or wearing cheap plastic ponchos that could be bought in just about every Quarter gift shop, but even they would give up after a few hours of cold misery and return to their hotels. Tonight would be a different story, though. Even if it was still raining, they would come out, eager for a fine meal in an expensive restaurant, for too many drinks in too many bars or the prurient entertainment to be found in the Bourbon Street clubs.

Tonight *he* would be home, dry and warm.

With Valery.

Who, with no more than a look, with no more than her mere presence, could make him entirely *too* warm.

His shoulders hunched against the rain that dripped from his hair, he entered the square through the side gate and did a quick sweep of the park. He spotted two men near the statue of Andrew Jackson, both wearing dark suits and overcoats, one under a black umbrella, pacing restlessly, the other—Remy—bareheaded and motionless.

As he approached, Remy spoke to his partner, then met Michael halfway. "Couldn't we have gone someplace a little less damp?" he asked in greeting, his voice as dry as the weather wasn't. "My shoes will never be the same."

A glance down showed that he was likely right. That kind of expensive leather wasn't meant for this kind of weather. "If you people dressed like normal folks, you wouldn't have to worry about such things. My tennis shoes won't be any the worse for wear."

There was a moment's silence while they studied each other. Remy looked tired, worried—and no doubt he was.

Whatever the problems between him and Valery, she was still his family.

"You still look like hell. Been getting any sleep?" Remy asked.

"Some." Michael rubbed one hand across his jaw, bristly and rough, then slicked his hair back. "You don't look much better."

"It's been a tough week."

After another brief silence, Michael asked, "Who's under the umbrella?"

"Wilson. He's working on Falcone with me."

Travis Wilson. Michael didn't know him well and didn't like him at all. It wasn't that he was a bad cop; he just wasn't a very good one. He was sloppy in a business where sloppiness could be a fatal flaw. Maybe he would learn something from Remy, but Michael wouldn't bet on it.

Shoving his hands into his pockets, Remy tilted his head back and raised his gaze to the leaden sky. "This weather is perfect. It matches the way everything else has been going lately." Finally looking back at Michael, he said, "My parents have been calling every day. This is the first time I've heard from them in fifteen years, and it's because of Valery."

Michael didn't ask if he meant it was Valery's fault that he hadn't heard from them in fifteen years or if she was the only reason he was hearing from them now. He didn't ask why there was both bitterness and regret in Remy's voice, both resentment and concern in his expression.

"They're sick with worrying about her, and it doesn't help that I don't have anything to tell them. Of course, they're used to my letting them down, so they're not surprised."

Michael glanced at Wilson, still out of earshot, then, just for good measure, he moved a half-dozen feet farther away. Remy followed. "You've got to promise not to do anything with what I'm going to tell you. You can't tell anyone, not even your parents."

Remy gave him a hard look. "If it involves this case, I can't—"

"Forget the damned case and promise."

"Michael—"

"You got me into this. Now you've got to play it my way."

The look got harder, edged with speculation. "You know something about Valery."

"Promise."

"Damn it, Michael."

"I want your word, Remy, or I'm walking away—from this, from you, from her." It was a bluff, of course. Although he'd sworn last week that he would ignore the visions of Valery, in the end he couldn't have, no more than he could turn her out now. He was in it for the duration, and not for Remy. For himself. For her.

After a time Remy scowled—the first resemblance to Valery Michael had found, other than the obvious blond hair and blue eyes. "All right. I swear I'll keep it to myself."

All too aware that Remy's promise meant more than his own, that Remy would die before breaking a confidence while he was about to easily—but not guiltlessly—do just that, Michael took a deep breath, then flatly betrayed both Valery and himself. "Valery is safe."

Remy took a moment to process that information before cautiously asking, "You've...seen her?"

He was referring to the visions. Michael shrugged. "Seen her. Talked to her." *Touched her.*

Emotion, dark and vital and carefully controlled, crept into Remy's eyes. "Where is she? How did you find her? How long have you known...?"

"*She* found *me.* Friday night."

"And you're just getting around to telling me?"

Anger. That was the emotion. He had so rarely seen Remy angry that he hadn't recognized it. But he made no effort to placate him. His friend was entitled to his anger. "Her terms, Remy, not mine."

"Where is she?"

Aware of what was coming, Michael stalled. "She won't turn herself over to you," he warned. "She doesn't want to be in protective custody. She doesn't trust the FBI any more than she trusts Falcone."

"Where is she, damn it?" Remy's voice rose, growing sharp enough to catch his partner's attention, softening before Wilson could react. "Where?"

"I tried to talk her into turning herself over, but the minute I mentioned the FBI, she panicked. She tried to leave. The only way I got her to stay was by promising I wouldn't tell anyone about her."

Remy walked a few feet away, stopping in a puddle that splashed over his shoes. Michael had always both admired and detested his friend's tremendous reserve of patience. If he weren't wet, cold and uncomfortable all the way from his soaked clothes to way inside his soul, he would have found it interesting watching Remy lose and seek to recover that patience. But he *was* miserable. He just wanted this over with.

Finally, as the rain continued to stream down, to soak the already-waterlogged ground, Remy turned to face him again. He was calm again. In control. "You said that *she* found *you*. You mean she just came to you? To a total stranger?"

Michael didn't reply. If Remy and Valery had been close, as two people who'd grown up the way they had should be, he would know about her premonitions. Her feelings. Her insight.

"She just came to you," he murmured. "Not to the police, not to me, but—" Abruptly he broke off, and his calm cracked as his gaze shot upward, seeking out the third-floor balcony that was Michael's. "She's at your apartment, isn't she?" he demanded. "All this time we've been out searching for her, and she's been at your damned apartment!"

Remy turned away, heading toward the gate, toward the building, but Michael caught his arm, forcing him to stop. He moved around, positioning himself between Remy and the gate—between Remy and Valery—and vented a little anger of his own. "You wanted her safe, and she is. You wanted her protected. *I* can protect her. You have to trust me, Remy."

He stared off into the rain, dark and bristly. "Does *she?*"

"As much as she can." Releasing his hold, Michael combed his hair back, then moved his hand in a futile swipe across his eyes. "She doesn't trust easily. It seems she's learned that's a good way to get hurt."

"Yes," Remy quietly agreed, and that quickly the anger was gone, replaced by bleakness. Michael recognized it immediately, because he'd lived so intimately with it. "She has."

On the street a horn sounded, and the squeal of skidding tires ended in the crunch of metal on metal. Neither of them even glanced in that direction. They just looked at each other.

"Damn." Remy shivered as rain trickled down inside his collar. "I'm going to have to go home and change before I can do any work today." He pulled the collar tighter, then sighed. "Does she know you're a cop?"

"Yes."

"Does she know that we're friends?"

"No. She wouldn't stay around if she knew...and knowing the extent of the plans she's made, if she takes off, she'll wind up in even more trouble." Michael glanced up at his apartment. He'd left only a small lamp in the corner burning; now other lights were on, giving the sheer curtains a luminescent quality in the morning gloom. "Give me some time, Remy. Let me talk to her. Let me see if I can help her." *Trust me.* He heard his silent plea for the very thing he'd recently decided was too big a burden to bear.

"All right. I'll give you time. But I can't promise how much. It might be a few days, it might be a little longer. But sooner or later, Michael, she's got to come in. Sooner or later, this *has* to be settled." With that, he walked away. After only a few feet, though, he turned back. "Thank you, Michael."

Michael waited until Wilson joined Remy, until the two of them—Wilson sheltered under the umbrella, Remy's head down against the rain—had crossed the park and exited through the Decatur Street gate. He waited a moment longer, until they had crossed the street and passed out of sight, before slowly heading toward his apartment.

When he let himself in, he found Valery at the French doors, leaning one shoulder against the jamb, the curtain lifted back a few inches and held in one hand. His first thought was to wonder what kind of view her position afforded her—just an overview of the square in general? Or maybe a bird's-eye view of clandestine meetings near the statue?

His second—and more dangerous—thought was that he could become used to scenes like this, to coming home and finding her waiting. Warmth, coziness, Valery—they went a long way toward chasing away the cold.

She smiled as he closed and locked the door, then shed his jacket and shoes on the small rug nearby. "That didn't take long," she remarked, her voice soft, sleepy, unfairly sensuous.

"What didn't?" Cautiously he crossed the room in his socks, going to stand beside her, looking out to see what she could see. Trees, the statue, rain and, in the background—always looming in the background—the cathedral. At the most she might have seen Remy walk away with Wilson. With the rain, though, she might not have recognized him. But she couldn't have seen Michael, couldn't have seen them talking.

"Your errands." She gestured to the note he'd left on the table.

He moved to the opposite side of the door, leaning as she was. That put the cathedral at his back and gave him a view that was by far easier on his eyes: the river, the rain, the distant lighted bridge—and Valery.

It was far easier on his soul, too.

"I thought you would sleep in," he remarked.

"I thought I would, too." She smiled one of her lovely warm smiles. "I slept well."

He had already guessed that. With only three good nights' sleep, the exhaustion that had given her an air of such fragility was gone. There wasn't so much as a line or a shadow on her face. Her eyes were clear, bright, her expression one of utter, bone-deep relaxation of the sort he hadn't felt in months. This was Valery as she normally was. Natural. Beautiful. Beguiling.

"You have a comfortable place here." Her gaze swept away, taking in all of the apartment that she could see from where she was. Michael didn't bother to look. He knew every small detail of his home, had chosen and placed every single item inside these walls. After the divorce, after his wife had moved out and moved on, it had seemed better that way—starting all over. Making what had previously been their home his, and his alone. He had repainted the walls, uncovered the wooden floors, had sold, traded or otherwise disposed of every single thing that Beth hadn't taken with her. He had taken down her heavy drapes, had gotten rid of her fussy plants, her floral sheets and ruffly curtains and white wicker. He'd made a place so personal that no one else could ever feel as much at home here as he did.

Except that Valery seemed to.

He could think of nothing more wrong.

And nothing more right.

"Can I ask you a personal question?" she asked, waiting until he shrugged in response before going on. "How can a cop afford an apartment like this?"

He could detect no suspicion, no doubt in her voice—only casual interest—but they were there. They were in the unspoken echoes of the question she *really* wanted to ask: How can an *honest* cop afford an apartment like this? It was a question he had been asked before by family and curious friends. It was an answer that Valery, who was putting her life in his hands, was certainly entitled to. "I have a deal with the management. I provide on-site security, and in exchange, they knock off a portion of my rent."

Only a moment ago, she had hidden her doubts well, but now the relief was evident in her eyes and in the soft beginnings of her smile.

Nothing more right, he thought again. *Absolutely.*

Remembering Remy's comment about time—limited time, a few days, maybe longer—he forced his thoughts to a more pressing subject. "What do you want from me, Valery?"

His question was simple, quietly spoken, certainly well deserved, Valery thought. If their roles had been reversed, she certainly wouldn't have been as patient as he had been. Still, it made the temperature in the room drop from cozy to winter-chilly. It made her comfort level plummet.

She stared out the window, her gaze fixed on St. Louis Cathedral, and she gave an answer, unplanned but honest. "I'd like to go to church." Although she wasn't Catholic, wasn't currently a member of any church, she longed for an hour of freedom to slip away inside the cathedral. She could sit quietly in a pew, could soak in the peaceful quiet, could ask for guidance, for help, for a simple reminder that she wasn't alone in this.

"Answers aren't found in churches," he replied, his voice still quiet but different now. Flat. Empty.

She gave him a curious look. "Some answers are," she softly disagreed.

"They're buildings. Nothing more, nothing less."

"Is that why you paint them the way you do?"

His gaze shifted quickly, jerkily, toward the armoire in the corner.

"I snooped while you were out Saturday. I'm sorry."

"You didn't like the paintings of the churches?" Now his tone was mocking, all the more effective for its subtlety. It was an effort for Valery to keep her tone even in reply.

"I only saw two. Are there more?"

He shrugged, a response she took as affirmative.

"No," she admitted honestly. "I didn't like them. They were disturbing."

"I was disturbed when I painted them."

By what? she wondered. What had happened to make him see a holy place in such an unholy light?

Anticipating her curiosity, he shrugged again. "It's a long story—and, under the circumstances, not a very reassuring one for you."

"I'd like to hear it anyway."

He considered the matter for a long, still moment, then abruptly gestured toward the sofa. "Sit down, Valery. Let me tell you what happened the last time I had one of these visions."

Chapter 6

He put water on for coffee, turned up the heat and warmed two sticky buns for her before finally settling in one of the chairs. Valery was on the sofa, snuggled between the over-stuffed arm and a giant-size pillow in dark crimson. Her feet in thin socks were tucked between two cushions, but her toes were still cold. Her hands were cold, too, although it wasn't because of the room temperature. The apartment was comfortably warm and growing more so with each moment. This chill came from inside.

From inside Michael.

He sat stiffly in the chair, unable—unwilling?—to relax. There was a frustrated look on his face that came from searching for the right way to say something he didn't want to say at all, and it tempted her to give him a way out, to tell him that it was all right, that she didn't want to know.

But obviously it wasn't all right.

And she *did* want to know.

"It was a little girl," he said at last. His beginning was rocky, but there was no doubt the tale would get rockier as it went. "She was eight years old. Blue eyes, blond hair, long curls—a tomboy, but you'd never guess it to look at her. She was the kind of kid you picture at Christmas wearing a red velvet dress, patent leather shoes and bows in her hair, looking like a little angel.''

Valery knew instantly the sort of child he was describing. Heavens, for most of her childhood, she'd *been* that sort of child, with red velvet one year, green the next, satin sashes and white tights. Being very much a tomboy herself, she had hated the dressing up, but it had pleased her mother so much to see her little Christmas angel, and so she had grudgingly cooperated.

Until the Christmas she was eleven. Then she had dressed willingly, even eagerly, convinced that her parents would miss her, supremely confident that they would come to see her. She would be good, she had promised God and herself. She would wear velvet and patent leather all year round if both of them—either of them—came back for her.

But they hadn't come. Her mother had sent her a card from a ski lodge in Colorado. Her father, on the road somewhere up north, hadn't done even that.

And she had never worn velvet since.

Drawing her thoughts back to the present and remembering the insubstantial figures—angels with a dark side— in his painting of the lovely white church, she offered a silent prayer. *Please don't let the little girl be dead. Don't let that be his sorrow.*

''The girl's name was Nicole. Everyone called her Nikki. Her parents were divorced, and she lived with her mother. Her father paid child support when he felt like it and forgot about it the rest of the time, and her mother was having trouble making ends meet. When she was approached by a friend of a friend who was interested in renting the second floor of their house, she agreed. She needed the money, and he was a nice guy, and the house had once been apartments, so it was already set up for separate tenants. There were kitchens and bathrooms on each floor.''

He was reciting the story in much the same way she had told him about Nate Simmons's murder: offering facts that were absolutely uncolored by emotion. That emotion—the feelings that accompanied these memories of his—was buried somewhere deep inside him, and he would never, Valery thought, *never* bring it willingly to the surface.

Not even if keeping it buried destroyed him.

"The guy was a great tenant. He always paid his rent on time, and he never made any demands. They got to be friends—Nikki and her mother and this man. Especially Nikki and him. She rarely saw her father, and Jeffrey—that was his name, Jeffrey Randall—was a willing substitute. He taught her how to ride a two-wheeler, how to throw a baseball and shoot hoops. He took her to the park and helped her with her homework, and when her baby-sitter canceled or her mother had a date, Nikki stayed with Jeffrey."

He broke off, and in the quiet Valery heard the bubble of hot water and for the first time noticed the rich aroma of coffee that drifted on the warm air. He noticed, too, and went into the kitchen.

Jeffrey Randall. The name didn't sound familiar, but that didn't mean anything. Although, until recently, she'd read the newspaper every day, New Orleans was a big city and, frankly, police stories had never much interested her.

But then, until recently, she'd never known any cops.

Until recently, she hadn't known Michael.

He returned with two mismatched cups, heavy ceramic for himself, translucent china for her. It felt fragile in her hands, delicate and old and easily damaged. Oddly enough, it, rather than the sturdy ceramic that could survive practically any amount of rough handling, reminded her of Michael. He had little enough strength now, all of it going to maintain that rigid control. She wished she could give him some measure of her own strength, wished that she could make him feel—as he had made *her* feel—that everything would be all right.

But she couldn't.

He picked up the story as if he'd never stopped. "One day Nikki's mother had to work late, and the baby-sitter couldn't stay over. Jeffrey said no problem; he'd take Nikki. And he did. Her mother came home around eight o'clock to an empty house. At first she didn't worry, even though it was a school night and Nikki was supposed to be in bed

soon. What was there to worry about? Her daughter was
with Jeffrey. She trusted him. She waited until nine o'clock,
then ten o'clock, and then she began to worry that something had happened to them—that they'd been in an accident—so she called the police. And while she waited for the
police to come, she went upstairs to Jeffrey's apartment and
found..." He shrugged. "Magazines. Photographs.
Videotapes."

Valery suppressed a shudder of distaste. Already she knew
too much of what he was about to tell her. She didn't want
to hear any more. She didn't want to hear that Jeffrey Randall was a deviant who found sexual satisfaction only with
young children. She didn't want Michael to confirm her
sixth sense that Randall had hurt that little girl, didn't want
to know how Michael had helped—or failed—the child. She
didn't want to know that someone—someone innocent—
had died, or that Michael held himself responsible for that
death.

But she knew, anyway, damn it, and she didn't stop him
from corroborating it.

"It turned out Jeffrey Randall was a sex offender. He had
a record in other states for doing dirty things to little kids,
and his preference ran to pretty little girls with long blond
curls." He paused and tasted his coffee for the first time.
Neither the richness nor the strength nor the warmth of the
brew seemed to touch him. "I had my first vision of Nikki
that night, right about the time her mother was discovering
what kind of man had disappeared with her child. I was
working, in the middle of a buy-bust, and all I could see, all
I could hear, was this terrified little girl crying for her
mother. My partner Evan had a soft spot for kids. He'd
been married for nine years, and he and his wife had been
trying to have a baby for the last five or six of them. He
wanted to help, and I let him. I figured with a kid involved,
it couldn't hurt to have backup. I found Jeffrey Randall and
Nikki—"

Valery interrupted. "How?"

He shrugged. "A combination of good detective work,
cop's intuition and—I don't know—the great psychic un-

known. It's a gift I have." Bitterness was heavy in his voice, but it faded away as he spoke again. "Randall was holding her at a house across the river. Ordinarily I would have gone to the department, but this time the visions were changing. They were fading…as if *she* were fading. As if she had given up. There was this sense of urgency that I'd never felt before, so we didn't waste any time. Evan and I went in after her, just the two of us. It took only a few minutes. When it was over, Nikki was all right—as all right as a kid in that situation could be—but Randall was dead and I'd been shot, and Evan…"

"Evan was dead, too," Valery finished in a whisper.

Michael was staring off into the distance, his expression so dull, his eyes so bleak. "He died so that I could have a chance to get that little girl out alive. He was my best friend, had been for half my life, and he died because of me."

In the silence that followed, she didn't point out the flaws in his logic. She didn't remind him that his friend had been every bit as much a cop as he was, that Evan had felt as strong an obligation to help Nikki as Michael had. Visions aside, they had both been sworn law enforcement officers who had known of a small child in trouble, and they had risked themselves to help her. That Evan had paid for his effort with his life was sad and tragic. It was heartachingly wrong.

But it wasn't Michael's fault.

"And that's when you lost faith in God."

He didn't respond, but she didn't need an answer. She could imagine the scene all too well. No doubt he had whispered panicked prayers for his partner, his best friend half his life. No doubt he had pleaded with God, had bargained, had made promises—anything to keep Evan alive. And God had let him die anyway. Evan had died and Michael had lived, and he had never forgiven Him for it.

Hence the pictures of the churches. He couldn't paint some unseen celestial being, couldn't take out his anger and bitterness and despair on something without shape, without form, and so he had chosen the next best thing: the church. The physical, spiritual house of God.

"I'm sorry." The words were insignificant, too small to hold even a measure of the sadness she felt. They meant nothing to him. What had he told her earlier? *Sorry is the most worthless word in the English language.* How many times had *he* said it before he'd reached that conclusion? she wondered. To himself, to Evan, to Evan's family? How many times had he tried to lessen the guilt he carried, only to find that words didn't help?

"What about the little girl?" Had she, at least, survived intact? Had something even remotely good come from Evan's death?

"Last I heard she was coping. She was seeing a psychiatrist. She'll probably be seeing one for a long time."

She started to speak, hesitated, then pushed ahead. "Did you consider that for yourself?"

"No. For a time I had my own means of coping, but I lost that, too."

"Your wife?"

The look he turned on her was mostly blank, only slightly confused around the edges. Then, abruptly, he understood what she was asking and shook his head. "We'd been divorced four years by then. No, I became a strong supporter of every distillery that could give me what I needed. I got intimately acquainted with every bar within staggering distance. I drank to forget, but getting your best friend and partner killed isn't easy to forget, and so I drank more. I drank until I damn near lost my job."

"And the fear of that made you stop?"

"No." His gaze went distant again, looking on unhappy scenes from his own life. "One of my friends, another cop— another friend of Evan's—came over one morning. I was hung over, sick as a dog, and well on my way to getting drunk again. He sat me down, put his gun on the table in front of me and suggested that I use it. It would be a lot more efficient and a lot less painful for me, my family and my friends, he said, than drinking myself to death one day at a time."

"And that was enough to stop you." This friend, this other cop, was a smart man, she thought silently, and a good friend. She missed having good friends.

"Not right away. But it was enough to make me want to stop. It was enough to make me try." Setting his coffee, now cold, on the table beside him, he linked his fingers behind his head and gazed up at the ceiling. In a voice so soft that she could barely make out the words, he murmured, "It's been the hardest nine months of my life."

"I'm not making it any easier, am I?" she asked regretfully.

Although she didn't expect an answer, he considered her question for a long moment before tilting his head so he could see her. "Since you came, I haven't had any more visions. Life is always easier without visions."

"Then why don't I just stay hidden away here forever? With me safe but my problems unresolved, you should be free of any future visions, and I wouldn't have to..." Her words trailed off, and she looked away.

Michael watched her, trying to ignore her man to woman and to concentrate fully as cop to... To what? Witness? She was definitely that. Victim? She was that, too. Suspect? Yes, in some ways—not that he believed her guilty of any wrongdoing, but she *was* hiding something. Things just didn't add up. She wasn't telling the full truth about something.

Two days ago he had promised that he would find some way other than turning her over to the authorities to help her. So far, though, he'd done nothing, and she had been more than content to let him do just that. Although her question—*Then why don't I just stay hidden away here forever?*—had been spoken in a light, teasing manner, he suspected that, to some degree, she seriously wished that were possible. Because here she could avoid more than just Falcone's men, more than just the FBI. Here she could also hide from whatever secret she was keeping.

"You wouldn't have to what?"

She continued to look away—he suspected because her blue eyes revealed her emotions all too clearly. Because if she met his gaze he might see more than she wanted him to know. "I wouldn't have to—to be afraid."

"Don't lie to me, Valery," he warned.

Then, defiantly she looked at him. "I'm not lying. I'm not afraid here. I feel safe."

"But that's not what you were going to say."

Predictably—guilty people were so often predictable—she turned away again.

"The last couple of days haven't been bad, have they? You've slept well, you've eaten regularly, you haven't had to worry or look over your shoulder or hardly even think about dying. I haven't asked you many questions, and you haven't had to give many answers. It's been kind of comfortable, hasn't it?" he asked.

Head down, she simply shrugged.

"Well, you can't stay here forever, Valery. I have a job—a *real* job—that I have no intention of losing. You have a life of your own to go back to. Sooner or later, you're going to have to face reality. You're going to have to deal with everything that's happened to you in the last week, and that means dealing with the FBI."

"I'm not doing it," she muttered fiercely, and then she once again met his gaze. That same fierceness was in her expression. "You promised that you wouldn't turn me in. You promised that you wouldn't tell anyone about me."

A promise he had already broken, he thought with regret.

"Have they caught the killers?" she demanded.

"No, but—"

"Do they know where they are?"

"I don't know. I assume, since there's been no arrest, they don't."

"Then why should I go to them? Why should I let the FBI lock me up someplace when the killers are still running around free?"

"Because they can protect you."

She settled more firmly on the couch and folded her arms across her chest. Her body language fairly screamed obstinacy. "I'm safe here."

Leaving his chair, Michael circled the low table between them and crouched in front of her. "'Here' is my home, Valery," he said quietly, insistently. "It isn't some safe haven people can run to whenever they're in trouble. It's my house. It's my life."

"And you want me out of it."

"No," he denied. Stung by the faint quaver in her voice, he lied. "That's not what I meant."

She studied him for a long moment in the same way that he tended to study her, and what she saw obviously disappointed her. Worse, it hurt her. "No, Michael. That's exactly what you meant. I—I'm sorry. I didn't mean to take advantage of your—your hospitality. Give me five minutes and I'll be out of your way."

"Valery—" He reached out, but she avoided his hand, scrambling to her feet and away from the sofa, heading toward the bedroom. For a moment he remained where he was, eyes closed, exhaling heavily, wondering why he made so damn many messes in his life. In a moment he would have to straighten this one out, would have to follow her into the bedroom, to apologize to her, to explain exactly what he'd been trying to say.

Which was, as she had so succinctly put it, that he wanted her out. He wanted her someplace safe—someplace *else* safe. He wanted out of this case before he got too deeply, too personally, involved. He wanted out before he had a chance to screw it up the way he'd screwed up the last time.

He wanted to walk away while he still could.

The squeak of rubber soles on the high-sheen wood floor caught his attention and made him bolt to his feet. He had expected her to be in the bedroom pouting, maybe even packing in preparation of leaving, but she hadn't bothered with that. She'd put on her shoes and her jacket—the jacket that held all her money—and was already at the door, unfastening the chain, twisting the lock, turning the key he'd stupidly left in the dead bolt.

She'd barely opened the door two inches when he slammed it shut again. She pulled against his greater strength but gave up when he relocked the dead bolt and pocketed the key. With a soft curse she pounded her fist once against the solid wood door, then slowly leaned her head against it, her face turned away from him.

He was standing close to her, close enough to hear her uneven breathing, to feel the tension that held her tight. He was close enough to smell her fragrance, subtle, enticing. The bathroom smelled of it after her bath each morning. It was in her clothes, on the air, in his bed. He wouldn't mind having it on him, he thought, transferred body to body, sheet to skin.

What a first-class bastard he was.

"Valery."

Somehow she stiffened even more. Inside the vividly colored jacket that swallowed her, she was still, coiled, ready to act, to react. Ready to shrink away from his slightest touch. He proved that when he touched her hair, just the end of a crooked strand that fell over her ear.

With a sigh he relinquished the contact, but he didn't move away. He didn't give her the space—the freedom from him—that she so clearly wanted. Instead he remained right where he was, close, too close. "I used to be good at this, Valery," he said quietly. "Once I got used to the visions, to having someone barge into my life, it got to be a game, like some sort of puzzle that only I had the clues to put together. Don't get me wrong. It was always serious. It was always people in trouble who needed my help. I never treated it lightly, but . . . it didn't scare me then. I had a one-hundred-percent success rate. Nothing ever went wrong. Until Evan died."

She was listening, he knew, but it would have been hard to prove. She didn't move so much as a muscle, didn't alter her breathing, didn't look at him.

"All I was supposed to do was find you and turn you over to the feds—see that you were safe. It was supposed to be that simple." He heard the regret in his voice, ached with it deep inside. "I can't guarantee your safety. I can't swear that I can protect you. I can't be responsible for you, Valery. I can't be responsible for another death. It would kill me."

"Then let me go," she whispered.

"I can't do that, either. Unless you'll go to the FBI. Unless you'll let them place you in protective custody."

Still leaning against the door, she slowly turned her head until their gazes met. "You're right, Michael. You're *not* responsible for me. Let me go. Let me walk away."

He shook his head bleakly. "If you leave and something happens, it's my fault for making you feel you couldn't stay. And if you stay and something happens, that's my fault, too, for letting you stay against my better judgment."

"And if you turn me over to the FBI and something happens? Are you responsible for that, too, for making me go to them when I didn't want to?" She waited for an answer that she knew he wouldn't give. "You're damned if you do and damned if you don't, aren't you?"

Again he said nothing.

"You're not God, Michael, and you're not my guardian angel. You're just a nice guy who got caught in something beyond his control. But it's not beyond *my* control. It's *my* life. It doesn't concern you."

It hurt, he reflected, having someone tell you in a roundabout way to get out of her life.

He should have thought of that before he'd said it to her.

Some cowardly part of him wished he could let her go. He could give her the keys to his car, in case leaving the state still seemed to her the best way to go, step back and watch her walk out. Would time and distance diminish his mental contact with her? If she made it safely to Mexico, would he know? If she got into even more trouble, more danger, would he know that, here in New Orleans, too far away to help?

You're not God, Michael. If he were, he could make things right. He would give Evan back his life, would give Valery back her peace of mind and an unfailing sense of security. He would reward Remy and Smith and everyone good, and he would reward himself, too.

He would give himself the gift of Valery.

Hesitantly, knowing she wouldn't welcome it, knowing he was crazy for doing it, he lifted his hand to her face, brushing her bangs into place, touching a damp spot at the corner of her left eye where, sometime in the past few minutes, a tear had worked its way free. "No," he hoarsely agreed. "I'm not God. If I were, I would change the last week of your life. I would undo every bad thing that's happened to you. And I'm not much of a guardian angel, either—even if I was named for an angel."

"You don't even believe in angels," she whispered.

For a time he hadn't. For a longer time he had. Right now, this close to her, all soft and fragile, trembling and vulnerable, he wondered. . . .

Damn.

Valery shifted her head slightly so that his fingers slid away. Perversely, the minute the contact was broken, she wanted it back. She wanted him to touch her again, wanted him to hold her, to simply hold her close, the way Aunt Marie had done when she was little and missing her parents and her home.

But how could she ask for anything from him when he wanted nothing—*nothing*—but to be rid of her?

Settling her gaze on his chest, on the navy T-shirt that bore the gold emblem of the New Orleans Police Department, she sighed wearily. "I *can't* go to the authorities," she said, trying to sound reasonable and logical when all she felt was emotional. "I'm not trying to be difficult. I'm not trying to impose on you. I just can't go."

"Why not? What are you afraid of?"

She opened her mouth, then closed it again. She had no answer to give but the truth . . . and she wasn't ready yet to trust him with that. She might never be.

"Talk to me, Valery. Tell me—"

He broke off when she grazed her fingers across his jaw. "I'm sorry, Michael," she whispered. "I'm sorry you got involved in this. I'm sorry I can't do the right thing and make it easier for you. I'm sorry . . . oh, God, I'm sorry about everything."

With that she walked away, going into the bedroom and closing the door behind her. She twisted the lock, knowing even as she did that it wouldn't keep him out if he were determined to come in.

But he wasn't.

Peeling off her jacket and kicking her shoes into the corner, she headed for the bed, then detoured to the chair between the tall windows. It was oversize, the only new piece in the entire apartment, but with its clean lines and beige-and-green stripes, it worked well with the older pieces. She settled in, knees drawn up, hands clasped and resting on her ankles, head down. Nothing like retreating into the fetal position in times of stress, she thought without a smile.

Michael's expectations were totally reasonable. He had put his life on hold, had taken personal time off from work, his own vacation time, to deal with her. He had every right in the world to ask her to move on. She owed it to him.

And failing that, she owed him an explanation. He had a right to know why she wouldn't go to the FBI. She didn't have to name names. She didn't have to give him specific details, although undoubtedly he would want them. All she had to do was offer some measure of the truth: I believe an FBI agent might be responsible for Nate Simmons's death, so my life might be in danger if I go to them.

Maybe he would believe her, maybe not. Either way, he would ask questions, and he would ask them in what she was coming to recognize as his cop persona. It wasn't a major change from the way he normally was, just that his eyes got harder and his questions developed an edge. She imagined he was an effective interrogator...except possibly with someone who had more to lose by talking than by keeping silent.

Like her.

But she did owe him some answers. He had been incredibly patient with her. Since she'd shown up on his doorstep, he'd done all the giving and gotten nothing but frustration in return. Besides, in spite of his promise to the contrary, he could have turned her over at any time, and there wasn't a thing in the world she could have done to stop him. All he needed to do was use the phone while she was otherwise occupied—during her morning bath, while she was asleep, even right now—and call someone at the FBI. He'd been a cop a long time; he had to have a friend or two there. He could call and say, "She's here, send someone to pick her up," and she would be none the wiser until men in suits and carrying guns showed up at the door. She would have no escape, no recourse, no option at all except to go wherever they took her.

But because Michael was an honorable man, he hadn't done that. Because he'd given her his promise. Because he felt responsible for her.

That responsibility weighed heavily on him.

And she could ease it.

Her muscles cramping, she changed positions, tucking her feet beside her, resting her head on the chair arm. If the drapes had been open, she could have turned the chair to the window and gazed out at the cathedral, where she knew she could find help that Michael swore didn't exist there. She could watch the rain and wait for the sun to break through the heavy clouds. She could watch people scurry around, wet and cold, and be grateful that she was here, warm and dry.

But the drapes weren't open. She liked the room dark when she slept, and the few times she went near the windows, she simply peeked out. She didn't want to draw attention to herself, didn't want anyone outside to be able to look in and see her. The resulting darkness made the room snug and evening-cozy. Coupled with the warmth from the heating system, it made her comfortable and drowsy. Unlike Michael, who suffered from insomnia, under normal circumstances she could sleep anywhere, even in this big chair.

Unlike Michael, who had been named for an angel. Letting her eyes drift shut, she tried to recall what she knew about the angel Michael from her churchgoing youth. The seven archangels, with powers exceeding those of other angels, had been considered to hold guardianship over the different nations. Michael had been the prince of Israel.

Her Michael considered himself the prince of nothing, and he had no desire to be guardian of anything but his own sorrow.

But he was *her* guardian, until she somehow managed to set him free, and then he could be her prince.

He could be her very own angel.

When Valery awakened, the room was darker, cooler, quieter. She must have been asleep awhile, judging from the stiffness in her joints and the crick in her neck, but she wasn't eager to wake up just yet. She'd been having a dream, a dream about angels—lovely, warm, ethereal beings who made her warm and gave her hope. She hated to release them, hated to let them go and return to wakefulness and the problems that had filled her life for the past week.

But she *was* awake, perhaps summoned back from sleep by the aroma of food, hot and enticing—or perhaps by the gaze, steady and undemanding, that was on her. She didn't open her eyes just yet, but in her mind she could clearly see Michael in front of her. Listening hard, she could just make out his breathing, so slow and measured, and she could smell the faintest scent of after-shave, applied early this morning before he'd gone out in the pouring rain.

"That chair's not made for sleeping." His voice was quiet, cautious—as if he wasn't sure how she would respond—but friendly enough. Soothing enough.

Sensual enough.

"I didn't intend to fall asleep. It's a gift I have—or a curse, depending on your outlook. I can sleep anywhere, anytime."

"Rub it in, why don't you?"

When she at last ventured to open her eyes, she saw in the dim light that he was kneeling in front of her. She also saw the faintest hint of a dry smile that matched the dry tone of his voice. A part of her would have liked to freeze the moment long enough to turn on every light in the room, so she could see the smile clearly. Another part was more than grateful for the darkness. There was something freeing about darkness, about shadows, about reading voices rather than expressions. It was easier to talk then. Easier to connect. "I don't imagine there's anything worse than someone snoring away when you can't sleep, is there?"

"I sleep alone. I wouldn't know." After a pause, he curiously asked, "Do you snore?"

"I sleep alone, too. I don't know." She wondered why he had come in. To tell her that lunch—or, probably, judging by the darkness, dinner—was ready? Or just to check on her, to make sure she'd given up her intention of running away?

Lifting her head in preparation for straightening, she winced as the muscles in her neck protested. Before she could move far, he came closer and began rubbing the knotted muscles with slow, easy movements. "Ah, that feels good. Where did you learn...?"

"I haven't always slept alone." Slowly he eased her into a sitting position, then used both hands to massage her. Her head fell forward, her breath rushing out in a sigh of pleasure, while he worked away the tension and strain.

"Your wife... What was her name?"

"Beth."

She couldn't keep the amusement from her voice. "Beth Bennett?"

"She didn't like it much, either. Now she's Beth Betancourt."

"That's worse."

"Betancourt's got money. That makes it bearable."

With a shake of her head, she returned to her intended question. "Did you miss her when she left?"

"I had stood in church in front of God and my family, promising to love her forever, and forever lasted only three years. I was disappointed."

"'Disappointed'," she repeated, mimicking his delivery. "The end of a marriage should be more than a disappointment. How about a tremendous loss? A heartache? A great sorrow? Where is your passion, Michael? What excites you? What inspires and inflames you? What stirs you to emotion?"

Slowly he ended the massage, dropping his hands to rest on his thighs, and waited for her to look at him. She did so just as slowly, raising her head, smoothing her hair back before meeting his gaze. Satisfied that he had her attention, he shrugged then, a simple raising of his eyebrows, a simple lift and fall of his shoulders. "Lately it seems *you* do."

His honesty made her catch her breath. It sent little shivers down her spine. It conjured heated images of bodies, of need, of hunger and satisfaction so sweet.

It made her want.

She opened her mouth but couldn't speak, lifted her hand but couldn't touch. She was trembling because she knew, in the way that she'd known to come to him, in the way that she'd known lots of inconsequential little things, that they were going to be lovers. That she could indeed stir his passion. That he could, for the first time in her life, teach her about passion. That he could teach her to trust—the deep, unyielding sort of trust that was essential to a satisfying life, exactly the sort of trust that her parents had stolen from her, that Remy had also taken.

She *knew* those things, not one of them inconsequential. She saw them in her future.

She also knew—no hocus-pocus this time, no great psychic unknown, but with pure, basic woman's instinct—that he could break her heart. Her parents' and Remy's abandonment had been painful, terribly, traumatically painful. Those losses had shaped her life, had made her into a woman who respected heartache, who respected love. She knew love could bring extraordinary joy.

She also knew it could bring extraordinary sorrow.

And Michael carried with him such an aura of sorrow.

He was waiting for her response, and she wasted a moment or two trying to determine what he most wanted—encouragement or discouragement. Did he want to hear that she found him appealing, too? Did he want her to tell him with all certainty that they *would* eventually become lovers? Or did he want her to push him away, to confirm what he probably already suspected—that an affair between them would be ill-advised at best?

She didn't know. She couldn't read anything in what little she could see of his expression, couldn't read anything in his mind. She couldn't foresee even the tiniest, most insignificant detail of her immediate future.

She was left to guess. To play it by ear.

And she'd never been very good at playing anything by ear.

Her voice came out a little soft, a little husky, but nothing that couldn't be explained away by her recent nap. "I don't believe I've ever inspired passion in any of the men I know."

"Then the men you know are fools."

"And what are you?"

His laugh was dry and bitter. "I'm the biggest fool of all."

He was disappointed, she realized. He had wanted encouragement of some sort, and she had protected herself by taking the neutral ground, by neither accepting nor outright rejecting his honesty.

"Dinner's on the table," he said curtly as he moved to stand up. "Come on out whenever you're—"

At last she touched him, her fingers wrapping around his forearm, finding it warm and strong. "Show me."

Slowly Michael sank back to the floor. When she had asked about passion, the truth had been the farthest thing from his mind—no, that wasn't true. He had known the answer before she'd finished asking; he just hadn't intended to say it aloud. It had come from someplace unexpected, from someplace that he'd been out of touch with for so long that he'd nearly forgotten its existence.

It had come from his soul.

And she had treated it . . . not lightly, but not seriously, either. Certainly not as if the interest, the connection—the desire—was mutual. That was exactly the reaction he'd needed.

But damned if it wasn't a world away from what he'd wanted.

And now she was asking for what he wanted. There was no denying the invitation in her voice, her words. No ignoring the heat growing between them. And no silencing the certainty that what he was about to do was wrong, but damned if he wasn't going to do it anyway.

You're damned if you do and damned if you don't, aren't you?

Yes.

Hell, yes.

So if he had to regret this tonight and tomorrow and a lifetime of tomorrows, he might as well make it worth regretting.

He touched her, drawing her forward, sliding his hands into her hair. It was soft and cool, and it feathered over his fingers as he picked up the massage he had earlier abandoned. She was surprised, he knew. She had expected something more immediate, more blatant, more demanding. With his fingers he silently coaxed her forward until her forehead was resting on his shoulder and her hair was cool beneath his cheek.

Gradually the surprise drained away, along with some measure of her tension. He continued to rub long after the need for it was past, finding a rich pleasure in no more than this—his fingers on her skin, her body close to his, her breath warm against his chest. In losing Evan he had also lost his ability to enjoy such simple things. He had survived, but he lived by routine. The color had gone out of his life.

But, for a time, Valery could bring it back.

For a time.

And for a man living in the worst time of his life, *for a time* was enough. She would bring him some color, some warmth, some healing, and when she was gone, he would be a better man for having known her.

Unless he failed her the way he'd failed Evan.

For an instant his fingers grew still and his heart beat too loudly in the still room. He'd told her he couldn't be responsible for her death, and he had meant it with everything in him.

So he would keep her safe.

Or die trying.

Setting aside such bleak thoughts for the middle of the night, when she was sleeping soundly as he roamed the darkened apartment, he turned his conscious thought to his artist's side. Not the man. Not the cop. Not the protector. Not the betrayer. He noticed the texture of her hair—soft but heavy, not silky or baby fine. He learned that the skin behind her ear was softer than her throat, which wasn't as soft as just below her eye. Closing his eyes, he compared her scents—perfume the strongest, shampoo nearly masking soap, which almost overwhelmed lotion. He stroked hair, skin, clothing and found incredible heat. He held her close and found incredible need. Incredible longing. Incredible fear.

His. Hers. Theirs.

He knew his fears. He wondered, for a moment, about hers.

Kissing her seemed the natural next step. He pushed her back, cupped her face in his palms, bent toward her. It must have seemed natural to her, too, for she anticipated the first touch. But it was his thumb, not his mouth, that made the first contact. He drew it along her lower lip, tickling, teasing, and she smiled, stopping him in midstroke.

Damn, when had he last seen a smile both sweet and seductive, innocent and tantalizing?

Not lately. Maybe not ever.

Reacting to that innocently seductive smile, he kissed her without further delay, without further play. He slid his arms around her, pulled her hard against him and took her mouth, sliding his tongue inside, kissing her as if he'd known her for all time, feeling as if he'd needed her for at least that long. And she responded—sweet damnation, yes, she responded with the same need, the same hunger, the same greed.

He kissed her until the heat between them was too much to bear, until he wanted more, needed more, needed it so much that he ached with it. He kissed her until he couldn't think, couldn't breathe, until he wasn't sure he could ever stop, until he wasn't sure—considering the way she clung to him, the way she welcomed him—that she would ever let him stop.

Finally, with strength born of sheer determination and nothing else, he pulled away—not too far away, just enough to completely break the contact. Slowly her eyes opened, and in the dim light they stared at each other. She looked startled, and he wondered if her surprise was reflected in his own eyes.

He wondered if she understood how badly he wanted her . . . and how badly he didn't.

He wondered if she knew that what he wanted didn't matter now. They had crossed the line. After one single extraordinary kiss, they couldn't go back to being two strangers sharing an apartment, to an off-duty cop protecting a witness.

They could only move forward.

And he could only hope that they both survived.

Chapter 7

The sun was shining on Tuesday, the day promising to be one of those bright, beautiful winter days that made life in the South worthwhile. Valery got up early, bathed and dressed in jeans and a snug T-shirt. She put on a little makeup, spritzed herself with cologne and for the first time regretted cutting off her hair and coloring it such a ghastly black. She regretted not giving Michael a list of clothing to bring from her apartment, so she could have something prettier to wear than this shirt that celebrated the blues in the Big Easy. She regretted being so damn restricted here.

But she didn't regret that kiss last night.

No way would she regret the follow-up that was sure to occur today.

She would never regret the lovemaking that would come after.

She left the bathroom, expecting to find him sitting at the table drinking coffee or in the kitchen making breakfast. Maybe she'd gotten up early enough to help.

He *was* sitting at the table, dressed as she was, only his T-shirt was solid black. But he'd obviously been up for a while—at least long enough to go to Café du Monde for *beignets* and coffee. Long enough to also go someplace else, it seemed, judging by the papers scattered across the table.

Valery sat down across from him. There were no *beignets* left in the bag or on the plate in front of him, she noticed, settling with a scowl for a taste of powdered sugar. Looking up from the papers—reports, she could see now; police reports?—he caught her chiding look.

"I wasn't sure when you'd be up. I'll make you a pancake in a minute."

"That's okay. Don't bother." She dipped her finger in the sugar again. "What time did you get up?"

"About five-thirty."

"Because you couldn't sleep, or because you wanted to run more errands while I was asleep?"

"Does it matter?"

"I'd hate for you to be losing any sleep because of me."

For the first time since she'd knocked at his door Friday night, he laughed, the genuine kind of laughter that she hadn't thought him capable of. It did wonders for him— eased the worry that seemed permanently etched into his face, lightened the shadows in his eyes, made him about a hundred percent friendlier, more approachable.

And a hundred percent more appealing, she thought, shifting edgily as the desire that had settled deep inside her last night twisted a bit, reminding her that it was there.

"Honey, I've been losing sleep over you since the first time you popped into my head. A little bit more here or there isn't going to hurt."

She settled more comfortably into the chair. "What are you looking at?"

He sobered, but a little of the openness remained. "Reports on Nate Simmons's death."

"Which you got from . . . ?"

"Smith."

Smith Kendricks. The old-money, blue-blood, high-on-the-social-ladder assistant U.S. Attorney. She would like to meet him sometime, would like to see what it was that drew him and Michael to each other. "Learn anything interesting?"

"Something." Sorting through the pages, he chose one and offered it to her. She had barely started to read it when he tapped one fingertip on the pertinent information, a name at the bottom of the page. The name of the agent in charge of the FBI's investigation into Simmons's killing. Remy's name.

She stared at it for a long time, knowing that Michael knew about her relationship to Remy, wondering for a moment how. Then she silently chastised herself. He was a cop, and she was a witness to murder. Right now, the cops in this city probably knew as much about her as she knew herself, and much of it was likely in these papers right here. Surely it was known that she'd been raised by the Sinclairs, that her home was their home and not anyplace she'd ever shared with her parents.

His voice was a shade gentler when he spoke again. "You want to tell me about him?"

She folded her hands together, resting them primly on the edge of the table. "What do you already know?"

"That he's your cousin. That it was his parents who took you in after your parents' divorce."

"How much more do you need to know?"

"Everything."

Everything. She thought back to the time when Remy had been one of the three most important people in her life, and she smiled bittersweetly. *Everything* was an awful lot for a cop to ask.

But it wasn't so much for Michael.

Her smile slipped away, and her fingers tightened together. "It's a long story."

"I've got nothing but time."

After another moment's hesitation, she glanced at the sugar-coated plate. "How about that pancake?"

He stacked the papers together neatly and laid them aside before going into the kitchen. She swiveled in her chair to watch him, expecting the kind of pancakes she made at home—a little baking mix, a little water, a hot skillet. Instead he gathered the essentials on the counter: eggs, milk, flour and sugar, mixer and bowls. When that was done, he turned on the oven to preheat, started a pot of coffee and began assembling her breakfast. He didn't prod her to start her tale, but he did glance at her curiously, so, with a sigh, she began.

"Remy's mother Marie is a Navarre. She's my—my father's younger sister. They were pretty close—our families spent a lot of time together—and that meant Remy and I were pretty close, too. He was the older brother I'd always wanted. He was my best friend. My earliest memories—and most of my *best* memories—involve Remy. He used to come down and spend weekends and part of his summer vacation with us in New Orleans, and I spent a lot of time with *his* family. I loved it at their house. It was so different from the city, so big and beautiful, so much a home."

She broke off for a moment, thinking of the house where she'd done much of her growing up. A Greek Revival built on the river that had made a fortune or two in shipping for the first Sinclairs in Louisiana, Belle Ste. Claire was as gracious as its name. Oftentimes she had spread a quilt under one of the giant live oaks out front and had simply lain there, chin cushioned on her hands, and stared at the house. She had marveled that *she* was welcome in such a place, that *she* who lived in a tiny apartment in a shabby neighborhood in New Orleans had a right to stroll the grounds, to relax on the gallery or to walk right inside.

She had always thought Belle Ste. Claire was a special place. Being there had always made *her* feel a little special.

Remy had always made her feel special.

"I told you about my parents' divorce. I thought I could survive my mother's leaving—after all, I still had my father, and I adored him. I figured we could get by. I could cook a little, could clean and help out so he wouldn't be overly burdened. I had everything all planned when I came home from school one afternoon and found everything I owned in boxes and my father waiting to take me to his sister's." Two heartaches in two days. She had cried herself to sleep every night for weeks, had tried to figure out what she had done wrong, why the two people who were supposed to love her most had both left her. How had she disappointed them? What could she do to make them come back?

She had prayed, had promised God everything she might ever have, had offered deals, if only He would bring one of her parents back for her. Eventually her father *had* come back, but only for a visit. He'd had no intention of taking her away with him.

His visits were infrequent from the beginning, but they had become even more so after he met a woman up in Vicksburg. For a time they had simply lived together—Valery had heard gossip at a Navarre family get-together—but after a few years they'd gotten married and started a family of their own.

He hadn't told Valery that he was getting married again, hadn't told her that they were having a baby, then another and then one more. She'd found all that out from Aunt Marie. *He* hadn't told her anything, except that there was no room for her in his life or his heart, and he'd done that with absence and distance, not words.

"The only good thing to come out of the divorce—that *I* could see, at least—was that I would be with Remy all the time instead of occasional weekends and vacations. He was my best friend, even if he was a couple years older. He looked out for me when we were together. He made me laugh."

She broke off to watch Michael pour the pancake batter into the skillet. It was unlike any pancake she'd ever seen, huge and fluffy, rising in peaks all across the skillet. He put it in the oven, but didn't come to join her at the table while it baked. After taking a package from the freezer and a carton from the refrigerator, he continued working, leaving her to continue talking.

"It was kind of funny, you know. I'd known Remy all my life. I thought I knew him better than anyone else, and I *knew* he knew me better than I did myself. But I'd never found out how he felt about being an only child. I hated it. I would have died to have an older brother. I would have died to have Remy for an older brother. But he didn't want me for a younger sister. As a cousin living off in New Orleans most of the time, I was fine. But living in his house, sharing his home and his parents, intruding on his life..." She shook her head, remembering the incredible anger and resentment he'd shown her, feeling the shock and the hurt she'd felt then. She'd been eleven years old, and her parents had deserted her, but she could have handled that, because Remy was there. Remy had never let her down. He'd always looked out for her. He'd always taken care of her.

Finally Michael finished in the kitchen and went to sit across from her. He really would have preferred to stay in the kitchen—it seemed that distance might make this easier for them both—but everything he could do had been done. The pancake was baking, the cream was sweetened, whipped and chilling, the coffee was cooling, and the strawberries were thawing. All that was left to do was wait...and listen.

"Aunt Marie and Uncle George did what they could to make things easier for me. They spent a lot of time with me, gave me a lot of attention—attention that used to be Remy's. That made him dislike me even more. He wouldn't play with me anymore, wouldn't include me with his friends. Sometimes Aunt Marie made him let me tag along, but he'd be so hateful that I stayed behind. As he got older, he wasn't so openly angry, but he still thought I didn't belong there. I wasn't part of his family, as far as he was concerned, and damned if he was going to treat me as if I was."

Remy had been a spoiled kid, Michael thought, but that wasn't unusual with only children, especially those onlies from well-off families, the ones who got pretty much whatever they wanted. But that didn't explain the fifteen-year silence between him and Valery. Surely two adults could look back with maturity and resolve their childhood differences. So Remy had been selfish and cruel; kids were sometimes like that. He had been reacting to major changes in his life; the Navarres' divorce had affected everyone in the two families, not just Valery. And his behavior then certainly wasn't a reflection on the man he'd become. So Valery had intruded on his life and, to some extent, had taken his parents from him. She'd been an unhappy, needy child whose own parents had abandoned her. It wasn't her fault that she'd needed the Sinclairs more than Remy had.

"So you guys never worked things out," he said, his voice neutral.

"No. We had other problems to tend to. We were both growing up, and we had all the usual teenage angst to deal with, and I was still seeing my father from time to time. It seemed as if every time I finally got used to having him out of my life, he came back for a visit. He'd stay a few hours, maybe even a day or two, and then leave again. It was hard—it left everything so unsettled—but I couldn't tell him not to come back. He was my father, and even if he didn't want me, I still loved him."

She paused a moment, gazing into the distance, the most exquisitely haunted look Michael had ever seen in her eyes. Damn her father for putting it there, and her mother and, yes, damn Remy, even if he had been just a spoiled, selfish kid.

Then the sorrow faded—didn't disappear, but simply faded back to the edges of her expression. "Anyway, things got better when Remy went off to college. He rarely came home, and when he did, he pretended I didn't exist. I missed him like hell, but I pretended it didn't matter. Then, on one of his visits, I overheard him arguing with his parents about his graduation. They were planning a big celebration, but he didn't want to include me."

Her voice quivered just the slightest bit, and her eyes were a touch too bright. "They said of course I would be there, and he responded with, 'Why *of course?* It's not as if she's actually family.' I'd heard that from him before, it wasn't anything new. But that time he went further. He was tired of the lies and the pretense, he said. Tired of the way everyone treated me. Tired of pretending that he didn't know good and well that I had no ties to the Sinclair family, that I didn't even have any ties to the Navarres. The whole family knew, every last one of them, that my mother had been pregnant when she'd met my father. Everyone in the whole damn world knew that he had agreed to pass her illegitimate daughter off as his own...everybody but me."

He saw her tears, heard them in those last sad words, and turned his gaze away at the same time that she bowed her head. He didn't want to hear any more, didn't want to see her cry, didn't want to sit there, as much a bastard as Remy had been, without any comfort to offer her.

After a moment she went on. "I walked into the room and confronted him. I was going to call him a liar, to make him admit that he was lying, but I knew from their faces that he was telling the truth. For the first time since I had moved in eight years earlier, he seemed sorry. He hadn't meant to go that far. He certainly hadn't intended for me to hear what he was saying. I was heartbroken. All I'd had, the *only* thing I'd had, those years was my father's family. I didn't even know my mother's family—she had left home before I was born and had lost touch—but the Navarres and the Sinclairs... *They* were my family. They were my life."

And Remy had taken that away from her, Michael acknowledged. In one angry moment, he'd stolen the last constant in her less-than-happy young life.

After one last, soul-weary sigh, she finished. "Remy's parents were furious. His father ordered him out of the house, told him he was ashamed of him, told him not to come back until he'd made a better man of himself. None of us have had any contact with him since." She offered a teary smile that Michael saw from the corner of his eye. "And that's *everything*, detective. Any questions?"

He had questions—he always had questions—but now wasn't the time. Shaking his head, he got up to check on breakfast. First, though, he stopped beside her chair, tilting her face up, wiping away a few tears. "There are different ways to define family, Valery. Blood is one. Love is another. The Sinclairs didn't take you in because they had to, because they were obligated by blood. They did it because they loved you. They're still your family. Remy didn't change that. Nothing ever can."

Bending, he brushed his mouth across hers, a simple gesture of comfort that hinted, far too quickly, at something more, something that was neither simple nor a mere gesture, something that could provide him with a hell of a lot more than comfort.

Something to be explored later, he silently promised as he went on into the kitchen.

Something to be explored in full.

And not too much later.

"Explain something to me."

Valery was lying on the sofa, her head tilted back, studying the textured tin ceiling, when Michael spoke. His voice was as quiet and lazy as the air, as quiet and lazy as *she* was this bright, warm, winter afternoon. They had shared breakfast—something of a cross between a pancake, an omelet and a meringue, mounded with whipped cream, warm strawberries and sugar—and had whiled away the rest of the morning watching old movies on TV. Although there had been little conversation, no touching—and no more kissing—it had been, she decided now, a lovely way to spend a morning.

Although she could think of much lovelier ways to pass the afternoon.

Rolling onto her side, she plumped the pillow underneath her head, then smiled sleepily at him. "What do you want to know?"

"When you left the police station last Monday, why didn't you go to Remy?" He raised his hand, stalling the response she was ready to give. "I understand that you two have had problems, but that was in the past. Last Monday you were afraid, you had nowhere to go and you thought your life was in danger. Don't the problems between you two seem rather insignificant in comparison?"

Of course he was right, she silently admitted. If the only thing standing between her and Remy was their childhood rivalry, yes, she probably would have called him, probably would have forgotten or forgiven everything in exchange for his protection.

But then, childhood troubles *weren't* the only thing between them.

"Why didn't you call him?"

She shrugged. "I couldn't. I just couldn't."

"Is he the reason you refused to go to the FBI? Because you thought he might be working the case? Because he let you down all those years ago and you were afraid he would do it again?"

"I thought he might be involved," she replied, choosing her words carefully. After a moment she asked a question of her own, one that hadn't occurred to her until just now. "Do you know him?"

Michael was silent for a moment, thoughtful. When he finally answered, it was with a sigh. "I know who he is. It's hard to be a cop as long as I've been and not have at least a passing acquaintance with most other cops, local and federal, in the city."

"But you're not friends." She was relieved by that. His self-imposed obligation to her would go a long way, but she didn't know how it would stand up against his loyalty to a friend. Thank God she wouldn't have to find out. "How long have you been a cop?"

"Fifteen years."

"Was it something you always wanted to do?"

He shook his head. "I didn't know what I wanted until I was in college. My dad had always hoped I'd take up one or both of his callings, but I'd had enough of farming, and I always thought I lacked the . . . goodness for preaching."

Interested, she sat up, giving him her full attention. "Your father's a minister?"

"He prefers preacher—says it sounds less stuffy. He's been pastor of the Titusville First Assembly of God for about thirty-five years now."

"Is it true what they say about preachers' kids being the wildest kids in town?" she asked with a grin.

"Not in Titusville," he responded dryly. "You don't have a chance to be wild when every single person in town, whether they're a churchgoer or not, knows you *and* your father."

She thought of the story he had told her about Evan, of the pictures he had painted, of the faith he had lost, and her amusement disappeared. "Does he know how you feel?

Does he know that you no longer believe . . . ?'' How that would hurt, after devoting his adult life to God and the church, to watch his son turn his back, to know that his own child, the son he had hoped would also become a minister, could find no peace with God.

Michael had also grown serious. "No, he doesn't. It would worry him and my mother, and I try not to worry them. And it's not that I don't believe, Valery. I still believe in God." Bleakness edged into his voice. "I just don't think He believes in me."

Wanting to erase that bleakness, even for just a moment, she steered the conversation in a slightly less serious direction. "Your being a cop—I assume that worries them?"

"I convinced them that it wasn't so dangerous once I made detective and was out of uniform. That blue uniform makes a pretty good target. It's hard to deny what you are when you're wearing it. When I worked homicide, they found the idea a little unsettling, but they liked it better than having me on the streets." He paused, then shrugged. "They don't know I work drugs now."

And the fact that he hadn't told them meant it was probably higher risk than homicide. What was it like, she wondered, to live with the knowledge that someone you loved worked a dangerous job? To know that every time you saw him might be the last? To know that someone, some low-life scum who didn't even have the right to exist, could take his life in an instant and leave you to handle the loss? How had Evan's wife dealt with the fear of losing her husband? Worse, how had she dealt with the reality of it?

It was apparent how Beth Bennett had dealt with the fear. She wasn't cut out for being a cop's wife, Michael had said. She had learned to stop caring, and she'd gotten out. Valery would bet next month's paycheck that Beth's new husband had a nice, safe, dull job, like accountant or stockbroker.

Could *she* do it? she wondered. Could she love a cop? Could she accept the uncertainty of that way of life? Could she marry a man who might not be there for her tomorrow, a man who could plan a future but couldn't guarantee he'd be there to share it?

Yes. Because if life had taught her anything, it was that there were no guarantees. Her father—the man she still called father even though he wasn't—had been a factory laborer, but he hadn't been there for her. Her mother, a frustrated housewife, hadn't been there for her, either. The job didn't matter. The uncertainties of life didn't matter. The person did.

Michael did.

Still, she casually asked, "Could you ever see yourself doing something else?"

He grinned. "You mean give up my badge and gun and wear a suit and sit in an office all day?"

"That's one option. Or you could buy a little piece of land and sit on a tractor all day. Or buy a folding chair and set up shop down there on the square, selling your paintings to tourists."

His chuckle was charming and warm. "I had enough of farming by the time I was sixteen. As for the other, honey, I'm too old to become a starving artist. Besides, I got the impression that you weren't particularly impressed with my work."

"I didn't say that," she protested. "I like the paintings on the walls in here. I just think the ones of the churches are depressing."

"They're meant to be."

"So you accomplished what you set out to do. I still don't like them."

"I don't either," he admitted at last. "It's just something I had to do." He gazed over at the studio, at the shrouded portrait on the easel. "You still haven't looked at the painting I did of you, have you?"

Flushing, she shook her head.

"Are you afraid I gave you two heads, or horns and a pitchfork or something?"

"Of course not." She wasn't sure exactly why she'd avoided the portrait. Maybe because it was a painting not of her, exactly, but of the visions he'd been having of her. Or maybe because she knew he hated the visions and she feared some measure of that might have come through. Maybe it was because she remembered the angels in the painting of the lovely white church.

"Come on." He got to his feet, grabbed her hand and pulled her along. She had no choice but to scramble to her own feet or be dragged off the couch and across the wooden floor. He positioned her in front of the easel, released her to reach for the cover, then caught her again as she started to turn away. Holding her with one arm around her waist, he lifted up the sheeting, then stepped back with her for a look.

The portrait was beautiful, far more beautiful than she could ever hope to be. The colors were soft, the details precise, the talent undeniable. And the passion...

She was impressed. Flattered. And just the littlest bit scared.

When a shiver passed through her, Michael, standing behind her, drew her closer and wrapped both arms around her waist. She felt safe in his embrace. Protected.

For the first time in practically a lifetime, she felt as if she'd found where she belonged.

"It's not so bad, is it?" he asked, his mouth near her ear, his voice soft and teasing. "No horns, no evil eye, and it even looks exactly like you."

"It bears a passing resemblance," she corrected. "She's much prettier than I am."

"How is that possible? She *is* you."

She twisted in his arms so that she was facing him. "She's your vision."

"*You're* my vision. You and she are one and the same. It's a perfect likeness."

She glanced at it again over her shoulder, unconvinced, then looked back at him. "I'm impressed. And I'm sorry."

"Sorry?"

"I thought your work lacked passion."

He smiled faintly. "Most of it does. I paint because I want to, not because I *need* to. I painted this one because I *had* to. The difference shows."

"Yes," she agreed in a whisper. She understood the difference between wanting and needing. For years she'd been wanting someone to hold her close, to make her feel wanted, but because it had simply been a desire, she hadn't felt compelled to find someone to do it. Right now, though, at this very moment, that wanting had turned to needing. She *needed* to be held, comforted, assured, and she wasn't ashamed to ask. "Michael...please..."

He understood and offered her wordless comfort, holding her tight, stroking her hair gently. Resting her head against his chest, she felt the soft knit of his shirt and the reassuringly steady beat of his heart beneath her cheek.

After a time, he tilted her head back and gazed down at her, so solemn, so intense. "You know where we're headed, don't you?"

She nodded.

"You know it might be a mistake."

Although she nodded again, she didn't agree, not deep down inside. She'd made enough mistakes in her lifetime; she could recognize one when she saw it. Michael didn't come even remotely close.

"I don't want to hurt you, Valery."

She wanted to assure him that he couldn't hurt her, but, of course, he could. What stirs you to emotion? she had asked last night, and he had answered, *Lately, it seems you do.*

Lately. As in right now, but maybe not in the future. Maybe not for long.

Seems. As in it appeared to be her. It was likely her. Possibly. Probably. But not definitely. Not beyond a doubt.

Oh, yes, he could hurt her, and the fact that it was done unwillingly wouldn't make it any less painful.

Forcing a faint smile, she reminded him, "I've been hurt before, and I've always survived." But how many heartaches could a person endure before it became one too many? Where did she draw the line and say no more? No more caring, no more loving, no more hurting?

She had drawn the line over twenty years ago, when Remy had let her down. And she had crossed over it when she had walked into this apartment last Friday night.

"We've both survived sorrow, Valery, but that's not living. I don't want to hear that you'll 'survive' whatever I do to you."

She smiled again, this time with genuine feeling. "I'm a grown woman, Michael. I'm willing to take a chance for something I want. And who knows? We might both come out of this just fine—better, even, than before."

And maybe they would. After all, there were only so many possibilities. Maybe sex was all either of them really wanted, and once their needs were satisfied, once they'd made up for all the hurt and emptiness in their lives, they would be happy to tell each other goodbye.

Or he could take what he needed and give what she wanted—but not what she needed—and break her heart.

Or he could take a few chances of his own and find out that sometimes the rewards *were* worth the risks, and these hours together could be the beginning of something long, happy and permanent.

Since she knew the first was impossible—for her, at least; sex was the least of what she wanted from Michael—that gave her a fifty-fifty chance of heartache.

And a fifty-fifty chance at happily-ever-after.

Those were better odds than she'd faced in a long, long time. Those were better odds than life usually dealt.

Michael brushed her hair back, tucking a strand behind her ear, thinking once again how soft and heavy it was. "Remember when I said that I liked your hair better this way?"

She nodded, and the motion tugged her hair from his fingers.

"It's nice . . . but I wish it was still long and blond."

"It'll grow back, and the color will wash out."

But would he be around to see it? he wondered. She was talking weeks, and they didn't have weeks. As Remy had reminded him yesterday morning, time was short. Sooner or later, things had to be settled. Valery couldn't stay hidden in his apartment forever, no matter how much she wanted to. No matter how much he needed her to.

He wished he hadn't lied to her about knowing Remy. Technically, he told himself, he hadn't. She had asked if he knew Remy, and he had admitted that he did. But technicalities didn't count when it came to lying. He had learned that lesson from his father. Either you told the truth or you didn't—simple black-and-white, no shades of gray. An answer that deliberately misled couldn't possibly count as telling the truth with Brother Mark Bennett—and it wouldn't count with Valery, either.

Wishes were futile. Standing here like this, his arms around her, her cheek against his shoulder, he knew that was true. His wishes, like the prayers he had once prayed, fell on deaf ears. If they hadn't, if they had ever come true, life would be different. *He* would be different.

He would deserve Valery.

But even though he didn't deserve her, he could have her. He shouldn't, but he could. He would. It was just a question of when.

Frankly, he thought with a wry grin, barring interruption, right now sounded damned fine.

As if summoned by his very thoughts, the phone rang, the sound shrill and intrusive. He thought about ignoring it—that was what an answering machine was for, wasn't it?—but then he considered the various messages that could be left, messages that could damn him in Valery's eyes. He had to answer it.

Before he could do more than lift his hands from her, she instinctively raised her head, took a step back and freed him to move.

The call was unimportant, someone he worked with wanting information on an old case he and Evan had handled. It was brief and uninteresting—that was a first; he had never before found cop talk uninteresting—and when it was over, he was more than willing to return his attention to her.

During the call, she had come over to sit on the arm of the sofa, one foot on the cushion, the other on the floor. Her legs were long, her jeans snug, her feet in familiar white socks. She had raided his sock drawer, he thought, liking the idea more than good sense allowed. There was something appealing about it. Something intimate.

"Business?" she asked, with a glance toward the phone.

"Hmm."

"Are you one of those people who doesn't like to talk about his work?"

Even the suggestion made him laugh. When she asked, with no more than the raising of an eyebrow, for an explanation, he gave it. "Beth and I used to spend a lot of time with Evan and his wife Karen. She used to complain that she could tell our cop stories as well as we could because she'd heard them so often. It's a hazard of the job, I guess. You relive the good cases for the glory and the bad ones for the commiseration."

"So you talk about it with other cops, not with . . . What do you call noncops? Civilians?"

"Citizens. People. Them—you know, us against them." He shrugged. "I guess so. But wives and girlfriends get to hear their share—too often more than they want to hear."

"Because it frightens them?"

"That and it bores them. It's hard to understand what it's like to be out there unless you've been there. There's nothing like being on the street to get your heart pumping."

"And you love it."

He considered that a moment. He'd told her before that he wasn't cut out for being anything but a cop, and just a short while ago he'd told her—more or less—that he couldn't see himself doing anything else. Both those things were true, but did he love the job?

He had, back when he was twenty-two, fresh out of the academy, naive and gung ho and out to save the world. It hadn't been a job then, hadn't been work. He'd been like a kid let loose on the giant playground of New Orleans, and he'd been proud, damn, so proud of what he was and what he did.

He had still loved it when he'd made detective, although he'd been less brash, less naive, less sure that the world could be saved. He had grown up some then—investigating murders could help you with that—and had long since lost the bright-eyed optimism he'd brought to the job, but he had loved doing it anyway. Even when his marriage had been falling apart and Beth had given him her final ultimatum: her or the job. He hadn't needed even a moment to think about it. It had been no contest. The job had won hands down.

But did he love it now? He did it. He showed up every day, followed leads, watched suspects, interviewed witnesses, cultivated informants. He prepared cases, planned buys and busts, and testified in court. He was still dedicated, but he'd grown up even more since his days in homicide. He knew now beyond a doubt that there was no saving a world that was intent on destroying itself. He, and everyone else in the world who worked narcotics, was fighting a losing battle. Arrest one dealer and five more would take his place. Bust a major supplier and someone was ready to fill his slot; business wouldn't be disrupted for more than a day or two.

It was an issue of supply and demand. As long as the demand for illicit drugs remained high, the supply would continue to flow. The so-called war on drugs was a failure, the just-say-no campaign a joke. His own work and the work of everybody in his division was about as effective as using a wad of tissue to plug a leaking levee when the Mississippi was rampaging.

Valery was waiting patiently for a response. He wondered if patience was a Navarre family trait, then, remembering that she was a Navarre in name only, wondered if she'd learned it from Remy.

So...did he love the job?

Damned if he could say. It was a part of him. Being a cop was both who and what he was. No matter how futile the work or how ineffective he felt, he would continue doing the job until he retired. He was dedicated to it. He didn't want to do anything else. But did he love it?

"It's a job," he said with a shrug.

She slid to the right until she was on the cushion. "A job you wouldn't trade for any other job in the world. A job you've given half your life to. A job," she added solemnly, "that you would give your life for."

Maybe he did still love being a cop, and he'd just forgotten it. That happened to people, didn't it? Sometimes couples who'd been together a long time began taking each other for granted, letting their love get lost in the work, the effort, the day-to-day reality of life. Sometimes, if they were lucky, they managed to rekindle the love. More often, it seemed, they drifted so far apart that they could never find their way back together.

He had wondered sometimes, in the early days of their marriage, if that would happen to him and Beth, if one day he would wake up beside her and wonder what he was doing with this person that he had somehow stopped loving. It was possible. The newness, the passion, the adrenaline rush of being *in love,* had to fade, and he had wondered if what took their place would be strong enough to last.

It hadn't been.

One day they had both awakened—figuratively, if not literally—and wondered what the hell they were doing there.

He couldn't imagine taking Valery for granted.

He couldn't imagine that any man lucky enough to win her love would be foolish enough to let it slip away again.

He couldn't imagine waking up beside her and wondering why he was there.

Unwilling to pursue thoughts of Valery and love, he deliberately changed the subject. "Would you do something for me?"

The wariness he expected didn't pop into her eyes, and she didn't attach any conditions—such as *"As long as it doesn't involve the FBI"*—to her answer. It was a simple, trusting "Sure."

"Don't you want to know what it is before you agree?"

"You've done a great deal for me in the last few days. I owe you."

His gaze narrowed. "Wrong answer. We're not trading favors here, Valery."

Her answering smile was sweet, innocent and smug as hell. "Okay. Right answer—beyond the obvious, I don't believe there's anything you could ask of me that I wouldn't do. *Anything*, Michael."

Possible responses flooded his brain: *Want me. Need me. Love me.*

Heal me.

God help him, yes. He needed healing, and she could do it. She could make things right again. She could make him whole again.

He sat utterly motionless, hearing again his own thoughts. *God* help him. He hadn't asked for help from God in nearly a year. He hadn't believed it existed, not for him. He'd long since given up praying for help or the blessed peace he had so desperately craved. But if prayer would bring him Valery—not for a time, which he was willing to settle for, but for always...

It would just be one more prayer to go unanswered. One more bit of proof that he'd been forgotten. One more piece of evidence to confirm that he wasn't deserving of an answer.

God answers prayers, his father had told him long ago, but sometimes the answer is no.

For a depressingly long time, *all* his answers had been no. He'd lost faith that there could ever be a yes for him.

"Michael?" she gently prodded.

Shaking his head to clear it, he looked at her—sweet smile, gentle patience. She was a better woman than he deserved. If he hurt her, or if he let someone else hurt her...

He would just have to see that it didn't happen.

"Go into the bedroom," he said at last, "and put on that dress I brought you."

She was a bit puzzled. "Don't you think it's a little bit much for the middle of the day when we can't go anywhere?"

"I'm going to paint your picture in that dress." And then he was going to remove it. He was going to make love to her the rest of the day and all through the night. Then, when she was gone, when this mess was over and life was back to normal and she had left him all alone again, he would look at the painting.

And he would remember.

He would always remember.

Chapter 8

Valery closed the bedroom door quietly behind her and walked to the closet, taking the dress from its place there. It looked out of place, the only garment that was even remotely feminine in a closet filled with men's clothing.

With Michael's clothes.

She wished she could look her best for him. At home she had lovely lingerie, including an ivory-hued full slip of the sort once associated with sensuous Southern women and steamy Southern nights, and a pair of sheer silk stockings that perfectly matched the dress. She had a satin ribbon choker and antique earrings, both purchased at the shop specifically to go with the dress.

But home was fifteen minutes away, and even home couldn't solve her biggest problems, she thought, looking at herself in the mirror, tugging despairingly at her short, black hair. She would never be as beautiful as the vision he'd painted, but she was a whole lot prettier with her own natural blond hair.

And this afternoon, she desperately wanted to be as pretty as she could possibly be.

After stripping out of her clothes, she carefully pulled the dress over her head. The fabric wasn't as fragile as its age might suggest, but still, she was always cautious with it. The dress had cost a small fortune, and she loved it. She had always thought, in a never-never sort of way, that she would be married in it.

Of course, that was when there'd been no one to marry.

No one to love.

No one to feel more than a passing affection for.

No one who hadn't been in her life one day and gone the next.

And what made her think any of that had changed? she wondered with a scowl as she fastened as many of the tiny fabric-covered buttons down the back as she could reach. Michael had been careful to make certain that she understood exactly what was ahead for them if they didn't stop: an affair, maybe a little heartache. He wanted her for now, but not always. He wanted intimacy and closeness, but not romance. He wanted to make love with her, but he didn't want to love her.

He wasn't offering her much, and he knew it—*It might be a mistake; I don't want to hurt you*—but, however little it was, she wanted it.

She wanted it with a greed she had never experienced before.

She wanted it with an intensity that frightened her.

After putting on the little leather slippers, she left the bedroom for the bathroom. There, a thick towel draped across her shoulders in front, she freshened her makeup, then brushed her hair. For a time she stared hard at her reflection, relentlessly ticking off flaws—her forehead was too high, her lower lip too full, her skin too pale. She wasn't beautiful, seductive, sensuous or any of the things that would appeal to the artist in Michael.

She probably wasn't more than a few of the things that appealed to the man in him, either.

"Take what you can get," she whispered, her voice no more than a rustle of sound. "Take it and appreciate it and consider yourself lucky for having that much."

At last, taking a deep breath, she left the bathroom. "You'll have to help me with the buttons," she said as she rounded the corner. "I can't reach—"

Abruptly she broke off. He was standing beside the easel, a small, flat box in hand, and he was staring at her as if... As if he very much liked what he saw. As if he very much approved of what he saw.

"Damn," he murmured fervently. "You're a beautiful woman, Valery."

Lazy, warm pleasure curled through her. Put that way, she could believe that he believed it. So his artist's vision was flawed. So he found beauty in the unexpected. *He* believed that *she* was beautiful.

She could be satisfied with that.

Feeling suddenly a little shy, she came a few faltering steps closer. "I can't reach all the buttons," she said, turning her back to him. She'd managed the top few and the bottom ones. The dozen or so in between were open.

His fingers brushed her skin, feathery touches, as he started with the highest button and moved down. This wasn't the first time she'd had to rely on a man's help to get into—or out of—her clothing, but this was the first time it had been so... sensual. So full of promise. By the time he finished, she was warm and tingly and couldn't have cared less about all the accessories that perfected the look of the dress. This time, no doubt, less was better.

Turning, she watched him while waiting for some instruction. She had never posed for anyone before, other than the occasional Sinclair family portrait, and those had always been photographs, not paintings. Brief as those sittings were, they had always been painful moments, with her and Remy separated physically by his parents, emotionally by a world of resentment and hurt.

But there would be nothing painful about this.

There would be only pleasure.

Anticipation.

"Do you always work in oil?"

"I prefer oils, but I do a little bit of everything—watercolors, pastels and pen-and-ink. I'm going to use pastels today." He lifted the lid from the box, revealing a palette of well-used crayon-type colors in a wide range of hues. They looked as if they would be fun to play with, she thought, soft and transferring their tints to paper so easily.

"So what are you planning to do? Me, just standing in the middle of your apartment?"

He fastened a heavy sheet of textured paper to the masonite drawing board that had replaced her portrait on the easel before looking at her and slowly smiling. "You," he agreed. "Just sitting in the middle of my apartment—for right now, at least. I'll add a background later."

"What kind of background?"

"A place I know." After finishing arranging his supplies, he left the room for a moment, then returned with a quilt. It bore an intricate design, shades of green and crimson, solids and prints, on an ivory background. To Valery, who knew little about quilts, it looked hand-pieced and finely made, the sort of thing that, once it achieved the grace of age, would be of heirloom quality.

"Pretty," she murmured, fingering one edge before helping him spread it across the floor. "You should use this, or at least display it, not hide it away in a closet."

"My grandmother made it for me. The pattern is called the double wedding ring." He glanced across it, found the section he was looking for and lifted it for her inspection. There, embroidered in the center of one loop in hunter green thread, were two names: *Michael and Beth*. Underneath that was a date. Their wedding date.

The quilt had been a gift to celebrate a marriage that had lasted, according to Michael, too long—and not long enough.

No wonder he kept it in a closet.

"It's still a shame not to use something so pretty. Maybe you can find another woman named Beth," she teased, "and marry on the same day, then get your grandmother to change the year."

"Another woman who wouldn't mind being Beth Bennett?" He shook his head. "I don't think so. Not this time. Come over here and sit down."

She obeyed him, taking a seat near the back edge of the quilt, folding her legs to one side as he instructed, supporting her weight lightly with one hand on the opposite side. The quilted cotton was pliable enough but lacked the softness of well-used fabric, and the batting was still thick, still as puffy as the day his grandmother had stitched it. So many hours of work, such a labor of love, only to sit forgotten in a closet. It was sad, she thought, as sad as the divorce that had relegated it to obscurity.

He crouched in front of her, shifting her body a little this way, her head a little that. After a time he walked back and looked, then returned and arranged the folds of the dress, smoothing it down her shoulders, across her stomach, over her legs. For a moment he fingered the hem of the dress, much as she'd just done with the quilt; then, as he got to his feet and moved to the easel, he asked, "Why antique clothing?"

"I graduated from college with a degree in business and no interest in going on to earn an M.B.A. I was tired of school, tired of being dependent on Aunt Marie and Uncle George. I had already cost them enough—" in terms far dearer, she thought, than money "—so I figured it was time to get out on my own. I wanted to live in New Orleans—in the Quarter, actually, though, of course, I couldn't afford that—so I began looking for a job, and I got this one."

"So it was just chance. You didn't already have an appreciation for old things."

She gave him a dry look. "How could I grow up at Belle Ste. Claire without developing an appreciation for fine old things?"

"How would I know, never having seen Belle Ste. Claire?" he retorted. "Do you like your job?"

After a moment's consideration, she nodded. "The only way I'd like it better is if the shop were mine, if I were working for myself instead of someone else. That's sort of a goal, I guess. The owner keeps saying that one of these days he's going to sell out and move to Arizona and that when he does, he'll give me first chance. When my mother died, she left me some money, and I've been saving, but...I don't know."

"What other goals do you have?"

"Other goals?"

"Do you want to get married?"

She watched him for a moment, so intent on the work before him, and felt an odd little twinge around her heart. She relieved it with a heavy sigh. "Like most little girls, I thought I would grow up and meet Prince Charming, get married and live happily ever after. When I did grow up, I found there weren't too many princes and they weren't too charming." Then, abruptly, she corrected that. "The problem wasn't with them. It was me. I don't get close to many people."

He gazed at her for a moment—seeing, she supposed, angles, lines, shadows and hues—before turning his attention back to the paper. "Not everyone's going to let you down, Valery."

Realistically she knew that, but telling it to her heart was a problem.

"What about kids? You only need a prince for a night for that. Surely you can be charmed for that long."

"No," she replied flatly, so flatly that he stopped what he was doing and looked at her in surprise.

"You don't want kids?"

"Not that way. I grew up without parents, Michael. Every kid deserves to have at least that much. I'll never have a baby without a husband, without a father for her." After a moment, she asked, "What about you and Beth? Didn't you want kids?"

"How do you know we didn't have any?"

"You would have mentioned it before now."

He nodded once in acknowledgement, then concentrated on his work for a time before finally answering her. "When Beth and I first got married, we decided that we wanted to stay in this apartment. Three years later we decided that we wanted a divorce. Those were the first and last things we agreed on during our marriage."

"You wanted kids and she didn't." It was a guess, but Valery was sure she was right. There was something about him—his gentleness, maybe, or his patience—that hinted at a good father in the making. And his background—small-town middle America, son of a preacher and farmer, big brother, protector—made him a natural for kids.

"So she said. As it turned out, she wanted them, all right. She just didn't want them with me." He broke off, exchanging a white tint for a richer shade of ivory. "She and her husband have a son and a daughter."

She wondered how he'd felt about that, if it had hurt when he'd found out. Even if he had no longer loved her, surely he must have felt a twinge of something—jealousy, regret, anger—at seeing her pregnant or hearing that she'd given birth to the baby she'd insisted to him that she didn't want. But she couldn't hear it in his voice, couldn't read it in his expression.

Michael worked in silence for a while, the minutes passing unnoticed, the sketch in front of him swiftly taking shape. Finally he stopped, standing motionless, studying his work so far. For a preliminary piece, it would do. Later he would fill in the background—a place so familiar to him that he could already envision the finished piece in his mind. Later still he would do it all over again, this time in oils—for their richness and intensity—on fine Irish linen.

By then he would probably be working from memory. She would probably never see the finished painting, but it was just as well, for it would represent *his* memories, not hers. She wouldn't know that the house in the background, with its deep shaded porch, was the house where he'd grown up, wouldn't recognize the distant fields as the Bennett family farm. The swing, a plank of weathered wood hanging from two ropes from a branch of a tall oak, would hold no special meaning for her; she would have no recollections of wading or fishing in the winding creek that ran nearby.

To her, the painting, if she ever saw it, would be no more than a pretty woman in a pretty place.

To him, it would represent *home*. A place, a woman, a feeling.

Peripherally he saw her shift a little and realized that she was probably tired, but he didn't tell her that she could get up and move around. He wasn't quite ready to stop, wasn't quite ready to move on to the indulgence, the pleasure—the commitment?—that awaited him when he was finished here.

Or was he?

With a shake of his head, he focused his gaze hard on the textured paper, on the shadings and shadows and degrees of colors, on the fluid lines of her dress and the effortless way the quilt colors blended one into another. Maybe he wouldn't use the farm for the background, he thought—or, at least, not that particular part of it. The age of it—the hundred-year-old house, the peeling barn, the leaning fences, the ancient trees—would complement the antique dress, the from-another-era look. The faded beauty of the farm would nicely balance the timeless beauty of the woman.

But maybe, instead, he would choose another location, someplace in the woods, a place where it stayed cool on the hottest summer day, where sunlight filtered through the tall trees to create a lace-edged pattern on the lush growth. A place where peace could be found, where privacy could be found—privacy for laying her down on his grandmother's quilt. For removing that lovely old dress, for stripping out of his own clothing, for...

His fingers clenched, and he felt rather than heard the breaking of the crayon he still held. He tossed it onto the worktable, then wiped his hands on a clean, white towel.

He couldn't take her to his parents' farm, couldn't show her that peaceful place in the woods. But they had privacy. He had his grandmother's quilt—or, better yet, a bed in the next room. He could remove that lovely dress. He could indulge her, could indulge himself. He could give her such pleasure and show her such need. He could make the last edgy, fearful week or so disappear, could give her something sweet and warm and tender to take its place in her memories.

For today, for this afternoon, he—who had been the cause of so much pain and sorrow—for once could make everything right.

Circling the easel, he walked over to her, extending his hand. He saw in her eyes that she understood the offer he was making. It was that simple: take his hand, and he would lead her into the bedroom to make love. Refuse it, and she refused him.

He also saw that she had no intention of refusing.

She laid her hand in his, and he pulled her easily to her feet. It was tempting to kiss her then, to undress her there, to make love to her right there on the quilt. But, holding both her hands in one of his, he delayed for the few seconds it took to reach his bedroom. At the door, though, he paused. "Last chance, Valery."

"It isn't a mistake," she said, referring to their conversation of that morning. She spoke with the seriousness of a child, so intense, so full of faith, that he almost found it possible to believe her.

Even though he had long ago stopped accepting anything on faith.

And then she smiled that sweet, seductive smile, and he thought that maybe he *could* take something on faith. Like that smile. Some bleak night, when she was gone and he was alone, he would start yet another portrait of her, he knew, wearing that smile and very little else. He would immortalize her for all those future bleak nights.

As if there were any need.

As if he would ever forget.

The bedroom was dimly lit, the afternoon sunlight blocked by the paisley drapes. The darker tones of this room—heavy fabrics, thick drapes, dark wood—had a practical purpose: many were the times when his evening shift lapped over into the night, when his hours for sleeping extended well beyond sunrise. Light was diffused, noise dampened, rest made easier.

But they also served another purpose, he realized for the first time. The room was cozy. Snug. Romantic.

It was the perfect place for this time with Valery.

Once inside the room, he released her to close the door, wanting no distractions—no phone calls, no unwelcome guests, no intrusions. Then, for a moment, he simply stood there, simply watched her as she removed her slippers, placing them neatly, side by side with his own shoes, in the closet.

Side by side. A memory came, unbidden, from the not-too-distant past, of words from a wedding ceremony—his and Beth's wedding. A couple should walk side by side, his father had instructed them. Not one leading, the other following, not one giving orders, the other taking, but together. Side by side. Sharing.

He and Beth had found it impossible. They had rarely even managed to be heading in the same direction, much less sharing anything along the way. They had both had their own goals, their own agendas, their own futures, and they had both naively expected the other to fall into line, to follow along. Until they had both stopped expecting anything at all from each other.

But he could envision just such a life as his father had described with Valery. He could imagine sharing his life with her. He could picture himself living with her at his side.

He could imagine himself loving her.

Always.

Forever.

Her hands clasped to still their trembling, Valery turned to study Michael. He was standing near the dresser, lost somewhere in his thoughts. Was he already regretting this? she wondered wistfully. Already looking for reasons why they shouldn't go on?

It was inevitable—their lovemaking. She knew it, and she suspected that, in his own way, he knew, too. The difference was that she accepted the inevitable, while he fought against it. His guilt over Evan's death, still intense after so many months, was proof of that. So was his struggle against the visions that had first linked them together. And his struggle against this. *Last chance, Valery.*

She knew there were no last chances. You could delay the inevitable, could postpone it time and again, but eventually it *would* come to pass. What was destined to be would be.

And this *was* destined.

"Michael?"

Her voice was soft, little more than a whisper, but it was sufficient to startle him from his thoughts, to bring his attention back to her. It was sufficient to coax a smile from him, gentle and sweet.

He came to her, sliding his arms around her waist, drawing her tight against his body. "No regrets?" she asked, and the surprised look in his eyes was genuine.

"No. I was thinking about promises."

"I don't need any promises from you."

He smiled again, then brushed a kiss across her forehead. "Maybe *I* need them from *you.*"

It was surprising, she reflected, how a few simple words could hurt. His settled, tight and sore and sad, somewhere in her chest, making it uncomfortable to breathe, making it damned near impossible to smile. But she did breathe, and she did smile, and she offered him his promises. "I won't make any demands of you. I won't think this means something. I won't expect more than you intend to give. I—"

He cut her off with a kiss, slow and lazy, taking away the breath she'd just reclaimed, increasing her heart rate, raising her temperature, making her feel both the most incredible power and the most luscious weakness. When he lifted his head again, he hoarsely said, "Wrong promises, sweetheart. Some demands are perfectly welcome. Even I don't know exactly what's left in me to give, and you'd damn well better believe that this means something."

"Then what is it you want?" she whispered.

"You. I want you, Valery."

She smiled unsteadily. "You've got me." For now. For as long as he wanted. For as long as he needed.

For as long as *she* needed?

He kissed her again, another long, slow, wet kiss that left her clinging to him for support. No man had ever kissed her this way, touched her this way. No man had ever made her feel this way. Only Michael.

Later, she thought, when she was alone, when she was calm and rational again, she would consider the significance of that. She would marvel over it, would be amazed that what they'd shared was so special, would be grateful for such a gift.

Or she would fear it. She would worry that he didn't feel the same, would fret over the heartache it could surely bring. She would fear losing it, losing him, losing herself.

But for now she would simply enjoy. Treasure. Take pleasure.

Tugging his shirt from his jeans, she slid her hands underneath, gliding them over his stomach. She felt scar tissue and remembered, from when he'd told her about Evan, that he'd been shot. She was sorry he'd been hurt, was sorry he carried this reminder of the worst time of his life. She was especially sorry she could do nothing to make it right for him. She wanted desperately to know that one day he would be all right, that one day his heartache would ease, that he would forgive himself and find healing. Faith. Love.

She would give him her own faith if she could.

She would give him her love.

If she could.

When he suddenly released her, she made a soft sound of protest until she realized what he was doing—not pushing her away, simply turning her away so that he could reach the buttons down the back of her dress. There were eighteen of them, each small and round and fitted through a narrow fabric loop, and he unfastened every one of them before pulling her back against him. His arms were around her waist, inside the dress, his hands seeking out her breasts. She didn't think even once about her precious dress. Only two thoughts ran through her mind, one behind the other, over and over: how wonderful this felt, and how she wanted more, more of his kisses, more of his caresses, more of *him*.

Michael squeezed her breasts gently and felt her nipples respond, hard little peaks pressing against the centers of his palms. Her bra—ivory, thin, lacy—provided a flimsy enough barrier, but he wanted it out of the way, wanted to feel her and nothing else, skin to skin, hand to breast, mouth to nipple. Sweet damnation, he wanted to see her, feel her, taste her. He wanted to crawl inside her body, the way she was crawling inside his soul. He wanted to get lost in her.

He wanted to find himself in her.

Hell. Not so long ago he would have said he didn't have a soul. Now he knew he did, and he knew it ached. For this. For her. For Valery.

Reluctantly he withdrew his hands and guided the dress off her shoulders, then drew it up over her hips, her waist, her breasts, her head. If it had been any other piece of clothing, he would have dropped it onto the floor and worried about it later, but he took a moment, one agonizingly long moment, to drape it across the nearest chair, and another moment—longer, sweeter torment—to look at her, to study and absorb her.

Paint her wearing a sweet, seductive smile and very little else? Try *nothing* else. In her ivory lace bra and matching tiny panties, she was lovely—winter pale, porcelain delicate. His artist's eye wanted to capture on canvas the well-proportioned lines of her body—long throat, rounded breasts, narrow waist, slender hips that led to long, long legs—while the man in him simply wanted—wanted to touch. Wanted to kiss. Wanted to thrill. Wanted to fill. His desire had turned sharp, had developed edges that scraped and left him raw with hunger. Thoughts grew jumbled, little making sense but that overriding need.

Not desire.

Not hunger.

Not wanting.

Need.

As if he couldn't live another moment without her.

As if he surely might die with her.

But it would be a sweet death.

With a smile, she unfastened the clasp of her bra and let it fall to the floor. He kicked off his shoes, peeled off his socks, pulled his shirt over his head and left it to fall where it might.

Hooking her thumbs beneath the elastic band of her panties, she drew the little bit of silky ivory down, bending, pushing, kicking it away, and then she lowered herself to the bed, one knee, one hand, slowly down, until she was lying on the green, navy and crimson cover.

Damned if she didn't look like she belonged there. Her nights in his bed had given her a claim to it.

And her days in his life had given her a claim to that, too. If she wanted it.

He unzipped his jeans, and Valery watched, unashamed of her curiosity. His jeans were snug, and he was hard—a tantalizing picture if ever she'd seen one. There was something impressive about a man's arousal, something so damned primitive, so damned powerful. A woman could hide her need, but a man's was impossible to disguise, impossible to ignore.

And Michael's...

He stripped off his jeans, and a fluttery little sigh trembled through her. Powerful. Oh, yes.

The mattress shifted when he joined her there, then shifted again as he moved over her. For a moment he simply looked down at her, his eyes clear—no shadows, she realized in some small, still-rational place—and then he moved, settling between her thighs, probing, finding, pushing, filling until she could take no more. The entire time his intense, dark gaze never left hers.

Unexpectedly her eyes grew damp, and she squeezed them shut, breaking that small contact. She had never felt so connected to another human being—not physically, mentally, emotionally. Certainly not spiritually. But if she told him, if she *tried* to tell him that, he would probably laugh in that dry way of his and remind her that he no longer believed in things spiritual.

But *she* did.

"Are you—"

All right? Opening her eyes again, she smiled, combed her fingers through his hair, brushed them across his mouth, brought her hand to rest on his chest. "I'm fine. I'm..." He moved just a little, seating himself a little deeper, and her body adjusted, tightening, stretching, easing. "Oh, Michael," she sighed.

Lowering his body closer to hers, he kissed her, sliding his tongue inside her mouth, tasting, teasing, tantalizing, and she welcomed him with her own tongue. At the same time he began moving inside her, withdrawing so gradually that she throbbed, then sinking deep again, until they couldn't get any closer, any tighter, any more intimate. His rhythm was slow, her response immediate. She was hot, on edge, quivering with need, with sensation, with emotion. Everywhere he touched her, seductively or not, intentionally or not, she ached.

As the tempo of his thrusts increased, as the fever built, she clung to him. She kissed him with more than a hint of desperation, with everything she needed and wanted, with everything she had to give, and she held him. She felt his muscles clench and tighten, heard his breathing grow ragged, felt his completion building, strengthening, demanding, as surely, as purely, as she felt her own.

When he emptied into her, it was with a groan, with a heart-stopping intensity that gave her the push she needed for her own finish. He held her so tightly, so fiercely, as if he might never let her go, and he kissed her as hungrily as if the last few minutes had never happened, as if satisfaction would be a long time coming.

Maybe it would be, she thought, shuddering, weakening, giving in to the lethargy that was slowly claiming taut muscles and quivering nerves.

Maybe satisfaction would take more than once, more than an afternoon, a night, a week, a year.

Maybe it would take a lifetime.

"Tell me something," Valery said.

Michael shifted, settling against the pillows propped behind him, drawing Valery with him so that her head remained cushioned on his chest. The room would have been a few shades darker if not for the bedside lamp, and the apartment was a whole lot quieter—no heavy breathing, no groans, no helpless cries. It was peaceful. Comfortable.

Valery made it comfortable.

After a moment, he pressed a kiss to her temple, then asked, "What would you like to know?"

She tilted her head to the side so she could see his face without leaving his embrace. "Have you ever done this before?"

"Made love?" He pretended to consider it. "I think I've done it a time or two."

"I could tell by your moves that you weren't a beginner," she said dryly. "I mean with one of... one of your visions."

His laughter broke free before he could restrain it. "Hell, no."

"Why so vehement? Am I the only woman who's ever come to you for help?"

The only woman who's ever come to you for help. He liked that phrasing, liked it better than visions, than people popping unwanted into his mind. But it wasn't entirely true in her case. He was beginning to believe that she had come to him—psychically, physically—for more than help.

He was beginning to think that maybe she was a gift, served up by the powers that be—by God?—as a reward for his years of enduring the other so-called gift.

"No," he replied, stroking the baby-soft underside of her breast. "You're not the only woman."

"But you've never been attracted to the others." She sounded smug, so sweetly, satisfyingly smug.

"We're not talking great numbers here. Over the years there have been twelve, maybe fourteen people. Four or five of them were women." Then he relented. "You're the only woman I've been attracted to in longer than you'd care to know."

"Since Evan died," she said softly.

Yes. Since Evan died. That was when *he* had stopped living, as well.

She turned onto her side, touching one fingertip to the scar that curved across his ribs. "Do you think he would have wanted that, Michael? Do you think that for one minute he would have wanted you to blame yourself, that he would have wanted you to punish yourself the way you have?''

Of course he wouldn't have. Michael knew that, knew it in his head as surely as he couldn't get it through to his heart. Remy had told him; Smith had. Even Evan's wife, Karen, had taken time from her grieving to come to him, to assure him that she didn't blame him, to remind him that Evan had loved him, that he wouldn't have wanted Michael to feel any guilt over his death.

And he'd felt it anyway, had tried to drown in it, along with the knowledge that, even after death, he was still letting Evan down.

''We met our freshman year in college—we'd been assigned as roommates. I'd never known anyone like him. Within minutes of meeting, I knew we were going to be best friends for the rest of our lives. He was a rare soul. Unique. Special.''

''No,'' Valery whispered against his chest. ''That kind of chemistry isn't one-sided. It takes two. You were both unique, Michael. Both special.''

That kind of chemistry. The closest he'd ever come to feeling anything like that since Evan was with Valery. He wondered if that meant she felt it, too. Did she agree that there was something special between them? Some sort of bond that might last the rest of their lives?

The rest of their lives. Forever and ever, till death do us part, amen. Now that was a thought.

''It's hard without him, isn't it?'' she murmured. ''You love someone, you build a special relationship together, you're always there for each other and then suddenly he's gone. It hurts. No matter how it happens, you can't help but blame yourself, but sooner or later you have to deal with it. You have to get on with your life.''

''Like you have?'' he asked skeptically.

Her hand had been stroking his stomach. Now it went still, and for a moment so did she. He couldn't even feel her soft little breaths. Then the moment ended, and her fingers began moving again. Her breast began rising and falling again. ''We're talking about you, not me.''

"You're talking about me as if you know what I've been through, and to some extent, I believe you do. Maybe it was even worse for you. At least Evan died. Your parents left you voluntarily. Your cousin turned his back on you of his own free will." He felt her stiffen and start to push away, and he held her tighter. "Don't tell me I have to deal with losing Evan. Don't tell me I have to get on with my life. Don't give me advice that you can't follow yourself."

"It's hardly the same, Michael." She succeeded in wriggling free of his embrace and sat up in bed, turning to face him. Her hair was mussed, her body all soft and enticing before she covered herself with the corner of the comforter. "You're still grieving for Evan. You're still convinced that if he can't be alive and happy and well, then you don't deserve to be, either."

"And you're convinced that everyone you love will leave you. First it was your mother, then your father—"

"He isn't my father."

"He is in your heart," he pointed out.

After a long still moment, she acknowledged that with a single nod.

"And then there was Remy."

"So I had a few bad years. I'm over them, Michael. I'm living a perfectly normal and happy life."

"Are you?" He reached for her hand, lacing his fingers through hers. "Who's sharing this perfectly normal, happy life with you? You told me before that you don't have any close friends, that the friends you do have aren't important to you. You don't know what it's like to lose a friend like Evan because you've never *had* a friend like him, have you?"

She didn't respond.

"You told me you don't need anyone in your life. Is that normal, Valery? Is that what makes you happy—being totally alone? How does it feel to be the object of a citywide—hell, a statewide—search and to know that, after all the years you've lived here, no one gives a damn whether you're found? No one gives a damn *if* you're found...except the cops and Jimmy Falcone."

She gave him a long, unfaltering look. "And you. You care."

The desire to smile at her quiet confidence was almost too much to control. "You noticed that, huh?"

"You wouldn't be here with me right now if you didn't care."

"You're right. I do." He hesitated, and his gaze shifted away, then back again. "I wish I could say the same about you. I know I don't make love with women who don't mean something to me . . . but I know you've been with men who meant nothing to you."

Valery felt cold inside, the sort of chill that settled deep inside and didn't go away for a long, long time. It was the sort of chill that a warm blanket or a hot drink couldn't touch. It was the sort of chill she had lived with night after miserable night when she was eleven.

What he was saying was the absolute truth. He was the kind of man who needed to be emotionally intimate with a woman before he moved on to physical intimacy. She had always started with physical intimacy, had always turned away before emotional needs could enter the picture. He had never made love to a woman he hadn't cared about. She had never had sex with a man she *had* cared for.

Until today.

Still, the fact that his words were true didn't make them hurt any less. Didn't make her feel any better. Didn't make her feel worthy.

"You're right," she admitted, a little sad, a little sore inside. "I've been with men who came into my life, and they stayed a little while, and then they were gone again. I never cared. I never missed them. I never wanted them again. But you're different, Michael. I'll always remember you. When you're gone—"

"Why do you assume that I'll leave, too?"

She stared down at her hand, still caught in his. "Because, in my experience, that's what people do." After a brief pause, she asked, "Don't you assume it, too? Don't you find yourself thinking, 'When this is over . . . When she's gone . . . When my life is back to normal . . .'?"

The guilty look that came into his eyes was answer enough for her. He was looking forward to the future—to a future that didn't include her. But quickly enough the guilt faded and was replaced by an intense stare. "Will you answer a question for me, Valery?"

She nodded.

"This afternoon, here in this bed.... Was it different from when you were with those other men? Was it the same, or did you feel something—" He broke off, raked his fingers through his hair, sighed exasperatedly. "Something *special?*"

She shrugged casually, as if she didn't know exactly what he meant. As if it hadn't almost brought her to tears. "Chemistry."

"Intimacy."

"Lust."

"Desire."

"Hormones."

He shook his head. "Emotion, Valery. And that frightens you, doesn't it? *I* frighten you. Trusting me enough to let me get close, letting me get close enough to hurt you, taking a chance on getting hurt—all that frightens you, doesn't it?"

Turning away abruptly, she leaned over the bed to grab the only clothing within reach—his T-shirt and the socks she'd left there earlier. She tugged the black shirt over her head, smoothing it down until she was modestly covered, then began straightening and pulling on first one sock, then its mate. "This is a stupid conversation," she said, choosing her words carefully, intending to offend, to bring an end to the talk. "I have sex with you once, and you start talking all this nonsense, as if you have a *right.*"

His voice, when he finally spoke, was steady but underlaid with a cool warning. "My feelings don't get hurt easily, Val, but don't push it. I know you're afraid of getting hurt. I know you've lived more than half your life afraid. But if you want to punish somebody for that, punish the people who hurt you—not me."

She sat still on the edge of the bed, feeling the mattress give and dip as he got up. She heard the rustle of clothing as he pulled on his jeans, heard the soft shuffle of his bare feet on the wooden floor as he walked away. She wanted to say something, anything, to stop him, but her throat was tight. No words could get out.

And she didn't have anything to say.

Again, he was right. It was easy enough to think that she was lonely, easy enough to envy him his friends, easy enough to want him in her life, to think of him in terms of love, when it was just that—thinking, wanting. No harm could come from thinking. A heart couldn't get broken just from wanting.

But faced with the prospect of possibly having what her heart wanted . . .

Frightened didn't even begin to describe the way she felt.

Chapter 9

Valery didn't know how long she sat there, not thinking, not moving, just doing her damnedest not to cry. After a time, though, realizing that she was cold, hungry and lonely—God, she was always lonely—she got up and got dressed. Still wearing Michael's T-shirt, she left the room, taking short, halting steps into the living room.

Michael was in the kitchen, still wearing nothing but jeans. He was gathering ingredients from the cabinets and the refrigerator, getting ready to fix dinner. His movements were controlled, his manner stiff and unapproachable. No doubt this was one of those times when he was thinking, *When this is over, when she's gone, when my life is back to normal...*

As she moved farther into the room, she saw that the quilt was off the floor, neatly folded and lying across the back of the couch. The easel was put away, too, along with the sketch he'd done this afternoon... and the portrait she had finally faced this morning. Tossed in the garbage, where he likely felt they belonged? she wondered. Or tucked into the lovely armoire with the disturbing paintings of the churches?

The possibility made her shiver.

Courage carried her only as far as the end of the galley-style kitchen. Her feet stopped where wood planks gave way to vinyl tile. A bowl of chopped vegetables—onions, peppers, celery—sat on the counter, along with dishes of shrimp, sausage and crabmeat, oil was starting to smoke on the stove, and he was in the process of mixing spices in a smaller dish. Three kinds of pepper, salt, several varieties of dried leaves. Her kitchen at home contained exactly three spices: salt, black pepper and garlic powder. Like his ex-wife, she was a lousy cook.

But she could be a hell of an assistant.

"Can I help?"

He didn't even glance at her. "No."

His curt tone stung, but she didn't have the right to complain, she reminded herself. Didn't have the right to mind.

"What are you making?"

"Seafood gumbo with andouille sausage."

She rested her elbows on the counter and watched as he started the roux, adding flour to the hot oil, stirring it constantly with a whisk. "If your wife was a lousy cook and you left home for good when you started college, where did you learn to cook so well?"

"Evan's aunt taught me after the divorce."

"I used to help my mother with dinner sometimes. I never actually cooked a meal, but I peeled potatoes and cut up chicken and made salads. Aunt Marie had a housekeeper who didn't much care for sharing her kitchen. Except for getting snacks, it was mostly off limits to Remy and me." Breaking off, she sighed, then took a deep, fortifying breath. "Michael—"

At last he looked at her. His expression was so hard, so unforgiving, that she wished he hadn't. "Go read the newspaper. Watch TV. Finish that book you started. Just get out of my kitchen and leave me alone."

Although his words—and, worse, his look—left her feeling raw, she withdrew with all the grace and dignity she could muster, withdrew all the way to the bedroom. There she hung up her dress, picked up their remaining clothing and straightened the bed. Then, after turning out the lamp, she went to the window, opened the drapes and the sheers behind them, and stood there, leaning one shoulder against the jamb.

She had come here—to this apartment, to Michael— needing time, and, she decided, she'd been given enough. Tomorrow, when she wasn't feeling quite so blue, she would tell him everything—what the two men had said after they'd killed Nate Simmons. Why she had fled the police station. Why she had refused to go to Remy for help. She would tell Michael, would place her life completely in his hands, and he would decide what to do.

She wondered what that would be. Would he go to his boss or whomever the appropriate people in the police department might be and tell them that an FBI agent might have been responsible for Simmons's murder? Would he arrange for the police department, rather than the FBI, to provide security for her?

Or would he call his friend Smith? As an assistant U.S. Attorney, Kendricks must have some pull within the local FBI office. Would *he* take over?

But what if Michael didn't believe her? What if he found the possibility that a federal agent would have someone murdered too absurd to accept? What if he insisted on turning her over to them anyway?

That wasn't likely, she comforted herself. No matter how angry he got, no matter how hurt he was, he wouldn't endanger her life. As long as there was the slightest, the most remote, chance in hell that Remy was guilty, Michael would protect her.

He had to.

If not for her sake, then for his own.

Michael stirred the roux in the efficient way Aunt Sirena had taught him, careful to avoid splashes, and watched it darken, but his mind wasn't on the job. He was thinking about Valery and how the best day in recent memory had turned so sour.

He had pushed her. Just so he wouldn't have to talk about Evan, just so he could avoid yet another conversation on how he should forgive himself and put the past behind him. He should have simply stated that he didn't want to discuss it. He should have distracted her with a kiss. He should have made love to her again.

He shouldn't have asked for some sort of declaration from her. He shouldn't have pushed for recognition that what they had shared was special. He shouldn't have brought her fears, her past, her other lovers, into the bed with them.

Those promises she had rattled off before they made love—*I won't make any demands of you. I won't think this means something. I won't expect more than you intend to give....* Maybe he had misunderstood them. Maybe she hadn't thought that was what *he* wanted to hear. Maybe it had been her way of telling him that that was what *she* wanted.

But he couldn't offer such promises.

He just couldn't.

Small, dark flecks in the pan in front of him caught his attention, and he muttered a curse. He had forgotten Aunt Sirena's first rule of roux making: pay attention. The high temperatures made burning roux an easy thing, and he'd just done it.

He moved the pan off the stove, pulled out another cast-iron skillet and measured oil into it. While it was heating, he went as far as the bedroom door. "Valery?"

She was standing in the dark, staring out the window.

"I just burned the roux. Want to make another one for me?"

Her voice seemed small and insubstantial. "I don't know how."

"I'll show you."

She hesitated so long that he thought she was going to refuse; then, slowly she turned away from the window. "I'll probably burn it, too."

"All it takes is oil and flour, and I have plenty. We'll keep trying until we get it right."

"What if it's never right?"

"Then we'll enjoy what we have."

She stopped in front of him, close enough now that the light from outside the room touched her face. She looked sad. Regretful. Wistful. Beautiful. "I'm sorry, Michael."

"No regrets, remember?" He brushed his palm across her hair, then pressed a kiss to her lips. "Come on. We missed lunch. Let's see about dinner."

He had never shared his kitchen with anyone—his cooking lessons with Aunt Sirena had taken place in her kitchen over in Slidell—but it was easy enough to get accustomed to. It would be easy, he acknowledged, to become accustomed to sharing a great many places in his life with Valery.

But maybe not on a permanent basis.

Maybe not until she someday realized that time had passed—weeks, months, years—and he was still around.

As soon as dinner—steaming gumbo ladled over hot rice—was ready, they ate, settling on the sofa with their bowls, napkins and drinks. Leaving their dishes for later, they made love there, too, as easily, as comfortably, as if they'd been together for years.

Made love, Michael thought with a scowl as he held her afterward. Someday she would acknowledge that. She would admit that it was more than just good sex. She would see that this wasn't an affair but a relationship. A commitment. It might not last forever—few things ever did—but if it didn't, it wouldn't be for lack of trying on his part.

Someday she would understand all that.

And when she did, he would be waiting.

They shared his bed that night. That was another pleasure Michael had forgotten—a warm woman close enough to touch at any time. It was another intimacy that Valery couldn't turn away from.

He slept soundly for seven or eight hours, rather than his usual three or four, or five if he was lucky. That was a pleasure he'd forgotten, too. Amazing, he thought with a grin, what the release of tension could do for a body.

Now he was watching Valery, asleep on her stomach, her face buried in her pillow. The case was white, old-fashioned, no doubt another find from her shop. His grandmother had pillowcases like that—linen or cotton, scalloped edges with lace or crocheted borders, and embroidered with flowers, different for each month of the year. He remembered dogwoods for April, mums in November and poinsettias for December. Valery's had violets in a dozen shades of lavender and blue.

His grandmother would like Valery. So would his parents. When this was over, maybe he could take her to the farm for a visit.

When this was over.

If she was still in his life.

If she didn't get scared and run.

But even if she did, he was a damned good cop. He figured he could find her. She might have a lot to fear...but *he* had a lot to lose.

Leaving the bed for a moment, he turned the heat on to warm the apartment. When he returned, she moved, murmured, shifted a bit closer, but continued to sleep. Slowly, as the room temperature rose, he edged the covers down, revealing the smooth, pale skin of her back. There was a symmetry to her body that appealed to him artistically, a sense of balance. Her back was long, her waist small, curving in nicely. Her hips flared out generously, a word that he used only in the most flattering way even though he knew she would hate it, and her legs...Her legs went on forever.

Symmetry. Balance. Everything needed it. In his work, good investigative skills were balanced by gut instincts; there was a time to be tough and a time to go easy, a time to negotiate and a time to act. Cooking required a similar balance of flavors, of textures, of proportions. Symmetry and balance were especially important in painting—lighter hues against darker, intensity against subtlety, shadows against light.

And in their lives. Stress demanded relaxation. To fully appreciate joy required an understanding of sorrow. Solitude led to a need for companionship. Distance from the people around you needed to be offset by closeness to the people who mattered.

Celibacy, he thought with a self-deprecating grin, led to a hellacious need for making love, as evidenced by his own arousal after doing no more than looking, admiring.

At last he let himself touch her, trailing his fingers down her spine, spanning her waist, stroking across her bottom. The changes in her body came gradually, so gradually that it took a while to realize that she was awake. The sleepy, relaxed air around her gave way to tension. Now, everywhere his fingers touched, chill bumps appeared. Her breathing had become shallower, more tautly controlled. The overall softness was gone, replaced by a tightening of muscles, a drawing up of nerves.

He leaned over her, nuzzling her hair back, seeking her ear. "I know you're awake, sweetheart," he murmured before kissing her there.

A soft sigh vibrating through her, she stretched sinuously, sensuously, then turned onto her side to face him. "Good morning." She sounded drowsy, hazy, as if the greeting required all her energy. Her eyes were still closed, her hair standing on end in places, mashed flat in others, and her face was soft, lazy, sleepy.

"Did you sleep well?"

"Hmm."

"Want to sleep some more?"

"Hmm."

"All right. Just a morning kiss, then I'll let you sleep." But it wasn't her lips he kissed. Bending lower, he cupped her breast in his palm and closed his mouth around her nipple. It hardened quickly, growing between his teeth, responding to his gentle bite and strong sucking kiss. She reacted quickly, too, catching her breath in a gasp, trying to speak his name but losing the second syllable in a deep, hungry groan.

Valery forced her eyes open, not an easy task when her body wanted nothing more than to lie back and let Michael have his way with her. The first thing she saw was his head bent over her breast. It was a lovely picture . . . a lovely sensation . . . a perfectly lovely way to start a day.

Then, before the thought was even completed, he ended the kiss and looked up at her. He looked well rested, she thought, smugly satisfied that she had played some small role in the accomplishment. His eyes were clear, his expression endearing—and his chin, where it rested against her breast, was bristly with a day's growth of beard.

"Good morning," she repeated, lifting one hand to stroke through his hair.

"You don't look so sleepy anymore."

"I don't know. It might take a few more kisses like that to get me fully awake."

"I have something better than kisses."

"I know. I feel it." She smiled appreciatively. His arousal was pressing against her thigh, hard and so hot. The heat generated between them was intense. She felt it everywhere he touched her, felt the ache for it everywhere he wasn't touching. She felt it deep inside, where she was hot, damp, empty, throbbing for his attention.

The look he gave her was serious and chastening. "I was referring to coffee."

With an uninhibited laugh, she wrapped her arms around his neck and wriggled a little closer. "Sure, you were. And this—" She rubbed against him, pressing indecently close, making him catch his own breath. "Am I supposed to ignore this?"

"Could you?"

"It's an awful lot to ignore."

"If you tried really hard . . ."

"It'd be easier to make it go away—and a lot more fun, too." Pulling him closer, she kissed his throat, his jaw, his chin, slowly working her way to his mouth. By the time she reached it, he was ready. He kissed her hard, filling her mouth with his tongue, taking, demanding, feeding. His passion was reserved for her, he'd said, and yesterday he'd proven it. He was showing her again this morning, stirring her own passion, making her hotter, needier, than she'd ever been.

She wanted him then, right then, wanted him inside her, wanted him to fill her hard and fast, then to do it again slow and easy. She wanted him deep, rough, tender.

But he had other desires, other plans. He intended to seduce her, even though she'd been ready, achy and hot since that first kiss. He suckled her breasts, making her nipples hard and sore, making her muscles strain, making her groan with helpless pleasure and mindless need. He left hot, wet kisses along her stomach, her hip and between her thighs, such sweet kisses that she nearly cried, creating such sweet torment that she nearly died. She begged him to stop, begged him never to stop. In the end, she simply begged.

"Please, Michael . . . please . . ."

He joined with her then, lifting her hips, seeking his place and filling her with one long, smooth thrust, pushing hard and deep until her body gloved him. Her senses feverishly heightened, she felt him—felt every inch, so intimately connected, so hard, so hot that it was a wonder, she thought dazedly, that they didn't steam. He took her hard, the way she wanted, and tender, the way she needed, demanding her passion—her body, her soul—and giving his own in return, and when she reached the edge, when the need for him shattered, when release washed over her with a hoarse cry and a relentless shudder, he filled her, hot and liquid, equally relentless, equally shattered.

For a long, ragged time they lay entangled—her body still sheltering him, his body pressing hers breathlessly down, their legs entwined. Finally he lifted his head from the pillow beside hers, gave her mouth a sweetly passionless kiss, then offered her a drained smile and a greeting.

"Good morning."

It was a few hours later before Valery got her morning bath and a few hours after that, over bowls of leftover gumbo, before she could keep the promise she'd made to herself the night before. They were sitting at the table, sharing the last soft drink in the house, when she finally spoke. "I need your help, Michael."

He studied her for a long time before mildly asking, "What kind of help?"

"Police help."

After another long silence, he shrugged. "To protect and to serve—that's my job. So far I've done the protecting. What about the serving?"

She took a deep breath and found that it didn't help. "You asked before why I was afraid to let the police turn me over to the FBI after—after I saw that man die. If my reason was personal."

"And it was. Remy."

"Yes." Betraying her cousin was harder than she'd expected, but she pushed on. She owed it to Michael—owed him the loyalty. The gratitude. The trust. "After I told you about growing up with him, you still wondered why I didn't go to him."

"I still don't understand that. In spite of all that's happened, he's still family, Valery. He's still your cousin— maybe not a great one, but..." He shrugged.

"Yes," she agreed again. "He *is* still family. His parents are really the only family I have left—by love, at least, if not by blood. That's why... That's why I didn't tell you everything. That's why I haven't told *anyone* everything."

Considering that, he left the table, taking their dishes into the kitchen. When he returned, he sat down not to her right, where he had been, but in the chair across from her, and he had that hard-edged look in his eyes. She was no longer talking to the man she'd made love with most of the morning, but to the cop who wore a badge and carried a gun.

"You have information about Simmons's murder that you haven't told anyone—not even the detectives who originally interviewed you?"

She nodded.

"What sort of information?"

She let her eyes drift shut, let the scene from that sunny Monday afternoon fill her mind. The misfortune of literally running into Nate Simmons. The pleasant half block's walk alongside him. The arrival of the two men. The guns, Nate's surprise, the shooting, her shock. And the words those two men had spoken as their friend lay dying. Oh, yes, their words.

"After the men shot Simmons, I told you they were in no hurry to get away. They were so calm, so deliberate about everything."

"They weren't interested in you. They didn't care that you'd seen them, that you could identify them."

"Sort of," she hedged. This was where she'd started lying, by omission if not with her actual words. "When they shot him, I was standing only a few feet away. I had his blood on my clothes. My first thought was to run, but there was a stoop behind me and a brick wall beside me. There was no place to go, no place to hide. I was terrified that they were going to kill me, too, because I could identify them. One of them pointed his gun at me and asked, 'What about her?' The other one—Vince—looked right at me, and he said, 'Forget her. Our deal—'"

She broke off and reached for the Coke, but found her hands were unsteady. Locking them together, she pressed them between her knees and continued. "He said, 'Our deal with Sinclair was only for him. Let's get out of here and let him know that the job's done.' And the other guy, the littler guy, just sort of laughed, and he said, 'Hell, Sinclair's a fed. He'll find out that Nate's out of the way soon enough.'"

He sat silent for so long that she began to worry, began to wonder if confiding in him had been the right thing to do. But finally he spoke. "Those were their words? You're not paraphrasing what they said? You remember their exact words?"

"Those were their words. It's not the sort of thing I'd be likely to forget."

"And you assumed they were referring to Remy."

"How many other federal agents named Sinclair are there in New Orleans?"

"I don't know of any," he admitted. After another of his thoughtful silences, he asked, "You believed them, didn't you? Remy's your cousin, Val, he's *family*. And you believed that he hired those two men to murder Simmons."

"I don't know. I don't know him anymore, Michael. I don't know if he could have someone killed." She felt disloyal for continuing. "I don't know if he could kill *me.*"

The idea that Remy could hurt her was so ludicrous to Michael that his first impulse was to laugh, but he controlled it. After all, she had a valid point. She didn't know Remy. But *he* did, and he didn't believe any of this. In all his years with the FBI, the greatest harm Remy had brought on anyone was to send them to prison, and that was a result of their own criminal activities, not any malice on his part. If there was no other choice, if push came to shove, he knew Remy was capable of killing a suspect, but *only* if there was no other choice, *only* if it was kill or be killed.

But murder?

No way.

No way in hell.

"You're sure you heard them correctly."

She nodded. She looked so serious, he thought. So troubled. She honestly didn't know whether to believe what those men had said. On the one hand, they were criminals, murderers—not exactly the most trustworthy sources in the world. On the other, why would they lie? She was a stranger, someone they hadn't expected to see, someone who'd just had the spectacularly bad luck to get caught up in Nate Simmons's trouble.

"Nate Simmons was one of Remy Sinclair's informants," he said quietly. "He was a hell of a lot more valuable to Remy alive than he is dead."

Pushing her chair back from the table, she brought her feet into the seat, then clasped her hands over her ankles. "I don't want to believe that Remy's responsible," she said softly. "But . . . when my parents divorced and my father took me to live with Remy's family, I expected him to welcome me. I knew him then, Michael, and yet his reaction to my moving in took me absolutely by surprise. I knew him better than I knew anyone, but I had no idea whatsoever how he really, truly felt about me. I don't know him at all now. He's as much a stranger to me as Nate Simmons was, as the men who killed Nate were. I don't know what Remy is or isn't capable of. I don't know the man he became at all."

"And you were afraid to find out. So when the detectives told you that the FBI was taking over the case, that they were going to take you into protective custody, you took off." He sighed. "Why didn't you tell the cops? Why didn't you come clean with them? They would have taken care of you. They would have seen that you were safe. They would have made sure that, guilty or not, Remy couldn't get close to you."

"If I had told them and it was true, his career would be destroyed, he would be in jail, he would end up in prison, and my aunt and uncle's hearts would be broken. If I had told them and it turned out *not* to be true... There's not really any such thing as 'proven innocent' in this country. No matter how convincing the proof that sets a person free, some people will always believe he's guilty. Remy's reputation would be tarnished, his career damaged anyway. He would rightly blame me, and our family would never have a chance to be made whole again."

"So you went into hiding." Which had led to his visions and, eventually, brought her here. Some clouds, he thought without mirth, did have silver linings. "Why are you telling me now?"

Was she simply tired of her secret? Had she decided to come forward and let the authorities sort everything out? Was she looking to escape her confinement here in his apartment, in his care? Was she eager to get her life back to normal—which seemed to mean without *him?*

Looking up, she met his gaze and offered a hesitant smile that faded as soon as it formed. "Because I trust you."

Her words caught him off guard and made him smile, even though he was feeling pretty damn grim. "Good answer, Val." Moving around the table, he kissed her hard and quick, then started for the closet.

He was halfway there when she asked, "Where are you going?"

Removing a jacket, he pulled it on. "Honey, you can't tell me something like this and expect me to just blow it off. I'm going to do some checking. I'm going to find out what the hell's going on.''

She left her chair and uneasily approached him. "Couldn't you let somebody else do that?''

He slid his arms around her and drew her close. "You're safe here, Valery. Nothing bad can happen to you here.''

"But—"

"No one has connected you to me. They'd search the mountains in Mexico for you before they'd ever think of looking here. Sweetheart, you're safe. You've been safe since you got here. Nothing will happen.'' He touched her hair, kissed her forehead, tilted her chin up coaxingly. "I'll do some snooping, pick up some groceries and be back in time for dinner, I promise. Okay?''

It was an effort for her to agree—he saw it in her eyes, felt it in her sigh—but she tried to hide it. "Okay. How about something sinfully rich for dessert?''

The desire that seemed permanently lodged in his belly immediately began building, tempting and enticing him. "Thanks for the offer,'' he said, his voice husky. "Believe me, by the time I get back, I'll be more than ready to take you up on it.''

She smiled slowly, chidingly, womanly. "When you come back, you'd better have chocolate, or you'll be sleeping on the couch again.''

He kissed her again, then pulled away. "Keep the door locked, stay off the balcony and don't answer the phone unless you hear me on the answering machine. I'll be back as soon as I can.''

She was still standing there in the middle of the floor when he closed the door and locked it. Damn, but he didn't want to go. As much as he needed to talk to Remy and Smith, he didn't want to leave the apartment.

He didn't want to leave Valery, not even for an afternoon. Not even for business.

And certainly not for business that, once resolved, might take her away.

His first stop was a pay phone in a quiet hallway at Jax Brewery, and all his calls were fruitless. Smith was in court and not expected back in his office today. Remy was also out of the office; there was no answer on his car phone, no response to his pager.

From there he went to the Vieux Carré District police station, where he spent the next few hours wading through records and computer files. He learned more about Simmons, more about the two men who had killed him, and he left feeling even more convinced that those men had lied. Friendship aside, Remy was a damned good FBI agent. His honesty and integrity were irrefutable. He simply wasn't capable of doing what Valery feared, what the men had suggested.

Michael knew it as surely as he knew he himself wouldn't do such a thing.

So why had the men lied?

He was on his way out of the building when a voice called his name. Recognizing it immediately, he considered not stopping, pretending he hadn't heard. But he knew better. It would be easier to shake a bulldog than Jolie Wade—and, besides, she knew where he lived. If he didn't talk to her now, she would come around later.

At the sidewalk, he stopped and waited for her to catch up. Under better circumstances, he didn't mind running into Jolie. He liked and respected her—which, considering that she was a reporter for the *Times-Picayune* who specialized in *his* work, was saying a lot.

But circumstances weren't better, and he had enough to worry about without adding Jolie to the picture.

"You're a hard man to find," she remarked, brushing her hair back from her eyes as she fell into step beside him. "It took me half a dozen calls just to find out that you were on vacation."

"If you didn't antagonize everyone, maybe they'd be more forthcoming," he pointed out mildly. "You're pushy, Wade. You do too good a job making law enforcement in this city look bad."

"They make themselves look bad, Bennett. I just give them the front page to do it on." She flashed him a smile. "Why were you at the station if you're on vacation?"

"I had business."

"Don't you know vacation generally means not working? Going out of town? Relaxing?"

"You're a fine one to criticize. I've worked here fifteen years, and you've been around thirteen of them. When's the last time *you* didn't work, when you went out of town and relaxed?"

She responded with a casual shrug and another smile, then—so quickly that it would have caught a stranger off guard—she turned serious. "Any news on the Simmons murder?"

"That's federal. NOPD isn't involved."

"Yeah, I know. I've been trying to talk to Remy, but he's been harder to catch than you." At the edge of Jackson Square, she drew to a stop and waited for him to turn toward her. "You're his best friend, Michael. Tell me something." She paused, looked away, then refocused on him. "Is Remy in trouble?"

If she had asked the question three weeks ago, three days ago—hell, three *hours* ago—he would have laughed. Remy in trouble? Not since he was twenty-two and wreaking havoc at home with Valery and his parents. But not on the job. *Never* on the job.

But coming on the heels of this afternoon's conversation with Valery, he didn't find anything the slightest bit humorous about Jolie's question. It seemed more than possible that Remy *was* in trouble—not that he'd done anything wrong, but that someone was trying to make it look as if he had.

"Why do you ask?"

"I've been talking to Nate Simmons's family. They're making some . . ." Again Jolie looked away. "Some claims. I've tried to get in touch with Remy—I want to talk to him before I go to his superiors—but he's not returning my calls."

Michael felt a shadow settle over him that had nothing to do with the clouds overhead. "What kind of claims?"

Stubbornly she shook her head. "I'm not discussing it."

"Then why tell me anything at all?"

"Because you're his friend. Because we're running this story—" She broke off, considered what she was about to say, then said it anyway. "Because I don't believe what I'm hearing, and I'd like to give him a chance to be prepared. Talk to him, Michael. Convince him to talk to me within the next day or so."

He didn't have to answer, didn't have to make any promises. He could walk away, and Jolie would let him go. She'd made her point. She knew now that he would do whatever was best—which was, obviously, exactly what she wanted: tell Remy. He would advise Remy to meet with her, to find out what she knew.

He did have one thing to say, though, before he left. "Thanks, Jolie."

She shrugged it away. "I'll be home all evening and around the paper most of tomorrow. I'll hold off as long as I can. But if he doesn't call me, Michael . . . the story runs anyway, and it just might hurt him." With those ominous words, she turned and headed back the way they'd just come.

Grimly he continued with his errands, making stops at the grocery store, the produce market and a little hole-in-the-wall bakery just down the block from his apartment. Valery had requested chocolate, and he got it for her in a cake, rich and just the right size for two. Then, stopping at a pay phone, he made one last set of calls. Remy still wasn't answering his car phone or his pager, which meant he was probably out of range. When he called the office, this time Michael asked to speak to Travis Wilson.

He didn't like dealing with anyone other than Remy—didn't even like leaving messages—but if he wanted to get back home anytime soon, he had no choice. He left a simple message with Wilson—*Tell Remy to meet me this evening around seven-thirty*—and he named a coffee shop near his apartment. The message was simple, unimportant to any casual observer, but Remy would understand its importance.

Remy would know it was about Valery.

* * *

"I wish you wouldn't go."

Her tone sulky, Valery murmured the words for the third or fourth time, then felt ashamed of herself. She wasn't the type to cling, she reminded herself. She was strong, independent and needed no one.

Except Michael, who was preparing to leave her alone for the second time today.

They had finished dinner, and she'd been anticipating the sinfully rich cake he'd brought for dessert when he had announced that he had to go out again. He hadn't answered when she'd asked where and why. He had only told her that it couldn't wait. He had to go now.

Now she watched as he took a heavy rubber slicker from the closet. It was raining again. Lord, she was tired of winter rain. Maybe it wouldn't be so bad if they lived someplace cold enough for it to freeze. Watching rain turn to sleet and then snow seemed a lovely way to spend a January evening, she thought. Watching it puddle and pool in the streets was just depressing, especially when she would be watching it alone.

"Let me go with you," she requested suddenly.

"You can't go out. You know that."

"I'll wear my coat with the hood. No one will be able to even see my face, much less recognize it."

He came to sit near her at the table and reached for her hands. "What's wrong?"

"I don't want you to go."

"Are you afraid here alone?"

She scowled at him. He sounded so reasonable, which made her feel pouty. "No, I'm not afraid," she denied. And she wasn't. But she *was* uneasy. Edgy. She had a feeling . . .

Abruptly she turned away from completing the thought. Maybe it was cabin fever. Maybe her nerves had simply worn through from the recent stress. Maybe . . .

Maybe it really was a feeling. A premonition. A sign.

He drew her out of her chair and into his lap. "I'll keep this short," he promised. "I just have to take care of some business, and then I'll come back."

"Business," she repeated skeptically. "You're on vacation."

"All our cases don't come to a sudden halt just because one of us takes some time off," he said with a chuckle. "I promise, Val, I'll be back soon."

With a kiss and a shiver, she let him go. As soon as the door closed, though, she longed to run after him, to beg him to stay or to let her go, to plead with him not to leave her alone.

She *was* afraid, she acknowledged, hugging her arms to her chest. This apartment that had been her safe place for days now felt too big, too bright and airy, too insecure. Without Michael here, she didn't feel the least bit safe.

It was silly. Nerves.

Still, she crossed to the door long after he'd left and double-checked the locks. She felt a little safer seeing for herself that they were locked, safer knowing that a solid door and two sturdy locks stood between her and the world.

Just as she'd done this afternoon, she wandered around the apartment. She stared out the windows and huddled for a short time in the cozy, dimly lit bedroom. Tiring of staring at shadows, she returned to the brighter lights of the living room, where she turned on the television for company while she rinsed the dinner dishes and contemplated making a cup of hot chocolate.

She was taking a mug from the cabinet when the phone rang. Startled by the sudden discordant noise, she let the cup slip from her fingers and watched as it shattered on the counter. It was just the phone, she admonished herself, but that didn't stop the trembling in her hands. It didn't slow the erratic beat of her heart.

The answering machine clicked on, the outgoing message played, then the incoming tape slowly turned, recording a few seconds of silence before shutting off.

A wrong number. A caller with a thing against answering machines. A solicitor who knew leaving a message was pointless. She waited for the silly little sense of relief that should come, but it didn't.

Something was wrong.

She tried to ignore the message as she cleaned up the broken glass. Nothing was wrong. Michael was at the police station, discussing some case with his colleagues; where could he possibly be safer? And no one in the entire world knew that she was here in his apartment; no one knew that they even knew each other. Michael had been right this afternoon: They would search for her as far away as Mexico before they would ever think to look here. Where could she possibly be safer?

The phone rang again, and again the machine played only silence. Valery glanced at the clock. It was a few minutes past 7:40. Michael hadn't been gone even twenty minutes.

With a heavy sigh, she went to the sofa, intending to concentrate on the TV. She hadn't settled in when the knock came at the door. Her heart rate, already none too normal, doubled, and fear drew her muscles taut. It was one of Michael's friends or one of his neighbors, she comforted herself, but she didn't believe it for a minute. The sound of metal working against metal confirmed it.

Something *was* wrong.

Someone was trying to break into the apartment.

Oh, God, where was Michael?

She rose slowly from the couch, looking around the room, knowing already that there was no place to hide, no place to go…but out. As the rattling continued at the front door, she moved swiftly, silently to the French doors. She unfastened the lock, turned the handle and opened the door only enough to slip through. She closed it carefully behind her to minimize the sway of the thin sheer curtains.

It was cold outside, still raining, and the balcony, narrow and long, held absolutely nothing of use—no furniture, no plants, no potted trees. There was nothing.

The rain fell in icy sheets, plastering her hair to her head, her clothing to her body. Already she was soaked, shivering. Jeans, no shoes and a T-shirt were less than ideal clothing for a rainy winter evening jaunt.

Peeking through the sheers from the corner, she saw the front door open, saw two men come in. In that instant, fear grew into sheer terror. It was Vince and his partner, the littler guy, the one who had laughed after killing a man. Every cop—city, parish and federal—in town was looking for these men, and here they'd just broken into a cop's apartment. Every cop was looking for *her,* but it was these two crooks—these two murderers—who'd found her.

Dear God, they had found her.

Frantic, she searched for some avenue of escape and found only two choices: a perilous climb from Michael's balcony to his next-door neighbor's or an even more perilous drop to the second-floor balcony beneath. Neither was anything that a person in her right mind would even consider…but desperation, she acknowledged with a dry smile, didn't exactly lead to rationality.

Leaning over the railing, she tried to estimate the drop, tried not to imagine the pain if she miscalculated and fell all the way to the ground. At the very least, she would break a few bones, most likely including her skull. Better that she try a lateral move, even if it did mean climbing around an ornate wrought-iron divider. Even if she did have to make the move on the outside of the railing. The wrong side. The one-misstep-and-you're-history side.

"Bathroom's empty," the little guy called inside. "I'll check the bedroom."

Taking a deep breath, Valery swung one leg over the rail. The metal was cold, wet, slippery. An instant later, before she could change her mind, before she could come to her senses and figure that taking her chances with those two men was better than no chance at all, she shifted her weight and lifted the other leg over, too.

So far, so good… but she was trembling head to toe, her hands were numb with cold, her knees were shaking, and her toes were curled so tight against the iron that she wasn't sure she could let go to move.

"Bedroom's empty. You sure he said she would be here?"

"Of course I'm sure." Vince sounded annoyed—and close. In the dining room, she thought, or just inside the kitchen.

"Well, she isn't. Now what?"

Valery sidestepped, left foot, right foot, left, right. The decorative curlicues that separated the two balconies extended beyond the rail, and it was all she could do to stretch far enough to hook her left foot on the opposite side. With another deep breath for courage, she swung her right foot around. Just as she found a toehold, her left foot slipped from the slick metal, swinging in midair. She swallowed a shriek, wrapped both arms around the railing and held on for dear life—for very dear life—until both feet were once again firmly connected.

Scrambling over the railing, she silently blessed Michael's unknown neighbor, whose balcony was as jumbled as his was empty. Ducking underneath a round table, she drew into a tight huddle, wriggled back close to a tree planted in a half barrel and adjusted a chair in front of her. Only an instant later, Michael's French doors swung open, spilling light onto the balcony. It shadowed Vince's face as he stepped outside and took a quick look from one end to the other.

"Nothing out here," he muttered. "Looks like our information was wrong. Damn. Some people..." He returned inside, the closing door cutting off the rest of his complaint.

Valery stayed where she was, cold and miserable but, at least temporarily, out of the rain. Even with her fears, she couldn't stop hearing their words again in her mind. *"You sure he said she would be here?" "Of course I'm sure."* Who? *Who* had told them they could find her there? Who was *he?*

Not Michael. She didn't consider that possibility for an instant. He wouldn't betray her. He cared too much about keeping her safe. He cared too much about not having to bear responsibility for someone else's death. He cared too much about *her.*

Maybe she had been followed the night she had come here. Maybe he had been followed the day he went to her apartment. Maybe Jimmy Falcone's people had had them under surveillance from the very beginning. Maybe...maybe they were watching Michael right now. Maybe they had followed him to the police station and were keeping an eye on him to make sure he didn't come back and interrupt Vince and his friend.

Oh, God, she had to find him, had to warn him.

She crawled out from under the table and to her feet, and a blast of wind off the river cut through her. Whispering a silent prayer, she tried the balcony door, and when it opened, she stepped inside the dimly lit apartment. The layout was similar to Michael's, only reversed—living room and kitchen on the right, bathroom and bedroom on the left. For a moment she hesitated just inside, listening for any sound that might indicate the place was occupied. She heard nothing.

She made a mad dash to the door, stopping to listen once again for noises in the hall. When she heard nothing, she carefully unlocked the door, opened it only a crack and peered out. The corridor was empty.

She was about to step outside when she noticed the shoes next to the door. They were canvas, bright red, probably a little big for her. For a moment she tried to talk herself out of taking them—it was stealing, after all—but only for a moment. She had to leave, had to find Michael. She couldn't do it barefooted in the cold rain, and no way was she returning to Michael's apartment for her own sneakers, not without him and his gun. She would return or replace the shoes, she promised the absent owner, along with her apology and her sincere gratitude.

Moving swiftly through the shadows, she took the stairs two at a time, formulating a plan as she went. She would stop at the first busy, brightly lit place she came to, and from there she would call the Vieux Carré District station. Someone there would track Michael down for her, and he would come and get her and take her someplace safe. He would take her someplace where Vince and his buddy could never find her, and he would protect her. She had faith in his ability to do that. She had faith in him.

Until she reached the first busy, brightly lit place, a coffee shop at the end of Michael's block.

Until she looked through the big plate-glass windows and saw him sitting there at a corner table, deep in conversation with another man.

With a man that she'd once known better—or so she had believed—than she'd known herself.

With a man Michael had claimed to know only in passing.

With a man who might be responsible for Nate Simmons's murder.

With a man who very well might want *her* dead.

Shrinking back against the brick wall, out of sight of the diners inside, Valery tried to control the pain. Her parents' abandonment, Remy's rejection—those episodes were nothing compared to the way she felt right now. It was more than just hurt, more than just betrayal.

This was how it felt, she suspected, when faith died.

Chapter 10

"I don't understand it," Remy said for the fourth or fifth time. "I just... Damn it, Michael...."

Reaching for his cup, Michael drained the last of his coffee. Remy had started out this meeting with coffee, too, but he had quickly switched over to beer. Michael had watched him drink half the bottle in one swallow, but he hadn't felt the old familiar longing. He hadn't craved just one taste, just one drink. He hadn't once again damned the weakness that had made him abuse alcohol. All he had felt was tension. Uneasiness. A gnawing desire to do his friend justice that was matched by a need to return home to Valery.

"Why would they lie?"

"I don't know," Remy answered with a scowl.

"Why would they want the best witness to their crime to know who had hired them?"

"I *don't* know. Hell, Michael... I need to talk to her."

He gazed out the window at the cathedral, bright against the night sky. He liked it at night, liked it especially when it rose so massive and strong out of the night fog. He had tried to paint it that way but had never been able to capture the eerie, shifting, menacing quality of the fog, had never been able to offset it with the goodness the church should represent.

I need to talk to her. His first impulse was to tell Remy no. Valery still didn't know that they were friends, and he couldn't help but worry about how she would react when she found out. She had so little trust to give; each time it was betrayed, she regrouped with even less. And knowing now what she knew—what she suspected, what she feared—he wasn't sure he could face telling her the truth.

But it had to happen sometime, and Remy had a legitimate need. It was his career, his reputation, maybe even his freedom, on the line here. He had a right to question her.

Why are you telling me now? he had asked her after this afternoon's confession, and she had given the only right answer, the only answer that could matter to him. *Because I trust you.* Would she accept the same answer from him now? Would she understand that, for her own safety, he'd had to keep his friendship with Remy secret? Would she see that he'd had no choice? Would she forgive his deception?

Or would she simply see that one more person whom she had cared about had let her down? That one more person whom she'd trusted had betrayed her?

"I don't know if she'll agree," he hedged.

"Damn it, Michael—" Aware of the curious glances from nearby diners, Remy leaned forward and lowered his voice. "She can't really believe I had that guy killed. She can't believe I'd hurt her. She *can't* be afraid of me! We're family, for God's sake!"

"You didn't always treat her like family."

Remy had the grace to look ashamed as he sank back in his chair. "No," he admitted bleakly. "I didn't. I've regretted that for longer than you can imagine." He picked up the bottle, then set it down again. "I need to talk to her, Michael. If she'll listen to you, tell her . . . tell her, please."

After a long moment, Michael nodded. It was time—time to be honest, for Remy's sake, for Valery's, for his own. "I'll talk to her, but I can't make any promises." Rising, he pulled some money from his pocket to cover his tab, then picked up the slicker. The water dripping from it had made a small pool beneath the chair leg. "I'll call you in the morning. Will you be around?"

"Either in the office or with Jolie. Page me."

After another nod, Michael headed for the door, leaving Remy alone with his beer. Once outside, he stopped under the awning to pull his jacket on, then, shivering against the chill, he turned toward his apartment.

He was only a dozen feet from the bottom of the stairs when the sensation hit him with a force that was almost physical. It was frightening in the abruptness of its onset, in its intensity, in its complete unexpectedness. It was just plain frightening—fear in its ugliest, most violent form. Panic. Near hysteria.

Dear God, something was happening—or had happened—to Valery.

The visions never passed quickly; they simply faded bit by bit until nothing remained but the lingering residue of dismay, of despair that it was happening again. This time the fear didn't fade at all—or if it did, it was replaced so quickly by his own fear that he didn't notice the difference.

He raced up the stairs, adrenaline flowing so strongly that he was barely winded by the time he reached the third floor. The hall was quiet. He had no sense of anything out of place, except for Valery's fear. That was still there, still constant, still haunting him.

Trading speed for stealth, he approached his apartment door, drawing his pistol from beneath the slicker, sliding the safety off. Then he stood utterly still, listening, feeling, seeking some clue, some hint, as to what he would find inside. He got no answers.

The door was closed, just as he'd left it, but close inspection revealed two scrapes, both recent, on the metal face of the dead bolt. Twisting the knob slowly, he encountered no resistance. The locks were undone. The door swung slowly in.

The minute he edged into the doorway, he knew the apartment was empty. There was no threat here, no danger. Whoever had broken in had gone away again.

Had they taken Valery with them? Was she their prisoner? Did that explain her fear? Or had she somehow escaped them? Was she once again out on the streets, on her own?

Despite his certainty that he was alone, he checked the apartment anyway, with the gun still clasped firmly in both hands. He found nothing out of place. This was his home, a place that he knew intimately, and if not for the unlocked door, he never would have guessed that someone had been here.

If not for the unlocked door, the vision and the fact that Valery was missing.

Standing motionless in the center of the room, he turned his attention inward. The fear was still there, but try as he might, he couldn't force an image to go along with it. He couldn't see her, couldn't see anything around her, couldn't hear so much as a whisper. All he could get was her fear and . . . something more. Despair? Pain?

His expression turned grimmer, bleaker. He would kill them if they had hurt her. He swore to the God he had long since turned his back on that he would kill them for whatever they'd done to her.

He was concentrating so intensely that it took a moment for the rapping on the still-open door to penetrate. When it did, he whirled around, relief so strong that he felt sick with it, only to lose it instantly when he recognized the woman standing there as his neighbor, Luisa.

Not Valery.

"Is this a bad time?" she asked hesitantly, her gaze straying from his face to his gun, then back again.

After a moment, he holstered the pistol, then combed his fingers impatiently through his hair, sending droplets of water down his back. "Yeah, it is." Then, reluctantly, he asked, "What's up?"

"Something weird happened tonight. Someone broke into my apartment, only—" She looked embarrassed as she continued. "Whoever it was came in from the balcony."

He fixed his gaze on her. "The balcony?" he repeated dumbly. "Someone broke in through the balcony doors?"

"Not exactly. The doors were unlocked. They just walked right in." Before he could comment on the foolishness of leaving doors unsecured, she hurried on. "I lock the front door every time I leave, but the balcony... Well, hell, Michael, we're on the third floor. It's not as if someone can just walk in."

He didn't point out that someone had apparently done just that. "What was taken?"

"That's the weird part." His dry look made her flush and, once more, rush on with her next statement. "The only thing that's missing is a pair of shoes—these little canvas sneakers that I gave maybe three bucks for last summer. My TV, the VCR, the stereo—none of that was touched. There were three twenty-dollar bills sitting on the table right in front of the French doors, and they're still there. I'd left the jewelry that I wore to work today—some nice stuff—on the coffee table, and it's still there. Just those cheap little worn-out red shoes—that's all she took."

Abruptly Michael moved toward the closet. "Why do you say she? What makes you think it was a woman?"

"Well..." She gave it a moment's thought as he looked for and found Valery's jacket, her money still inside, hanging between a couple of his own coats. "I guess because of the shoes. They're women's shoes." Her tone of voice indicated that she found her own reasoning somehow faulty.

Michael didn't.

Leaving her for a moment, he checked the bedroom closet next. Valery's shoes—all three pairs—were there, neatly lined up in a row. If someone had broken into the apartment, she'd had only two choices: wait to be discovered or flee via the balcony. There was no way she could climb from there to the roof, and going down in the rain and the dark would be treacherous. But climbing across... That would seem manageable. Plus, there was all that clutter on Luisa's balcony to form a hiding place, unlocked doors to escape through once the danger had passed and a pair of shoes just waiting to be taken.

For a moment he closed his eyes and pictured her as she'd looked when he had left to meet Remy—dressed in jeans and a thin cotton T-shirt, wearing no shoes or socks, nervous and uneasy. Had she known in that way of hers that something was going to happen? Had she asked him not to leave because she'd had one of her premonitions?

Damn it all, he wished she had told him. He never would have left her if he'd known. He would have taken her edginess seriously, would have packed their bags and taken her someplace anonymous and safe.

As long as she was out on the streets, she would never be safe. And he had no doubt that that was exactly where she was, looking for him, maybe waiting for some signal that he'd come home again. It was the only possibility. She had no money, no coat and only a pair of stolen shoes. There was no place she could go. She couldn't rent a hotel room, couldn't buy a cup of coffee. Hell, she couldn't even afford a telephone call to track him down.

"Michael?" Luisa called from the living room. "Should I call the police? It's such a petty thing that I hate to bother them. Still, someone *did* break in and—"

"No." He returned from the bedroom, joining her at the door. "Don't worry, Luisa. I think I know... It's no big deal. You're not in any danger. You don't need to bother the cops with it. I'll handle it." He ushered her out as he spoke, then pulled the door shut and locked it behind him. He waited until she was inside her own apartment, the door locked between them, and then he took the steps two at a time.

He had to find Valery, had to find her before anyone else did. Once he did, he would take her someplace safe. He would ease her fears. He would make her warm.

And he would never leave her alone again.

Not ever.

The rain had stopped sometime around eleven o'clock, but Valery had long since given up hope of ever being warm and dry again. Her clothes were soaked all the way through to her skin, and from there it seemed that the water and the chill had seeped into her very pores. She would ache if her nerve endings weren't frozen.

If her heart wasn't frozen.

She huddled on the steps of the shop where she worked, wishing futilely that she'd had time to grab her jacket, her own shoes, her money, her keys. There was a key to the shop on her ring; she could let herself in and hide in relative comfort in the back room, then be on her way long before her assistant came to open up in the morning.

For more than three hours she had wandered around the Quarter, sticking to the shadows, looking furtively over her shoulder with every other step. Finally, cold, wet, miserable, her feet aching and blistered from the shoes that didn't fit, she'd come here. No one would look for her here, she had reasoned; it was too obvious. And, so far, she'd been right. The occasional passersby hadn't even noticed her huddled on the top step, protected from the rain by the awning overhead, from the wind by the shop windows that extended on two sides.

Lord, she was tired—not the sort of physical exhaustion that she could recover from with ten hours of sleep. This weariness went deeper. It came from her soul.

Michael had lied to her.

For four and a half hours she had refused to think further than that. Now she was too tired, too disappointed, too despairing, to stop the thoughts.

He had told her that he knew who Remy was only because he'd been a cop so long, because it was hard to be a cop in this city and not have a passing acquaintance with other cops.

He had told her that they weren't friends.

He had promised to keep her presence in his apartment a secret, had promised that he wouldn't tell anyone, not the cops, not the FBI, not *anyone,* that she was there.

He had lied to her.

Just like everyone else, he had made her believe he cared about her, and then he had let her down.

He had made her start to care for him. Then, like her mother, like her father, like Remy, he had betrayed her.

A tear slid down her cheek, leaving a warm trail before it dissipated. And she had felt she would never be warm again, she thought with a bitter smile as another tear followed.

Was it coincidence that Vince and his partner had discovered her at the same time Michael was meeting with Remy? Maybe... but not likely. It was just too lucky. Too convenient. Michael must have told Remy that she was there, and Remy had taken advantage of their meeting tonight to send his thugs over to pick her up.

Which meant that Remy *was* guilty of ordering Nate Simmons's murder.

Right now, right this minute, she didn't care. Later would be soon enough to worry over that. She had other worries now.

Michael.

What was *he* guilty of? she wondered. Bad judgment? Misplaced trust? Or something worse, something more sinister? Had he simply been foolish in trusting Remy enough to confide in him?

Or was he a part of their crime?

She wanted to believe the worst of him, wanted it with every bit of pain she was feeling, but she couldn't. He had suffered too much with Evan's death. She knew—*knew*—he'd meant it when he'd said that being responsible for another death would kill him. He wasn't a murderer. He was just a foolish man who had believed that because Remy was a cop like him, he could be trusted.

He was a man who had lied to her.

A man who had broken his promises to her.

A man who had broken her heart.

With a heavy sigh, she raised her gaze to the small slice of sky that she could see above the buildings opposite her. The rain clouds had passed, leaving a clear sky that was dotted with distant stars. It wasn't really such a bad night, weatherwise, if you were dressed for it. It would be a perfect night for zipping up a warm jacket and lacing on comfortable shoes and taking a long, quiet walk along the river. Of course, solitary midnight strolls along the river weren't advisable, not if you wanted to stay safe. But if you had someone to go with you, someone to hold you close, someone to protect you…

Bad line of thought, she admonished herself as the tears welled again. The only protector she'd ever had was Michael, and he had destroyed the trust she had so naively offered him. Now who would protect her from her protector?

From down the street she heard footsteps, slow steps, tired steps. She didn't try to make herself into a tinier little lump to avoid detection; she was already as unnoticeable as she was going to get. She didn't worry, either, that the person might mean her harm. At this point, she was beyond caring. Her cousin was a murderer, and the man she had fallen in love with was a liar who couldn't be trusted.

That was two heartaches too many.

Slowly the steps came to a stop right at the point where the jewelry shop next door ended and her shop began, and he stood there, motionless, looking at her through the plate-glass windows.

Michael.

She didn't need to look to know that it was him. She knew. She felt it way down inside.

Clasping her hands tighter around her knees, she tried now to make herself smaller, less obvious. She would have crawled right inside herself if it meant not having to deal with him now, when the ache was so fresh, but, of course, she couldn't.

He came closer, shrugging out of his jacket, wordlessly offering it to her. When she didn't take it, he bent and covered her with it. It smelled of him, and it was almost warm enough to make her sigh with comfort. But she didn't make a sound. She didn't move. She didn't draw the jacket tighter to absorb its heat—*his* heat. She just sat frozen, inside and out.

After a moment, he sat down on one of the lower steps, his back to her, resting his arms on his knees. Staring out at the street, he finally spoke, his voice low, quiet, empty. "What happened at the apartment?"

Her voice was just as quiet, just as empty. "Right after you left, the men who killed Nate Simmons broke in. They were looking for me. They knew I was staying there. Some-one had told them I was staying there.''

For a long time he continued to stare off into the dis-tance; then finally he looked at her. When he did, she felt the weight of his bleakness. ''And you think it was me.''

''No. I think you told Remy. I think he told them.'' Emotion crept into her last words, and she stopped to con-trol it before going on. ''I saw you with him tonight, Mi-chael. You lied to me about knowing him. You lied about keeping my whereabouts a secret. Why?''

He lowered his head, resting it in his hands. The posture spoke silently, eloquently, of sorrow, of despair. It begged for comfort.

But she had no comfort to give.

After a time, he straightened a bit, lifted his head and turned on the steps so he could see her. ''I've known Remy since we were eighteen years old. He, Evan, Smith and I were best friends. Since Evan's death, Remy and Smith are all that's gotten me through. They're my family. Remy didn't kill Simmons, Valery. I swear to God, he wasn't in-volved.''

''You don't believe in God,'' she murmured.

''I believe.'' After a moment, he bleakly added, ''But He doesn't believe in me. And you don't, either, do you?''

She didn't say anything. Not answering was easier and more effective. It added another degree of desolation to his expression.

''Remy knows about the visions. He and Smith both do. After what happened with Evan, I swore I would never get involved again. And then the visions of you started. Remy came to me, told me your name, told me that you were a witness to the Simmons murder and that you were missing. I told him I couldn't help. I didn't care if you died, but I wasn't getting involved. The next day Smith came, and he told me that you and Remy were cousins. Remy hadn't told me himself because he knew I would feel obligated to help. I owed him a hell of a lot. He saved my life after Evan died.''

She remembered his story about the aftermath of Evan's death, about how he had tried to drink away his guilt and his grief, about his friend who had shaken him up enough to make him stop. At the time she had silently reflected that his friend had been a very good friend.

Now she knew that it was Remy.

"When you showed up at my apartment, I had to tell him. He was worried. He was afraid something had happened to you. I had to tell him that you were safe. He's known since Monday morning."

Monday. Michael had made his promise to her on Saturday morning. He'd kept it barely forty-eight hours. He had broken it before he'd kissed her, had betrayed her before he'd held her, before he'd made love to her.

And she'd never had a clue. Not a single clue.

"He didn't kill Nate Simmons, Valery. And he didn't hire those men to do it for him."

She shifted position a bit on the cold brick step and, catching it as it slid, tucked his jacket a little closer around her, blocking off the night chill. "And how do you know that?"

"Because I know *him*. Maybe he's a stranger to you, Val, but I *know* him. If you would give him a chance, if you would just talk to him, you'd know it, too."

"If Remy isn't involved," she asked wearily, "how did those men find me? How did they know to come tonight? How did they know I would be alone?"

He shook his head. "I don't know. Something went wrong."

"Yeah. I trusted you."

Michael clenched his jaw so tightly that his teeth ached. It had been a hell of a night—first the meeting with Remy, then the vision, the worry, the unspeakable fear. The certainty that Valery was in danger, that she was out there somewhere in the cold and the rain, afraid, needing him, looking for him, followed by the slow realization that she wasn't hiding from only the men who'd broken in but also from him. She *wasn't* trying to find him, wasn't trying to somehow connect with him, wasn't looking to him to protect her. She was hiding—hiding from *him*.

The realization had damn near broken his heart.

He wanted to shake her, to yell at her, to make her understand that he couldn't do anything to hurt her, that he couldn't let anyone else hurt her because he loved her. But shaking her and yelling wouldn't do any good. This was Valery, who even before tonight had believed that everyone who loved her would leave her, would somehow betray her.

And, damn it, she was right. He *had* betrayed her. He had hurt her.

But he still loved her.

And he wasn't going to leave her.

Feeling older and wearier than any man ought to, he got to his feet and extended his hands to her. "Come on. We can't sit out here all night. We need to find someplace safe for you to stay."

Seconds crawled by as she simply looked at him. He knew she was debating whether she trusted him enough to go with him, debating whether she cared anymore about someplace safe. Her answers, whatever they might be, didn't matter. He wasn't letting her out of his sight again. He wasn't reneging on his promise to protect her. He wasn't letting anything else happen to her.

Just when he'd decided he was going to have to take her along by force, she slowly rose to her feet. She moved stiffly, as if she'd been sitting there on the hard steps too long. As if warmth hadn't yet found its way from his jacket into her body. As if she, too, felt older and wearier than a person should.

Avoiding his hands, she put his jacket on, fastening the snaps all the way up to her chin, curling her fingers so that her hands disappeared entirely inside the too-long sleeves. Ignoring him, she awkwardly descended the steps and turned automatically in the direction of his apartment.

They walked back in silence, then climbed the stairs and covered the length of the hall, still in perfect silence. He checked the door, making sure both locks were still secured, before using his keys to let them in, and then he locked it again immediately behind them. "Change into some dry clothes," he instructed, "then pack the rest of your things. We won't be coming back here for a while."

She disappeared into the bedroom, then the bathroom, a dry set of clothes folded over her arm. While she was in there, he took care of his own packing, hauling a seldom-used suitcase from the back of the closet, filling one half of it with his own clothing, leaving the other half for hers.

For the first time since she'd shown up at his door, he took his credentials and badge from the closet shelf, along with the extra clips for his pistol and an unopened box of shells. The credentials went into his hip pocket, everything else underneath his clothes in the bag.

Valery came out of the bathroom just as he was leaving the bedroom. At least she had on dry clothes now, but she still looked cold and pale, the color seeming permanently drained from her face. Her hair, still damp, was combed straight back from her forehead, and her eyes were cast down. He wanted to hold her, to warm her, but he knew she wouldn't welcome his touch, though she wouldn't pull away, wouldn't push him away, if he tried. Worse, she would just stand there stiffly, unyielding. As if she didn't care enough to stop him.

He went to the kitchen without speaking, clearing the way for her to enter the bedroom. Muttering a curse, he grabbed a shopping bag from the narrow space between the refrigerator and the wall and packed the few remaining items he wanted.

She was ready to leave in less than five minutes. Michael carried the suitcase in his left hand, keeping his right hand free, and she took the shopping bag. Once again, in damning silence, they made their way downstairs and to the narrow courtyard where his car was parked. They made only one brief stop on the way: at Luisa's door, where Valery carefully set down the rain-soaked red sneakers.

For tonight's refuge he chose a motel off the interstate that led to Baton Rouge. He borrowed cash from Valery so he wouldn't have to use his credit card, registered under a false name and got the key to a room that was clean, if a little shabby. A room with only one bed.

He watched her take note of that with more than a little cynicism, but he didn't apologize, didn't make excuses, didn't lie. Double rooms had been available; he simply hadn't requested one. Like it or not—like *him* or not—she was still sharing a bed with him.

At last he pulled off his jacket, tossed it over one of the two straight-backed chairs, then turned his attention to her. "We need to talk."

She faced him from across the bed, wearing her own coat now. Her hair was starting to dry in unruly wisps; together with the jacket that swallowed her, it gave her a waifish look. A lost little girl look.

When she made no response, he went on. "Remy wants to meet with you tomorrow. I told him I would ask you."

She still said nothing.

"The silence between you two has gone on too long. You need to talk. You need to settle what went wrong."

Still no response, not even the flicker of an eyelash.

"If it would make you feel safer, we can include someone else."

That roused her interest enough to make her ask, "Who?"

He shrugged. "Smith? The assistant U.S. Attorney?"

"Yours and Remy's best friend?"

"Jolie Wade." He saw recognition flash across her face. "She's a reporter for the *Times-Picayune*. She's covering the Simmons murder. She's doing a story right now regarding that and Remy."

"Invite them both. We'll talk." She started to turn away, then swung back. "If you're wrong about Remy—"

"I'm not."

"But if you are..."

Slowly he circled the bed, not stopping until he was right in front of her. "I would kill anyone who tried to hurt you," he said quietly, deliberately.

She gave that a moment's thought.

Then, with a single accepting nod, she walked away.

Thursday morning looked like another of those wonderful winter days, although it was hard for Valery to be certain, peeking out through rubber-backed drapes as she was.

The motel parking lot had emptied out early; now only Michael's car remained at this end, along with one or two closer to the office.

Soon they would be having company. She had listened from the bed, just before Michael went to shower, as he called Jolie Wade and arranged the meeting. He had warned her to be careful, had asked her to pass on the information and the warning in person to Remy and to Smith. He had insisted that the three of them take whatever precautions were necessary to ensure that no one else knew where they were going or who they were meeting. He had assured *her* when he got off the phone that they would be careful. That they, too, would protect her.

She was nervous about seeing Remy—about *seeing* him, not about confronting him. Sometime in the long night just past, she had begun to believe in him at least a little, had begun to accept Michael's belief in him. He had earned from Michael the sort of loyalty and trust that she had always longed for, the sort of unwavering faith that she had never inspired in anyone.

Maybe he *was* innocent.

Maybe she was wrong.

God, she hoped so.

Behind her, the bathroom door opened and Michael came out. He was already dressed in jeans, but his shoulders and back were still wet, and his hair was dripping. She looked for only an instant, then turned her gaze to the parking lot again.

He had lain with her last night—not slept; she couldn't say either of them had slept much, if at all. But he had lain behind her with his arm around her waist, holding her close even when she had tried to keep her distance. In the end she had let him hold her because it was easier. Because she had needed it. Because...hell, because *she* had needed *him*. Even though he'd lied. Even though he'd made her a promise and only forty-eight hours later had broken it.

"Anything interesting out there?"

She shook her head, then let the panel fall back into place and turned to face him. "I wish you'd asked them to bring breakfast."

"No need. Sit down."

As she took a seat on the edge of the bed, he got the shopping bag he'd given her to carry last night. She hadn't looked inside to see what it contained. She'd been too numb to care. Now she watched as he removed two saucers, both delicate old china, the patterns mismatched, two forks and a small white bakery box. She recognized it as last night's dessert, the one they'd never gotten the chance to share because he'd had to go out and then she'd had to leave, too. Some part of her was touched that he'd thought to bring it.

The first part of the cake disappeared in silence. If she tried hard enough, she could pretend they were simply too busy savoring it to bother with conversation. It was that good—dark chocolate layers separated by sweet chocolate cream, all of it covered with rich fudge frosting and decorated with thick milk and white chocolate curls.

But indulgence wasn't the reason for the silence. It was nothing so simple. Nothing so easily overcome.

"I'm sorry."

Pushing her saucer aside, she used her fork to hook a white chocolate curl off the cake remaining on the cardboard tray and lift it to her mouth. After swallowing it, she sneaked a look at Michael, who was watching her from the other side of the dessert box.

She wished she could be cold, wished she could ignore his apology or, better yet, throw it back in his face.

She wished she didn't hurt worse every time she saw how he was hurting.

She wished she could hate him for what he'd done.

She wished . . .

Oh, God, she wished she could take away that sad look.

"I should have told you the truth from the beginning, but I knew that if you didn't trust Remy enough to go to him, you wouldn't trust one of his friends. I had to do whatever was necessary—including lying—to protect you."

"Because of Evan?"

"In the beginning." His gaze held hers, refusing to let her go, refusing through sheer will to let her look away. "But not anymore."

He wanted her to ask what his reason was now, but she was afraid to. Afraid of what he might say. Afraid of how she might respond. Still, the question came out, was dragged out against her will. "And now?"

"I'll do whatever is necessary now because I love you." He waited only long enough for the words to sink in, not long enough for her to come up with a response—something lighthearted to brush him off, a declaration of her own feelings, a denial. "I'm sorry I lied to you. I'm sorry I broke my promise. I'm sorry I'm not a better man, sorry I don't have more to offer you. Damn it, Val, I'm sorry as hell that I hurt you, but I'm not perfect. I'm just trying to do what's right...and I'm not very good at it. But I can promise you three things—I do love you. I'll always be here for you. And I will never leave you."

She wanted to believe him, wanted it, God help her, so badly that she hurt inside.

She just didn't know if she could.

One moment slid into another, and for Michael expectancy passed into despair, which gave way to resignation. Disappointed, he returned what was left of the cake to its box, then began gathering the dishes. Once everything was back in the bag and the bag had been returned to its place beside the suitcase, he turned to her. "I can wait, Valery," he said quietly. "However long it takes to gain your trust— a few weeks, a few months, a few years, a lifetime. However long, I'll be here."

After another long silence, she rose from the bed and went to the suitcase to gather clothes and toiletries. On her way to the bathroom, she had to pass him, and she came to a stop beside him. She didn't say anything, didn't look at him, for a time didn't do anything at all. Then her hand sought his, and for a moment, one all-too-brief moment, she moved closer, resting her cheek against his chest, letting him touch her, hold her.

Then she was gone, disappearing into the next room, closing the door behind her.

As encouragement went, it wasn't much...but for now, Michael reflected, it was enough. It was enough to hope, enough to believe.

Things were going to be all right.

Sometime in the future—a few weeks, a few months, a few years—everything was going to be fine.

And until then he would be patient.

A knock at the door drew him from his thoughts. He gave the room a quick once-over to see if anything was out of place. The bed was rumpled, but it didn't look as if anything more intimate than conversation had gone on there. They had slept in their clothes last night, hadn't even bothered to pull the spread down or untuck the pillows from the covers.

After checking out the window, he opened the door to find Remy standing there alone. His friend looked impatient, troubled and worried as hell. Without a greeting, Michael stepped back so he could enter; then he scanned the parking lot. "Where are—"

"They were following me in Jolie's car. We got separated in traffic. What about Valery?"

"She's taking a shower."

"Jolie said Falcone's men almost got her last night. What happened, Michael?"

"You tell me." He was starting to close the door when a flashy little sports car pulled into the lot. Jolie, with Smith beside her. Leaving the door open a few inches, he sat down on the bed, leaning back against the wall.

"I don't know. I don't know anything, because that's the way you've wanted it." Remy combed his fingers through his hair. "What happened last night?"

"Yes, by all means, fill us in." Jolie pushed the door open with her hip and came in, carrying two bags from a local doughnut shop. Behind her, Smith had his hands full with a cardboard holder and five tall cups of coffee.

Michael waited until everyone was settled and the food had been passed around before he quietly related the events of the night before. He had no sooner brought them up-to-date than Jolie and Remy, at the same time, asked, "How did they know—" They both broke off, and she scowled at him before continuing. "How did they know where to find her?"

Michael responded with a question that he didn't want to ask but knew he had to. "Did you tell anyone, Remy?"

Remy's scowl became darker and more intense than Jolie's could ever be. *"No."*

"Could someone have followed her there and been watching the apartment ever since?" That came from Smith, near the door.

"I suppose," Michael replied. "But why wait so long? Last night wasn't the first time I'd left her there alone. I met Remy one morning, you another, and I was out most of the afternoon yesterday, when I ran into Jolie."

"And if they had known enough about her movements to follow her," Jolie added, "why not take care of her then? Why wait until she'd gone into hiding in some cop's apartment?"

In the bathroom the shower shut off. Valery was in there, drying off, getting dressed, Michael thought. In a few moments she would gather her courage and come out here into this roomful of strangers. He wished she didn't have to, wished her life could be safe and normal again, with no talk about dead men or killers stalking her. He wished he could take her away from her problems as easily as he'd taken her from his apartment.

It *was* only a moment until the door between the rooms opened, and she stepped out. She was wearing jeans that were faded and fitted and a shirt—one of his—that didn't fit at all. He wondered if she'd grabbed it out of the suitcase by accident or design. He preferred to think the latter.

All conversation broke off, and all eyes turned in her direction. She stopped short and returned the stares, her gaze moving from one stranger to the next, lingering longest on Remy before finally reaching Michael. He offered her a faint smile that, though she tried, she couldn't return.

With a casualness that he was far from feeling, he performed the introductions. "Valery Navarre, this is Smith Kendricks, Jolie Wade and..." He shrugged. "Remy you used to know."

Smith nodded in acknowledgment, and Jolie said hello, but they were perfunctory greetings. Their attention—and Michael's and Valery's—was on Remy, and his was on her. He rose from the dresser where he'd taken a seat and took a few steps toward her before coming to an abrupt stop. For a moment he simply stared at her; then he moved in a slow circle around her. When he was finally in front of her again, he took one step closer, then lifted his hand before letting it fall back to his side.

Shaking his head in disbelief, he found only one thing to say in greeting. "Good God, Valery, what happened to your hair?"

Chapter 11

When he asked the question again a few moments later in the privacy of the bathroom, Valery offered him a frown and a defensive reply. "I cut and colored it. Since everyone was looking for a woman with long blond hair, I figured short and black was a better way to be."

"Damn. Even when you were the worst tomboy I'd ever known, you wouldn't let your mom cut your hair."

"I didn't have much choice this time. I needed to hide."

Sobering, he settled more comfortably on the small bench in the open end of the room that served as a closet. "You could have come to me, Valery."

She gave him a doubting look. "Could I? It seems I made the mistake of counting on you in the past, and look what it got me."

He had the grace to look ashamed, something—if she'd considered it—that she might once have expected to enjoy. Instead she just felt petty.

With a sigh, she dropped the brush she'd been fiddling with and turned away from the mirror. The bathroom was small and lacking in comfortable places to sit. Spreading the last dry towel, she settled on the floor, her back against the side of the tub. "What happened, Remy?"

"I don't know. I swear to God, I didn't tell anyone where you—"

"To us," she interrupted. "When we were kids."

With no regard for his suit, he moved from the bench to the floor, too, mimicking her position, resting his arms on his knees. They were on the same level now and closer than they'd been in twenty-four years. Only an inch or two separated her bare feet from his Italian leather shoes. They were almost touching, something they hadn't done in so long that they'd almost forgotten how.

"You didn't like being an only child, did you?" he asked. "You always thought it would be neat to have a brother or sister, so you'd always have someone to play with or to fight with or to scheme with. You figured two kids would be twice the fun, twice the opportunities. You would never be lonely, never be alone."

She nodded. She had wanted an older brother—had wanted Remy—but since that was impossible, she would have been happy with a younger sibling. She would have made a fine big sister, she'd always thought. She would have done the things for a kid brother or sister that Remy had done for her—teach them how to throw a curveball, to slide into second and tell truly awful jokes. She would always have been there to stand up for them when other kids were picking on them, to make sure that they were treated right.

"Well, *I* didn't feel that way," he continued. "I liked being the only kid. I liked my family exactly the way it was— Mom, Dad and me. I didn't want anyone else around, not on a permanent basis. I didn't want *you* around."

Even after living with that knowledge for so many years, she still felt a twinge of pain at hearing it stated so bluntly.

"You were so damn needy when you came to live with us, Valery. For weeks—months—our entire lives revolved around you. When you were around, Mom and Dad were constantly fussing over you. When you weren't around, they were endlessly worrying about you. All my life I'd been the center of the family, and suddenly there wasn't a damn thing

I could do to get my own parents to notice me. They gave you everything—attention, time, affection. By the time they were through with you, there wasn't anything left for me.''

His words brought to mind a memory that Valery had long since forgotten of a pretty spring day. It had been her mother's birthday, her first birthday since the divorce, only she was off in places unknown, far from Valery and Belclaire. Valery had dreaded the day, had mourned it for weeks before, and to cheer her up, Aunt Marie and Uncle George had suggested a trip to Baton Rouge. They would make a day of it, would shop and play tourist and cap it off with dinner in the fanciest restaurant Valery had ever seen.

There had been just one problem: Remy, who was first baseman for the Belclaire High team, had an important game scheduled that same Saturday afternoon—a game that he was counting on his parents to attend. Valery could have been generous about it and agreed to postpone the trip one day, but she hadn't been feeling generous. She'd felt abandoned and unloved and desperately unhappy, and she hadn't been willing to accept one more disappointment.

So Remy's parents had missed his game and taken her to the city. It was no big deal, Aunt Marie had explained to him. After all, he would play in plenty more games and, besides, Valery *needed* this trip. She needed *them*.

They had gone to the city, and Remy had won the game with a grand slam homerun. He had finished out the season, and he hadn't gone out for any sports during his remaining years in high school. There had been no more games for his parents to watch him play.

So damn needy. Yes, she had been, so needy and so desperate for a family to belong to that she had taken his.

"I was selfish," he acknowledged. "I understood that at the time. I just didn't know what to do about it. And I resented you. I wanted you to go back where you came from. I wanted to go back to just being long-distance cousins. I didn't want you living in my house or disrupting my life. I didn't want to watch you take my place in my own family."

"If I'd had more of *your* attention, Remy, I wouldn't have needed so much of your parents'," she murmured.

"You're right. I *was* needy. In the space of a few days I lost my mother, my father and my best friend. I didn't know why, all at once, nobody loved me anymore. I didn't know what I had done wrong. Your parents were all I had left, and I was terrified of losing them, too, so . . . I clung to them. I held on tight so they couldn't leave me, too."

He rubbed one hand over his temple; then, with a sigh, he went on. "You read about families where one kid has some fatal illness and the other kids are healthy. The sick kid gets all the time and attention and, it seems, all the love, because the parents realize they won't have him around for long. The healthy kids are worried and afraid, but they can't help being a little resentful, too, because they've been pushed into the background. Their problems don't matter anymore, because, hell, what kind of problem can a normal kid have that can compete with impending death? They get jealous and wish things could go back to normal, and they wish they could have just a moment to be the important one, and then they feel guilty for being jealous and selfish."

"And that's how you felt," Valery said, her voice soft. Then she smiled tightly. "Only you didn't have the luxury of knowing that I was going to drop dead sometime soon."

He smiled, too. It wasn't the easy, teasing grin that she remembered painfully well from the first third of her life, but it was a start. All too quickly, though, it faded, and he became serious and grim again. "I'm sorry, Valery. I'm sorry I went from loving you to hating you to being such strangers that you could be afraid of me."

That made twice in one day that a man had spoken of loving her. It was funny that she found it easier to believe that Remy, this stranger, *had* loved her than that Michael *did*—and not so funny, too, because it was partly due to Remy that she found it so hard to believe in Michael.

"I didn't distrust you completely," she said in her own defense. "If I had, I would have told everything to the detectives the day of the shooting."

"I shouldn't have given you reason to distrust me at all." His tone and expression were glum, reminding her of the teenage Remy she'd grown up with.

"If it's any consolation, Michael never doubted you, not for an instant. He has tremendous faith in you."

"I'm not surprised. All Michael's doubts are reserved for—"

When he broke off abruptly, she smiled faintly and finished for him. "For himself. For God."

For a moment, he looked surprised—that she was sensitive enough to pick up on Michael's doubts or that his friend had trusted her enough to confide in her?—and then he shook his head. "I guess you had to do something all those hours you were together."

"Yes," she agreed with a tiny smile. "Something." Before he could comment on that, she got to her feet. "We have a roomful of people waiting to discuss the trouble we've gotten ourselves into. I don't guess we should keep them waiting any longer."

He also stood up and touched her gently, stopping her as she reached for the doorknob. "I'd like to be friends again, Valery. I'd like—" He broke off and sighed. "I'd like to make things right. Tell me honestly, do you think that's possible?"

Honestly. Honestly, while she was pretty much convinced that he'd played no role in Nate Simmons's death, a part of her still didn't completely trust him. He had hurt her deeply once before. Could she give him a chance to do it again?

Honestly, she harbored a little resentment of her own. Maybe she *had* been needy and demanding, maybe she *had* usurped his place in the family, but she had been a *child,* for heaven's sake—a terribly hurt, terribly frightened child whom he had turned his back on. His rejection had helped make her into the woman she was at this very minute—still hurt, still frightened . . . and still so damn needy.

Honestly, they *were* strangers. He might not like the woman she was. She might not care for the man he had become. They might have nothing in common.

"I don't know," she replied, meeting his gaze head-on. She saw the disappointment flash there, and it touched something deep inside her. It prompted her to go on. "But I'd like to try. When this is over...."

After a moment he withdrew his hand and nodded resolutely. Ending on that note, she opened the door, and they rejoined the others in the bedroom. Michael was still sitting on the bed, a pillow behind his back. Smith had settled in one of the chairs, and Jolie sat cross-legged on the dresser. While Remy took the other chair, Valery settled a few feet from Michael on the bed.

Smith seemed to step naturally into the role of moderator, and the others let him. They were an interesting group, Valery thought—three strong-willed men and an even stronger-willed woman, and yet there was no struggle for control. They worked well together. They fit well together. They all, Jolie included, seemed to understand something that she didn't—the workings of the criminal mind, perhaps? The harsh realities of life?

Prompted by the assistant U.S. Attorney, Valery repeated her story—the details they all knew and the ones she had kept to herself. After a few questions, Smith turned to the reporter and asked for her input.

"I covered Simmons's murder from the start," she explained for Valery's benefit; the three men already knew it. "A couple of days ago I got a call from his family—his mother and two uncles live in the area. They had some new information on his death, they said, and they wanted to share it with me. What they have is a lot of speculation, a lot of say-so and suspicions. What they don't have is proof."

"Fortunately, as a reporter, you don't need proof," Remy said dryly. "That's why you people invented the word 'allegedly.'"

Jolie ignored him and went on. "The family story is that Nate was a good boy who took a few wrong turns and got in with a bad crowd. They admit that he wasn't perfect—all that time in prison probably had something to do with that—but he had his own code. There were things he simply wouldn't do, not for any reason—honor among thieves, that sort of thing.''

"And what was it in particular that Nate wouldn't do?" Remy asked, skepticism in his voice.

"Lie to trap a friend. According to the family, he'd been asked to do just that. It seemed that he'd gotten hooked up with an FBI agent who wanted to use Nate to bring down his friend and sometime employer, Jimmy Falcone. Now, keep in mind, the work Nate did for Mr. Falcone was on the up-and-up, strictly legit. As far as Nate knew, *all* of Mr. Falcone's business was legit. He told the FBI agent that, but the agent wasn't satisfied. He pushed hard, but Nate wouldn't give. Finally—''

Jolie broke off to rummage in one of the white bakery bags beside her. "All that's left is an apple fritter and two glazed," she said, turning her gaze to Valery. "Which do you want?''

"The glazed.''

Jolie fished out the fritter, then crumpled the top of the bag and sent it sailing to the bed, where it landed between Valery and Michael. When Valery reached for it, she caught his grin and knew he was thinking about all that rich cake she'd eaten little more than an hour ago. With a scowl, she took out one of the glazed doughnuts and, while Jolie returned to her story, devoured every crumb.

"Anyway, finally the agent got threatening. He told Nate that if he couldn't get Falcone, he would settle for *him*. He would set him up for some crime or another and send him to prison. Nate knew that, of course, he could do that, and since he'd already seen more than his share of prisons across the South, he didn't much care to take up residence in another one, so he agreed to cooperate. He agreed to help the agent falsify evidence implicating Mr. Falcone in various crimes, agreed to plant the evidence on Falcone—at his house, in his records, whatever was necessary—for the agent to find. Then Nate's conscience got the better of him. He was going to come clean. He admitted everything to Jimmy, who accepted his sincere apologies, and he called the crooked FBI agent to tell him that he wasn't going to play his game any longer. The agent threatened him, tried to talk him out of it, and when he couldn't change Nate's mind, he demanded a meeting the next day. Nate reluctantly agreed.''

Jolie caught her breath, glanced around the room, then settled her gaze on Remy. ''Unfortunately for ol' Nate, the agent didn't show up for the meeting. He sent his goons instead. Ironic, isn't it? the family asked. The same pair of thugs working for both Mr. Falcone *and* the fed trying to put him away. Whatever happened to loyalty?'' she asked with a doleful shake of her head. After another brief pause, she finished. ''The last thing Nate told his family before leaving to meet the agent was that if anything happened to him, anything at all, he wanted them to know who was responsible. He wanted them to remember the name of the FBI agent who was threatening him. He wanted them to see to it that Remy Sinclair was punished.''

In the silence that followed, Michael muttered a curse. Remy sat absolutely still, his expression one Valery could recognize a mile away. Worry. Dread. Just the slightest bit of fear.

After a time, Smith turned toward him. ''How much of it's true?''

Valery stiffened. Michael had assured her that *none* of it was true, that Remy couldn't possibly be guilty of what she—and, apparently, the Simmons family—had suspected. But here was the assistant U.S. Attorney, one of Remy's best friends, asking as if he knew—as if he *knew*—that at least part of it *was* true, that Remy *was* at least a little guilty.

''Simmons was a source,'' Remy replied. ''You make deals with sources—work with us, and we won't send you to prison, give up your buddy and save yourself. As far as setting him up... Hell, Smith, you know people like Nate Simmons. You've prosecuted them. There wasn't any need to set him up. He had two or three crooked deals going at any given time. Yes, it's true that we cut a deal with him. I suppose you could even say I threatened him—I did tell him that if he didn't help us, he was going down. But falsify evidence? Murder?''

"What about the phone call?" Michael asked.

Remy nodded. "He called me the day before he died— wanted to change a meeting we had arranged earlier. It was supposed to take place Monday afternoon, but he said something had come up, that he needed to reschedule. We agreed to meet Tuesday instead."

"And, of course, no one can corroborate your version of the conversation." Michael's voice was flat, not questioning, and he sounded grim. "So it's your word against the family's."

"Did they actually hear the conversation?" Smith asked. "Or is their version what they claim Nate told them was said?"

"It's secondhand," Jolie replied.

"So the family believes that Remy killed Nate because he wouldn't cooperate?" Valery asked. "Isn't that a little extreme?"

Again it was Jolie who answered. "Because he wouldn't cooperate and because he supposedly intended to stop Remy by going public. Instead of helping Remy prove that Falcone was dirty, according to the relatives, he was going to prove that *Remy* was dirty."

"So," Remy mused, "according to their theory, I killed the guy to stop him from destroying my case *and* my career. The family has no proof, but, like Jolie here, they don't need proof. Just the allegation, even unsubstantiated, is enough to get me pulled off my cases and stuck behind a desk, completely out of the game."

"Which is probably their goal," Michael pointed out. "They don't care if you're fired or if you go to jail. They want you off this case."

Once more Smith spoke up. "How do you figure that?"

"Timing. Jolie, when did you say the family contacted you?"

"Tuesday afternoon."

"More than a week after Nate's death. Why wait? If you suspected that a cop was responsible for your son's murder, would you wait more than a week to tell someone?" Michael shook his head. "I'd be in Smith's boss's office as soon as I heard the news. I'd be demanding an investigation and an arrest, and if I didn't get it right then, I'd be on the ten o'clock news that same night, making my accusations public. So why did the Simmons family wait a week?"

"Because it took that long for Falcone to come up with the idea?" Remy suggested.

"No." Slowly Michael turned his head until his gaze locked with Valery's. Her eyes were shadowed and dark, and worry was etched into her face. There was also, underneath all that, a glimmer of understanding. She knew what he was thinking, knew where he was heading, and she agreed. He knew it, felt it, and she confirmed it when she spoke.

"It took Falcone that long to give up on me," she said softly. When everyone's attention was on her, she continued. "I was supposed to tell the police everything—how those men murdered Simmons in cold blood, how they let me live even though I could identify them, how they just happened to identify the man who had hired them. It wasn't coincidence. It wasn't bad luck or timing. I was *supposed* to be there. I was supposed to hear what they said, and I was supposed to be hostile enough toward Remy to tell the detectives."

He nodded. "A person could watch you for a few days and have your schedule down pat. It never varied. You went to work at nine o'clock. You left at three. You walked the same route to your car at the same time every day."

"Routine," she murmured, then repeated something he'd told her earlier. "If I weren't so predictable, chances are five out of six that I wouldn't have been on that street at that time. And if it wasn't coincidence that *I* was there, it wasn't coincidence that Simmons was."

"No coincidence at all," Michael agreed. "Simmons canceled his meeting with Remy because something had come up. Because someone—likely Falcone—had told him to be on that block of Chartres shortly after three that day. He had probably been shown a picture of you, had probably been instructed to strike up a conversation with you. I would imagine that was all he was told."

"No," she said quickly. "He knew to expect those men. Remember—I told you that he wasn't surprised to see them. I didn't think much about it then. I just assumed that it was an area where they all lived or worked or hung out—you know, a place where one would expect to see the others. He expected to see them there…but he was surprised when they shot him. He didn't expect that."

It was Jolie who broke the silence that followed Valery's words. "So you're saying that Jimmy Falcone had Nate Simmons killed so he could set Remy up for it and thereby get him pulled from the investigation into his own activities. And he arranged it in that way and on that street at that time so Remy's own cousin could be the prime witness against him." She shook her head, setting her blond hair swinging. "That's cold."

"Falcone is cold," Remy pointed out. "You know that better than most, Wade, you've been writing about his organization for years." He left his chair, paced to the opposite end of the room, then back again, stopping in front of the door. "One problem—getting me pulled off the case wouldn't stop the investigation. The bureau would simply assign another agent and continue. Some of the evidence that I've gathered might be tainted, but if it could be corroborated in other ways, that might not be much of a problem. So where's the benefit—other, possibly, than time—to Falcone?"

"Who would be most likely to replace you?" Michael asked, expecting his answer, finding it fit perfectly.

"Travis Wilson's been working with me. He's most familiar with the case, so I imagine it would go to him." Anticipating their reactions, Remy raised one hand to stall them. "I know you guys don't think much of him, but he's a good guy."

"He's careless," Smith said. "His cases have holes big enough for the Mississippi to flow through. No one in the office likes to prosecute his work."

"He's shifty," Jolie added. "He won't look you in the eye. And he's evasive."

Remy responded with sarcasm. "That's because he's not supposed to even be talking to you, Wade. Look, I know Travis isn't the best agent in the office—"

"Not even close," Smith interrupted.

"But he tries. He wants to do better. He's learning. He—"

This time it was Michael who interrupted, his voice quiet, his tone cold. "He was with you when I told you that Valery was in my apartment. He was the only one besides you who knew I would be gone last night, who knew where I was going and what time I was leaving."

That silenced Remy. He opened his mouth to protest, closed it again, then let his head fall back until it banged against the door. When he finally did speak, it was in a flat, dull voice that offered a futile protest. "He wasn't close enough to hear what we were saying."

"No. But he must have known why we were meeting. He probably saw that we were arguing. That you wanted to leave and I stopped you." Michael didn't go on. He didn't remind Remy how he had looked up at the apartment, how he had headed in that direction before Michael had stopped him. Wilson was a bright man. He knew about Remy and Michael's friendship. He could easily find out where Michael lived. He'd probably heard rumors about Michael's visions, probably knew that he and his visions had helped Remy out on more than a few cases. Add in the emotion Remy had displayed that morning, and Valery's location would be a simple conclusion to reach.

Simpler than the conclusion that they were reaching here.

"He's a cop," Remy said bleakly.

And that always made it harder, Michael acknowledged silently. Cops expected bad guys to be bad. They expected generally decent people to sometimes do wrong. But they expected their fellow officers to be good and noble and above temptation. A cop's crimes, in and of themselves, might be no worse than the same crimes committed by people like Falcone, but the fact that the laws were being broken by people who were sworn to uphold them made them worse. A dirty cop was a slap in the face—or a stab in the back—of every good cop out there.

After a moment's grim silence, Jolie asked, "Why would he do it?"

"Money. Power. Blackmail." Smith shrugged. "'Why' isn't important. 'How' is."

Michael stared off into the distance. Smith was right. The reasons behind Wilson's betrayal—greed, weakness, whatever—didn't matter. What did matter was how—not the logistics of it, not the details of how the first contact was made, how the offer was approached, how the information was passed, but the moral issues. How could Wilson try to destroy the man he worked with, the man he probably considered one of his better friends? How could he put an innocent woman in danger? How could he turn his back on everything that being an FBI agent meant? How could he do the job without being dedicated to it, and if he was dedicated to it, how could he ever sell out? How could he show so little regard for the laws he'd sworn to uphold?

And most of all, the biggest question of all: How could he live with what he'd done?

"I don't understand," Valery said slowly. "If this plan had worked, if Remy had been suspended and Wilson put in charge of the investigation, how does that help Falcone? Wilson can't decide on his own to drop the investigation, can he?"

Smith answered with a shrug. "No, but the case agent can have a tremendous influence on how the investigation is handled, on what direction it takes, how extensive it is and so on. A really aggressive agent is generally going to put together a much stronger case than someone like Wilson. If a case agent wants to screw up without being too obvious about it, it's simple enough. He misplaces a little evidence, overlooks a witness or two, or makes a few mistakes in his reports. He neglects to read a suspect his rights because he's sure someone else has already done it, or he doesn't get a search warrant, or he fouls up the chain of custody for crucial evidence. The case is shot, and he's sorry, but, hey, he says, everyone makes mistakes. And he's right—everyone

does make mistakes. Even if you suspect that his mistakes
were deliberate, you're going to have a hell of a time prov-
ing that what he did was criminal and not careless, over-
eager or just plain stupid.''

"If Travis Wilson already has a reputation for carelessness," she said, "then messing up this case would be blamed
on his incompetence and not—"

"Collusion," Smith supplied. "Conspiracy. Criminal
wrongdoing."

"So what's to stop the FBI from replacing him with another agent? What's to stop them from firing him?"

Jolie laughed. "Valery, we're talking the federal government here. Getting rid of incompetents has never been a
high priority with them."

"So..." Michael looked around the group, starting with
Valery and ending with Remy. "What do we do now?"

Jolie would write her story and get it in the evening paper. Smith would talk to the Special Agent in Charge of the
FBI field office and, for show, have Remy officially suspended from his investigative duties pending an inquiry into
the Simmons family's claims. At the same time, the three of
them would pool their resources and dig up whatever information they could on Wilson and Nate Simmons's family,
searching for something, anything, to link them to Falcone. Michael would continue to watch over Valery, and
she...

Valery sighed. She had nothing to do. Nothing but sit and
wait and go quietly crazy.

It had been two hours since the others had left. Two hours
of near-silence with Michael. She hated the uneasiness,
hated the discomfort, hated the silence, but she didn't know
how to break it. She didn't know how to approach him. She
didn't know what she wanted to say to him.

Mostly, she thought gloomily, she wanted him to just hold
her, but she didn't know how to ask for that, either.

"Valery, come over here."

She pulled her gaze from the TV and looked at him on the
bed. For the past fifteen or twenty minutes he'd been over

there fiddling with his gun. Now it was lying on the spread in front of him.

Leaving the chair, she settled at the foot of the bed, facing him, the gun between them.

"Pick it up."

She glanced at it, then back at him. "I've never touched a gun before."

His smile was faintly sardonic. "I figured. Pick it up."

Hesitantly she did so. It was black, cool and surprisingly comfortable in her hand.

"This is a Beretta nine millimeter. It's a good gun. These particular bullets make it even better." Leaning across, he inserted the clip into the gun, and the weight increased significantly. "There's a round in the chamber, so all you'd have to do to fire is slide the safety off—" he did so "—and pull the trigger. It might be kind of hard for you, so to make it easier, you can pull the hammer back, *then* pull the trigger. Understand?"

She did. She understood entirely too well. Very carefully, very gently, she laid the gun on the mattress, then got up and went to the window, staring out through the small crack between the drapes and the wall.

"Val?"

"Nothing's going to happen," she said belligerently.

"I know. But just in case . . ."

"No! There *is* no 'just in case.' There's no reason for me to learn how to shoot your gun. You're not going anywhere. You promised that you would be here, and you have to keep your word, because you've already broken one promise, and although I've never bothered to figure it out, I think two is probably my limit."

"Valery." He was closer now, behind her, sliding his arms around her waist. She stood straight and unbending for a moment, but only a moment. Only until he brushed a kiss across her ear. "You're right, sweetheart. Nothing *is* going to happen. You're safe, and I'm safe. But—"

Twisting in his arms, she pressed her face to his shoulder. "Stop it, Michael," she demanded, her voice breaking.

"Honey, I just want you to be prepared for whatever *might* happen," he murmured, stroking her hair.

"Nothing's going to happen. Remy and Smith and Jolie will take care of it. They'll get it all straightened out."

He pushed her back so he could see her face. "You're probably right. They probably will take care of everything. But probably isn't good enough, Val. From the beginning, we all assumed that Falcone wanted you dead because you could identify his men, but we were wrong. He wanted you to come forward with your story, with the evidence that would incriminate Remy. Now he's gotten the family to come forward. Now you know that Remy wasn't involved, that it was a setup from the start. *Now* you're a liability to Falcone."

Stubbornly she lowered her gaze, refusing to meet his, refusing to accept what he was saying. Instead she insistently repeated, in clear, concise tones, "Nothing is going to happen, Michael."

"If they come looking for you, if they find you, they're going to try to kill you. Right now I'm the only protection you've got, and if they kill me—"

She tried to twist away, but he held her tighter.

"If they kill me, Valery, you won't stand a chance unless you have some means of protecting yourself. Understanding the mechanics of firing that gun just might save your life, sweetheart."

At last she managed to wrench free of him, and she crossed the room, putting the bed between them. "Damn you, stop it!" she demanded, then wiped a tear from her eye. "If they kill you, do you think I'll care about saving myself?"

He stood motionless for a long time; then he came a few steps closer before answering. "So, out of some misplaced sense of guilt, you would let him kill you, too."

She gave him a long, hard look. "You should recognize misplaced guilt, Michael," she said quietly. "You've been mourning Evan all these months, blaming God, blaming yourself, and his death wasn't even your fault. *It wasn't your fault.* But if Jimmy Falcone kills you for the simple reason that you're standing between him and me . . . that *is* my fault."

"So you would let my death be for nothing," he said flatly. "At least Evan knew that, in dying, he gave that little girl and me a chance. You won't even give me that much."

He sounded disappointed. Tired. Bleak.

He sounded hopeless.

Valery closed her eyes, sighed and swallowed hard past the lump in her throat. He was getting so much more out of this conversation than she was putting in. He was receiving messages that she wasn't sending, somehow translating her concern for him into selfish concern for her own guilt. Why couldn't she just be honest? Why couldn't she simply say, Michael, I'm afraid for you?

Because she was equally afraid for herself.

Only he was at risk of losing his life, and she was afraid of losing her heart.

God help her, she was such a coward.

Hearing him move, she opened her eyes again and saw that he had the pistol in hand now, that he was working it into the holster clipped to his waistband in back. "Wait," she whispered. When he stopped, she moistened her lips. "Show me again what you want me to know."

After a moment's hesitation, he gave her another explanation, this one terse and clipped, of the workings of the gun. When he was finished, when she was sure that she could fire the pistol with no problem—although what she might hit, Michael admitted, was anybody's guess—he returned the Beretta to the holster, then started to turn away. She stopped him, clasping both his hands in hers. "I want one more promise, Michael."

He didn't say anything but simply waited for her to ask.

"Promise you won't get yourself killed on my account."

His look was hard. "I have no intention of dying at any time in the near future."

"Intent isn't a promise."

"I've already broken one promise."

"Telling Remy about me was no big deal. This is. Promise."

He studied her for a time, then shook his head. "I can't, Valery."

Thoughts of his visions, of threats and death, sent a chill rustling through her. "Because you think something might happen?"

"Because I don't make promises I can't keep. I can promise you that I won't kill myself, that I won't step in front of a speeding car, that I won't carelessly walk into a dangerous situation. I can promise that I'll drive safely to try to avoid accidents, that I'll take the proper precautions at work and that I'll never start drinking again. But I can't control what other people do. I can't promise that someday someone won't try to kill me. I can't promise that they won't succeed. And I can't promise that, in some way, it won't have to do with you."

I don't make promises I can't keep. Which meant he only made promises he *could* keep. And just this morning he'd promised her three things: to love her, to always be there for her—as much as it was in his control, she silently added— and never to leave her.

He raised his hand to her hair, his touch so light that she barely felt it. "I can tell you this, Valery—whatever time we both have left, I want to spend it with you. I don't want to be alone because you're afraid to trust me."

Tears welled in her eyes. "You might change your mind after you've spent more time with me. People tend to get tired of me after a while."

"Maybe I will," he agreed, pressing a kiss to her temple. "Ask me in..." His next kiss landed on her cheek. "Oh, about fifty years or so." His third kiss covered her mouth, taking possession of it, sending warmth through her all the way down to her toes. He interrupted it only long enough to pull her shirt over her head, to strip off his own, and then he claimed her again, murmuring as he gently lowered her to the bed. "Maybe I'll have an answer then."

Chapter 12

Friday evening found Michael standing at the window, gazing out across the winter-dark sky. Behind him there was a murmur of conversation as Valery, Remy, Smith and Jolie finished the take-out fried chicken dinner the reporter had supplied. What would soon be a serious meeting at the moment resembled nothing more than an indoor picnic. The food was lined up on the dresser, paper plates were balanced on knees and laps, and the drinks were in chilled cans that came from a cooler, also provided courtesy of Jolie.

Remy, Smith and Jolie had been busy the past two days. He knew from his own experience the vast wealth of knowledge you could pick up through legal channels, but he never failed to be amazed at the amount of information Jolie could learn through her own less-than-official sources. She had more informants on the street than any ten cops, Remy had grumbled. His respect was grudgingly given, but Michael outright admired her. She was damn good at what she did.

And a large part of what she was doing now was making things easier for Valery. Realizing just how restricted to the room they were, she had made several trips out to bring food, a cooler full of drinks, some books and an armload of women's magazines. She took time on each brief visit to chat with Valery, woman to woman rather than reporter to subject. She made Valery laugh.

This morning, earning Valery's undying friendship, she'd shown up with a stash of sweets, including enough chocolate to last at least a week. Right now they were sharing gooey marshmallow-and-walnut brownies, diet sodas and gossip from the latest *People*.

Things were coming to a head. Another twenty-four or forty-eight hours, and Valery would be safe. She would be free to go back home.

He hoped she understood that she would also be free to stay.

He hoped she trusted him enough to make that choice.

At last the rustle of plastic and paper signaled that dinner was over. Now business would begin. Turning from the window, he went to his usual place on the bed, close to Valery...but not close enough. He could never be close enough.

Jolie started. Her story had run on the front page of Thursday's paper, and Remy had been officially removed from his duties soon after. It wasn't easy for him, Michael knew—having his co-workers look at him with suspicion and worse in their eyes. It wasn't easy letting his friends think he was dirty, playing a role he detested with everything in him.

But it was only for a few days. By Monday morning he would be cleared. There was no such thing, Valery had told Michael once, as being proven innocent; once an accusation had been made, an idea planted, some people would always believe in your guilt. But that wouldn't be the case for Remy. With his boss, Smith and Smith's boss standing behind him, Remy would come out of this with his reputation intact.

Michael hoped *he* came out with everything intact.

"I couldn't find anything other than Nate himself to connect his family to Falcone," Jolie continued. "However, according to the neighbors, Mrs. Simmons is getting a new car sometime in the next couple of weeks, and she and her brothers have been flashing a lot of cash in the past week. She told the lady who was nosy enough to ask that it was from Nate's life insurance policy. Funny. I never knew a con artist and small-time thief who spent any of his profits on life insurance.''

''I don't know,'' Remy disagreed dryly. ''In a sense, Mrs. Simmons is telling the truth. When Nate's life ended, Falcone came up with cash to ensure the family's cooperation. What about Travis?''

''He's so clean, he squeaks,'' Smith replied. ''His finances are in line, his neighbors all like him and think he's such a fine young man and he hasn't had so much as a parking ticket since he moved to Louisiana. He lives comfortably, but he doesn't have any expenses that can't be covered by his salary. He votes in every election, pays his bills on time and takes care of his landlady's cat when she's gone.''

Across the room Jolie was grinning like the aforementioned cat with a canary in its sights, but she didn't speak until, with an exasperated sigh, Smith prompted her. ''And what did you find out about him, Ms. Wade?'' he asked sardonically.

''Don't you guys have to have background investigations or something before you're allowed to go to work?''

''Of course.''

''Don't you ever do periodic reviews?''

''Yes. Wilson's due for one next year.''

Shaking her head, she made a clucking sound. ''Well, let me give you a heads-up—Special Agent Travis Wilson, Federal Bureau of Investigation, has a little gambling problem.''

Smith was studying Jolie with a narrow-eyed gaze—probably wondering, Michael thought, exactly where and how she had come across such information. Remy accepted the news with no real outward emotion, although his gaze seemed to grow more distant, his jaw a little more taut. Even though he'd never liked Wilson himself, Michael sympathized with him. Remy had been more than friendly to Wilson. He'd done his best to help Travis become a better investigator; he'd defended him and trusted him, and Travis had repaid him by turning on him. By trying to destroy his career. And all because he had a fondness for the horses, the cards and probably every game of chance that came along.

"Your source—probably some government computer—says Wilson's finances are in line," Jolie went on smugly. "That he lives comfortably but within his salary. *My* sources—only some of the better patronized bookies in the city—say he's got problems. He likes to bet, only he hasn't got a clue. His instincts are so bad that you could bet against him and make a fortune. If he says the Saints will win, they'll lose. If he picks the first horse out of the gate, it'll be the last one across the finish line. He can put money down on a team that's on the hottest winning streak in the history of the game and still manage to lose."

"So he's in debt—"

She interrupted Smith. "Oh, no, no. He *was* in debt, so deep in debt that no one would take his action. And then one day he showed up and had a wad of cash for everyone he owed. Since then, he's won a little, lost more, but he always covers his losses promptly. The bookies love him."

"And he's getting the money from... ?"

"According to your computer, not his paycheck. My money's on New Orleans's friendly neighborhood banker. Jimmy Falcone."

Michael finally turned his attention from Remy to Jolie. "When did he find this source of money to pay off his debts?"

"About eight weeks ago. He explained it to each one as winnings from a bet placed elsewhere. Said he got lucky on a long shot."

At last Remy stirred from his moodiness. "He got assigned to the Falcone case eight weeks ago."

"So he didn't exactly lie," Jolie said with a shrug. "For someone with his talents, that *was* a long shot."

Valery changed positions, making the mattress shift beneath them. "How did it start? Did he approach Falcone, or was it the other way around?"

"It doesn't matter." Remy's tone was harsh, his scowl unforgiving.

Reaching for her hand, Michael laced his fingers through hers and explained in a quieter, gentler voice, "All that matters is that Wilson took the money. He committed the crime. He sold out."

Gradually he became aware that the tenor of the brief silence had changed, that the attention had shifted subtly from the problem of Travis Wilson to him and Valery. It was because he was holding her hand, he realized. In two days, neither of them had touched the other, had barely spoken to or even looked at the other in front of their friends. It wasn't anything they had planned, just an unspoken agreement, he supposed, to keep their relationship private.

So they were holding hands. So what? They'd been more intimate than that before they'd ever even met. And the others would have found out eventually, when he convinced Valery to move in with him permanently. When they couldn't come to his apartment without finding her there. When he finally talked her into marrying him.

Once again it was Jolie who spoke, getting the conversation back on track, drawing attention away from something no one was going to comment on. "We've got a murderer or two to catch, folks. Let's make some plans."

Making plans. He liked that idea. They would work out a plan to send Jimmy Falcone and his thugs to prison, to get Travis Wilson in a cell he couldn't wiggle out of and to clear Remy's name.

Then *he* intended to make some plans of his own.

Plans that involved no one—for a while, at least—but him and Valery.

Plans for a long and happy future.

Together.

* * *

After a few days away, Michael's apartment felt more like home to Valery than her own place ever had. She walked in Saturday evening, happy to unpack her clothes and toss them into the laundry hamper with his. She looked forward to sleeping in his bed in his cozily dark bedroom, and to the pancakes and coffee he had promised her for breakfast Sunday morning.

She was happy to be home.

Even if Michael wasn't.

Even if all she had for company was Jolie Wade and, outside the door and down in the square, an undisclosed number of unidentified cops.

"You might as well sit down and get comfortable," Jolie said, curled up on the sofa with a magazine and a candy bar. "The meeting won't even start for another half hour. It might be midnight or later before Michael gets back."

With a scowl, Valery dropped into the chair where he usually sat. "I don't understand why he had to go along," she said grumpily.

"Yes, you do. Remy's his friend. A cop doesn't send somebody else for backup when his friend's in danger." After a moment, Jolie relented, put away the magazine, tossed half the candy bar to her and smiled. "It isn't easy, is it?"

Valery bit into chocolate-coated peanut butter. "What?"

"Falling in love with a cop. I don't think I could do it. Of course, I'm not going to fall in love with *anyone,* at least not before I win my Pulitzer, but when I do, it won't be a cop."

"A Pulitzer? You don't ask much of yourself, do you?"

Jolie's answering smile was easy, serious and tremendously satisfied. The reporter had already asked a great deal of herself, Valery knew instinctively, and she had met every challenge. Someday Jolie Wade would be a name that stirred recognition all over the country, not just in New Orleans, Louisiana. Someday she probably *would* win her Pulitzer.

"What are your ambitions?"

"Falling in love with a cop certainly wasn't one of them," Valery replied dryly. "I'm not sure I ever had any. Oh, I'd like to buy the shop where I work if the owner carries through with his promise to sell, but that's not some burning goal. Mostly..." Her voice grew soft, thoughtful. "I've tried to be independent, not to get involved with anyone, not to get too close to anyone and not to let anyone get too close to me."

Jolie gave a low whistle. "Boy, have you failed miserably. You need to set some new goals, Valery—like marrying a cop and raising a bunch of little cops. Like resolving things with your cousin, healing your family, healing Michael. Like getting close to someone who's already close to you. Like living your life instead of watching it pass you by."

Marrying Michael. It was a lovely proposition...and one that was within her reach—if she found the courage to try.

Marrying Michael in that little white church that he'd painted so bleakly, in his father's church in Titusville, Arkansas, with his father officiating and his entire family— *their* entire families—in attendance.

Marrying Michael and living happily ever after, raising a brood of little cops, and artists and gourmet cooks.

It was a wonderful ambition, one she wanted so desperately that it hurt.

It would be a dream come true.

Provided that she could stop waiting for the dream to turn into a nightmare.

"Explain to me what they're doing tonight." She had sat in on the meetings, had listened to them plan and organize, but she'd heard the words danger and risk, and the rest had sailed right over her head. She'd been too cold and afraid inside to let anything else penetrate.

Jolie was more than willing to comply. At Smith's request, Travis Wilson had been summoned to the U.S. Attorney's office that morning, where he'd been met by Michael, Smith and his boss, and Remy and his boss. They had confronted him with what they knew, and they had offered him a deal.

"It wasn't much of a deal," she mused thoughtfully. "The terms weren't particularly favorable. I mean, with Nate Simmons, it was 'Help us bust Falcone, and we won't send you to prison.' With Wilson, it's 'Help us bust Falcone, and we won't send you to prison for the entire rest of your life—just most of it.' Anyway, Wilson caved in, confessed everything and agreed to help."

His help, in this case, had consisted of playing out the game with Falcone. He had called the man, had told him that Remy's career was over, that Remy was angry and bitter and looking for some payback. He had valuable services to offer, Wilson had reminded Falcone, and after the way the bureau had treated him, he was in the market to sell those services to the highest bidder. He was looking for a job that would make use of all his years of FBI experience, something that would pay handsomely and, most of all, something that would give him the satisfaction of thwarting the very department that had cut him loose.

It had taken some doing, but Falcone had at last agreed to a meeting, scheduled to begin in another fifteen minutes, at a wharf a short distance down the river. Michael and Smith were already there, Michael as part of the backup team, Smith to listen to the conversation via Remy's wire and let them know when the conversation had gotten incriminating enough.

"You think Travis will cooperate fully?" Valery asked.

"He has no choice. He's screwed either way. He's got to work the best deal he can get, and that's playing with the bureau. When it's all over, Remy's name will be cleared, Falcone and his thugs will be on their way to jail and you'll be safe again."

If everything went according to plan, Valery considered.

Everyone, including Jolie, had seemed confident that it would, but their plan, she thought uneasily, counted on Jimmy Falcone being a fool. He would have to be a tremendous fool if he believed that Remy would sell out.

But hadn't she believed the same thing herself—sort of— less than two weeks ago?

She had been a fool, too.

But no more. Doubting Remy had been one of her last mistakes.

Doubting Michael *was* the last.

When he came back tonight, she was going to tell him that she loved him. She was going to ask him to marry her. She was going to warn him that she would hold him to his promises, especially the ones of the forever-and-ever-till-death-us-do-part variety.

With a deep breath, Jolie finished. "So they get their bad guys, you get Michael back and, even though I'm here baby-sitting you, *I* get the story first."

"And how will that work when they're at the wharf and you're here?"

"Smith promised to call the *instant* it's over. I'll leave you to your bodyguards, and I'm hightailing it to the scene."

"He just agreed to do that," Valery said with some skepticism.

Jolie's smile was filled with self-pride. "Actually I talked him into it. After all, here you are, Remy's cousin and Michael's sweetie. Naturally you'd be worried sick about them, and letting you know they were safe was the least he could do in return for all the help you've been."

Valery rose from her chair and headed for the kitchen. "I realize you didn't do it for me," she called over her shoulder, "but thank you anyway. I do want to know."

Opening the freezer door, she began searching through plastic-bagged and foil-wrapped packages, seeking something for dinner. She had just settled on a heavy-duty bag labeled crabmeat gumbo when her stomach gave a slightly disorienting heave. Straightening, she closed the freezer door and set the bag on the counter, then rested her hand on her waist. Maybe she wasn't hungry, after all. Maybe her stomach was reacting to all the rich food Jolie had been bringing around the past few days. Maybe she was . . .

Unbidden, Jolie's comment about Travis Wilson drifted into her mind. *He's screwed either way. He's got to work the best deal he can get, and that's playing with the bureau.*

The little flutter of unease moved from her stomach up high into her chest, making it hard to breathe. Wilson was incompetent. He wasn't much of an investigator. He was foolish and had no control over his gambling. But none of that made him stupid.

None of that could make him forget that he had helped Falcone set up Remy.

Or that the setup had included murdering a man in cold blood.

Surely Travis would never forget that Falcone had sacrificed Nate Simmons for his own selfish gain, that he had ordered Simmons's death as easily, as carelessly, as he might have squashed an annoying bug.

Travis Wilson *was* screwed either way. He had to work the best deal he could get. But there were more than the two options Jolie had considered. It wasn't a matter of helping the FBI and going to prison for a long time or not helping them and going for the rest of his life. The question was simpler than that: What was he more afraid of? Arrest, trial, conviction, imprisonment?

Or Jimmy Falcone?

The tightness in her chest fluttered again. She was all too familiar with it, all too afraid of it. She had felt it about a block and a half before her one and only car wreck. She had endured it through a series of misfortunes a few years back. She had experienced it only minutes before the phone call notifying her that her mother had died.

Anxiety. Dread. Apprehension.

Foreboding.

Oh, God, no.

Nothing was going to go according to plan. She knew it, knew it as surely as she'd known to come to Michael that Friday night a lifetime ago. Their plan counted heavily on Travis Wilson's cooperation, and he wasn't going to cooperate. He was going to weigh his options—betray the bureau once more, an act that he obviously hadn't found too difficult the first time, or betraying Jimmy Falcone, an act that would likely get him killed for his efforts—and he was going to make the logical choice for a man in his position.

He was going to warn Falcone, if he hadn't already, that the meeting was a setup.

He was going to try to save himself by joining forces with Falcone.

He was going to expose Remy and Michael and everyone else to danger and the threat of death.

Leaning against the counter for support, she considered her own options. She could try to convince Jolie, could try to convince the cop outside the front door. The cop who had taken strict orders from Michael that he was to allow no one other than Michael, Remy or Smith to enter the apartment, that under no circumstances was he to allow Valery to leave. The cop who had that do-or-die look about him.

Or she could take matters into her own hands and warn Michael and Remy herself.

"Are you all right?" Jolie came into the kitchen, stopping beside Valery, giving her a concerned look. "You look like a ghost. Come and sit down. Don't worry about dinner. I'll take care of it."

When she started to slide her arm around Valery's waist, Valery pulled back. "No, I'm okay. It's just..." Her stomach heaved again. "Too much rich food, too many sweets."

"And too much stress, too many nerves, too little peace. Come on..."

"I'll be fine."

"You don't look fine."

She managed a weak smile. "Michael's got some of the pink stuff for upset stomachs in the bathroom. If you could just get it for me..."

Jolie left to search the bathroom cabinets. The instant she was out of sight, Valery made a beeline for the balcony, opening, then closing, the French doors with the quietest of clicks. It was a chilly night, and, just like before, she had no coat. Unlike before, she was wearing her own shoes, it wasn't raining and she was at least a little experienced in climbing from one balcony to another.

A quick glance over the railing showed what she assumed was a normal number of people out and about on a January Saturday night. They were alone or in groups, in a hurry or taking a lazy stroll. Some just stood and talked, some were reading papers and maps, some were enjoying the sights.

Some, she knew, were cops, there for her benefit. But which ones?

Inside she heard Jolie call her name. "Valery, I couldn't find—" Hastily she climbed over the balcony rail. If any of the cops below noticed her—if anyone at all noticed her—they weren't obvious about it. She moved quickly, competently. It wasn't so bad this time. Of course, dry metal and shoes made a tremendous difference, to say nothing of the fact that this time her fear wasn't for herself. She wasn't afraid of her own death. It was Michael and Remy she was worried about.

She swung over the rail onto the neighbor's balcony just in time to duck under the table as Jolie opened Michael's doors. "Valery, are you okay? Where the hell did you go?"

When Jolie returned inside, Valery wriggled out and, whispering a soft prayer for help, tried the doors. Bless this neighbor's heart, she hadn't learned a lesson from last time. The doors were unlocked.

She hurried across the room to the front door, figuring that about now, Jolie was alerting the cop outside. Being a man and a cop, he wouldn't take her word that Valery had simply disappeared; he would want to search the apartment himself. Opening the door just a crack, she saw that Jolie was, indeed, talking to the officer, that he was, indeed, insisting on seeing for himself.

"There's nothing to check. I'm telling you, she just vanished. You need to get on the radio and..." As she followed the officer inside, Jolie's words faded away.

Valery shot out the door. She hit the stairs at a run and, a scant moment or two later, she was home free. Once she reached Decatur, she slowed to a fast walk, trying not to stand out among the crowd, but as soon as Michael's building was out of sight, she broke into a run.

The wharf wasn't far away—a half mile, maybe a mile. She prayed as she ran.

Please let me get there on time.

Please let Falcone be late.

Please keep Michael and Remy safe.

Please, God.

Please, please, please.

Michael was cold, his muscles cramped, his nerves on edge. It seemed he'd been waiting forever in this dirty niche formed by tall wooden packing crates, listening to the lap of the Mississippi off to his left and the sounds of the city on his right. Now it was time. Showtime, Evan had always said with a grin and a flourish, even that last time.

Remy was standing about fifty feet in front of him. Travis Wilson waited another ten feet or so away. They were dressed much the same, looking, even out here, like FBI agents in their suits and overcoats. But that was the extent of the similarities. Wilson was scum. He didn't know the meaning of honor. He was the worst kind of cop there was.

At least, he had been. No matter what happened here tonight, Wilson's career in law enforcement was finished. Even if he somehow managed to escape jail—a distinct possibility; earlier Michael had heard someone mention the federal witness relocation program—he would never be a cop again.

Wilson lit a cigarette, then, after only a few puffs, tossed it to the ground. He didn't bother to step on it, and Michael watched its faint glow until the sound of a finely tuned engine caught his attention. It was a limo—long, black, tinted windows. Jimmy Falcone liked to travel in style. He liked to flaunt his money, his power. If he couldn't have respect, which lately he'd gotten a taste of, he would damn well have flash.

Showtime.

The car came to a stop some distance back, and the driver got out to open the door. Falcone's bodyguards exited first, then the man himself. More suits, more overcoats. It was getting so you couldn't tell the players without a program, Michael thought without a smile. He felt downright conspicuous in his jeans and leather jacket.

The three principals came together, forming a loose triangle, too far away for Michael to hear their words. Smith was in the surveillance van parked inside the warehouse, listening to the conversation as it was recorded. They each had their limitations: Smith could hear but not see, and Michael could see but not hear.

And from this particular spot, he couldn't see a hell of a lot. Falcone was in shadow, and Remy stood at an angle, his profile hazy. Wilson was the only one Michael could get a good look at. Travis was nervous, too damned nervous. Michael had been in favor of using him only to arrange the meeting; he hadn't wanted him here, hadn't wanted him acting as a go-between. But he'd gotten voted down by the others. He could do it, Travis had insisted. He could handle it.

But the truth was, he couldn't. He was obviously nervous, obviously troubled, obviously afraid. All they could do was hope that Falcone would put it down to Remy's presence and nothing else.

Michael shifted, trying to ease the stiffness in his legs, trying not to think about how cold his fingers were, how damp and uncomfortable his clothes were. Winter weather in New Orleans was unpredictable. One day might be sunny and warm, the next uncomfortably chilly. There was only one constant: it was always damp. In one form or another—fog, rain, humidity or the rare snow—there was always moisture in the air.

He'd just found some semblance of comfort when all hell broke loose inside his head. The images flashed in quick succession—Valery, Remy, the bitter odor of gunpowder, a lingering pain. He tried to rise, but his legs wouldn't support him; he had to lean against one of the crates with its prickly wood. Sweat popped out on his forehead, and his lungs burned with each breath, burned as if he'd exerted himself too hard, as if he'd used every last breath in him, as if he would collapse any moment now.

Then he saw her—Valery—*really* saw her. Flesh and blood, no visions, real this time. She was here, running toward Remy, running hard. Remy didn't see her, though, and neither did Falcone or the others. Their attention was on Travis Wilson, who suddenly started backing away from the group, drawing his gun from underneath his coat as he went. "Jimmy, it's a setup!" he shouted, turning the pistol on Remy and pulling the trigger. "Damn it, Jimmy, it's a trap!"

Then all hell really did break loose.

Valery watched as the paramedics loaded the stretcher into the ambulance, watched as they took Remy away, lights flashing, siren wailing. He was going to be okay, they'd told her—Michael, the paramedics, Remy himself. Still, she felt cold and empty and terribly afraid inside.

Michael came up behind her, laying his hands on her shoulders, squeezing the taut muscles there. "Are you okay?"

Unable to make her voice work, she nodded.

As he'd done only a few nights ago, he removed his jacket and offered it to her, sliding her arms inside, zipping it up. "Before we go to the hospital, there's something I want you to see."

Numbly she followed him across the busy pier to the tall wooden box where she'd taken refuge during the gunfight. He crouched beside it. "This is where you were, sitting right here."

She didn't comment.

"They were shooting at you—did you know that?"

She shrugged. There had been so many shots—hundreds of them, maybe more. It had reminded her of childhood Fourth of July celebrations, when she and Remy and some of the cousins had tied giant strings of Black Cats together,

then lit them all at once. After their mothers had endured
the one or two thousand firecrackers blasting off within
minutes, they had always chased them away with the ad-
monition not to do it again. But that had been harmless fun.

Tonight people had gotten hurt.

Remy had gotten hurt.

"I was over there—" he pointed to the corner of the
warehouse "—and I saw them shoot at you. I saw the wood
splinter. I thought..." He looked away from her, blew his
breath out, then grimly finished. "I thought they were going to kill you."

She huddled deeper in his jacket. "I had cover. I was
safe."

"Honey, this is a simple wooden crate with some packing material and furniture from Taiwan inside. All it did was
slow them down. Every bullet that went in on their side
came out again over here. Except one." He motioned for her
to come closer, and she did, kneeling beside him. "The way
you were sitting, your head was about right here. I remember most of this label was hidden behind it." He fingered a
rectangle of poster-board-type paper that had once been
fluorescent orange but had long since faded to a soft peach.
Lifting one corner of the paper, he revealed a hole in the side
of the crate that was plugged with a small chunk of metal.
"Do you know what that is?"

She leaned closer. It was misshapen, a dull silvery color,
squished-looking.

"That's a slug. That's the part of the bullet that kills you.
The only thing between this slug and your head was this
piece of paper. The only thing that stopped it was this paper."

Her knees weakened, and she slowly slid to one side until
her bottom was on the ground. Her voice was hoarse and
shaky when she finally spoke. "I guess I was lucky."

Michael shook his head. "Not lucky. Blessed. Protected.
Watched over." He released the paper and took her hands.
"I've been damned angry and bitter the past nine months,
Valery. I lost my faith in God, in prayer, in miracles, in me.

But I prayed tonight when I saw you here—me, the great unbeliever. For the first time since Evan's death, I prayed. I prayed for you to be safe, and God heard me. You should have died here, Valery. Only a miracle could have kept you alive. I asked for a miracle, and I got it."

She smiled nervously. He might have gotten more than he bargained for. "Michael—"

With a shake of his head, he silenced her. "I know life hasn't been fair to you, Valery. You've been hurt too many times by people who should have done their damnedest to protect you from pain. But bad things do happen. How you deal with them determines what kind of life you'll have. You can give up and close yourself off from everyone else, or you can learn from the bad times. You can learn to appreciate the good when it comes along. You can learn to value it that much more. You can—"

"Michael." She kissed him, stopping his words, then cupped his face in her palms, meeting his intense gaze. "I love you."

He stared at her for a long still moment; then slowly, oh, so slowly, he smiled a faint smile. "I know you do. I just didn't think *you* knew it."

"I knew. I was just afraid."

"And you're not now?"

"I am," she whispered, tears coming too easily to her eyes. "I always have been. But I'm less afraid *with* you than I am *without* you. I never want to have any regrets, Michael. I never want to get hurt again, never want to be left again. But there could be no regret, no pain, no loneliness, that could ever equal the way I would feel if I lived my life without you."

"Do you know what you're saying?"

She nodded.

"I'm not as generous as you. I'm not going to give you a chance to break a first promise, much less a second. You make a vow, and I'm going to hold you to it."

"I'm counting on that."

"For the rest of our lives," he warned as he drew her into his arms.

"I'm counting on that, too."

For one serious moment he searched her face; then, at last, with a smile, he kissed her. Somehow, Valery reflected, it was different from all the other kisses they'd shared. It was as sweet, as passionate, as proprietary, as the others, but it was also full of promise. It was a commitment. It was a vow.

When he raised his head, he studied her face again. She didn't wonder what he saw there. She knew; she saw it reflected in his own expression. Hope. Love. A future worth living. A future worth sharing.

Getting to his feet, he pulled her up, too, wrapped his arm tightly around her waist and started toward the cars parked inside the warehouse. "You know," he remarked thoughtfully, "there's something to be said for the power of prayer. I asked for one miracle, and I got two. I got you."

Epilogue

At the sound of the phone, Michael eased out of bed, away from Valery's side, tugged on his jeans and left the bedroom, closing the door behind him. A quick glance at the clock showed that it was nearly ten o'clock. They hadn't gotten home from the hospital until shortly before five, and it had been closer to seven before either of them had managed to fall asleep.

He stopped beside the answering machine as it came on. If it was something important, he would pick up. Otherwise, he didn't want the stillness of his morning disturbed with conversation just yet.

"Hey, Michael, it's Smith." His friend sounded weary. Michael doubted that he'd gotten any sleep at all. "I just checked with the hospital, and Remy's fine. Falcone got away clean. His people aren't talking, not even the two we got for killing Simmons. The man inspires some loyalty, doesn't he?"

More like fear, Michael thought.

"Anyway, I'm going to tie things up here, then go home and sleep until tomorrow. Once you're up, if anything changes with Remy, let me know, will you?'' He hung up, and the machine reset itself, the zero on the message counter changing to a one.

Michael went into the kitchen and started a pot of coffee. They had waited all night at the hospital—he and Valery, Smith and Jolie, and George and Marie Sinclair. Even once the doctors had told them that Remy's injuries, while serious, weren't life-threatening, they had remained until, finally around dawn, they had each been allowed to see him for a moment or two. They had left him with the parents he hadn't seen in fifteen years, the parents whose only contact with him in that time had been brought about by their concern for Valery. It had taken a too-close encounter with death to get them there on Remy's behalf, but now that the silence between them had been broken, Michael had no doubt they would stay in touch. Their love for their son and their regret over the estrangement were obvious; they had gone a long way toward removing that perpetual sadness from Remy's eyes.

He drank his first cup of coffee on the balcony, even though, shirtless and shoeless, it was a chilly place to be. The sun hadn't yet burned away the morning fog. It hung in low wisps around the square, obscuring the ground here, revealing it there. It gave the Quarter a softer, gentler look.

His entire future had a softer, gentler look this morning.

''Good morning.''

He turned from the rail to see Valery standing in the open door, wearing one of his shirts and nothing else. Definitely softer, he thought with a smile. Infinitely gentler. ''I was wondering when you might wake up,'' he said, although it was a lie. If he'd given the immediate future any thought at all, his plans likely would have been to return to bed with her, to let her sleep until the lines of weariness that etched her face were gone, and then to wake her with kisses, to make love to her when she was soft and drowsy, and again when she was awake and passionate.

''I was wondering when you might come back to bed.'' She folded her arms over her chest, shivering with a chill.

The cotton was pulled tight across her breasts, outlining their rounded shape, revealing their erect nipples.

"You plan to sleep the day away?"

She smiled sensuously. "I didn't say anything about sleeping."

"Good. Because I want to talk."

Immediately she sobered. "That phone call...Remy...?"

"He's fine. I want to talk about us."

Leaning against the doorframe, she crossed one ankle over the other, drawing his attention to her legs, her incredibly long, bare legs. "We can talk in bed where it's warm."

Emptying his coffee cup, he started toward her and wrapped his arms around her, drawing her snugly against him. "If we go back to bed, sweetheart," he said while nuzzling her ear, "talking is going to be the last thing on my mind."

With a delicate shiver and a rueful sigh, she nudged him back. "All right. You can have five minutes. Then we go to bed. What is it you want to talk about?"

"Five minutes, huh? All right. The wedding."

"As soon as Remy's out of the hospital."

"Where?"

"Your father's church."

He grinned. "Good answers. Living together."

"We already are."

"Officially. As in giving up your apartment and moving all your stuff over here."

"Tomorrow." With a lascivious smile, she reconsidered that. "Or the next day."

"Okay. The balcony."

That one puzzled her. "What about it?"

"Quit climbing off it. I always thought it could be a problem with kids, but, honey, you're thirty-four years old. Give my heart a rest and only leave by the door from now on."

"I promise," she replied solemnly, but the effect was diminished by the grin that immediately followed. "Michael?"

"Hmm." He was gazing down at her, noticing yet again how clear and blue her eyes were, how stubborn her jaw was, how utterly kissable her mouth was. Feeling a slow burn starting deep inside, he began to think that her request to return to bed was more than reasonable. More than desirable. It was quickly becoming downright necessary.

She touched his face, claiming his attention, not going on until she was certain she had it. "I love you, Michael."

Taking her hand from his jaw, he pressed a kiss to her palm, then wrapped his fingers tightly around it. "I learned to hate the visions after Evan died," he said quietly, fiercely. "I was convinced that nothing good could ever come from them again. But I was wrong. When the visions of you started, I was in despair. I thought I couldn't bear it again. I didn't know that they were different this time. I didn't know how I would need you. I didn't know how I would love you. I didn't know that they were visions of my future."

"Of *our* future," she corrected him in a husky whisper.

Yes, he silently agreed as he kissed her. Visions of their future.

Visions of life.

Visions of love.

*   *   *   *   *

Dark secrets, dangerous desire...

Take 4 bestselling love stories FREE

Plus get a FREE surprise gift!

MONTANA
Mavericks

Stories that capture living and loving beneath the Big Sky, where legends live on...and the mystery is just beginning.

This September, look for

THE WIDOW AND THE RODEO MAN
by Jackie Merritt

And don't miss a minute of the loving as the mystery continues with:

SLEEPING WITH THE ENEMY
by Myrna Temte (October)
THE ONCE AND FUTURE WIFE
by Laurie Paige (November)
THE RANCHER TAKES A WIFE
by Jackie Merritt (December),
and many more!

Wait, there's more! Win a trip to a Montana mountain resort. For details, look for this month's MONTANA MAVERICKS title at your favorite retail outlet.

Only from **Silhouette®** where passion lives.

Fifty red-blooded, white-hot, true-blue hunks
from every State in the Union!

Look for MEN MADE IN AMERICA! Written by some of
our most popular authors, these stories feature fifty of
the strongest, sexiest men, each from a different state in
the union!

Two titles available every month at your favorite retail
outlet.

In August, look for:

PROS AND CONS by Bethany Campbell
(Massachusetts)
TO TAME A WOLF by Anne McAllister (Michigan)

In September, look for:

WINTER LADY by Janet Joyce (Minnesota)
AFTER THE STORM by Rebecca Flanders (Mississippi)

You won't be able to resist MEN MADE IN AMERICA!

HE'S AN

AMERICAN HERO

Men of mettle. Men of integrity. Real men who know the real meaning of love. Each month, Intimate Moments salutes these true American Heroes.

For July: THAT SAME OLD FEELING,
by Judith Duncan.
Chase McCall had come home a new man.
Yet old lover Devon Manyfeathers soon stirred familiar feelings—and renewed desire.

For August: MICHAEL'S GIFT,
by Marilyn Pappano.
Michael Bennett knew his visions prophesied certain death. Yet he would move the high heavens to change beautiful Valery Navarre's fate.

For September: DEFENDER,
by Kathleen Eagle.
Gideon Defender had reformed his bad-boy ways to become a leader among his people. Yet one habit—loving Raina McKenny—had never died, especially after Gideon learned she'd returned home.

AMERICAN HEROES: Men who give all they've got for their country, their work—the women they love.

Only from

IMHER09

MORE GREAT READING FROM
BARBARA FAITH

If you enjoyed Barbara Faith's DESERT MAN, you'll want to join her in November as she visits the dark side of love with DARK, DARK MY LOVER'S EYES, Silhouette Shadows #43.

When tutor Juliana Fleming accepted an assignment in Mexico, she had no idea the turn her life would take. Kico Vega—her solemn, needy student—immediately warmed to her presence, but Kico's father, Rafael, showed her nothing but contempt. Until he took Julie as his bride, ravishing her with his all-consuming desire—yet setting in motion Julie's worst nightmare.

Take a walk on the dark side of love with Barbara Faith—only in **SILHOUETTE SHADOWS**
